YOUNG GUNS GONE BAD

A TERRENCE CORCORAN WESTERN

JOHNNY GUNN

WOLFPACK
PUBLISHING
— EST 2013 —

WOLFPACK PUBLISHING
— EST 2013 —

Paperback Edition
Copyright © 2020 Johnny Gunn

Published in the United States by Wolfpack Publishing, Las Vegas

Wolfpack Publishing
5130 S. Fort Apache Road, 215-380
Las Vegas, NV 89148

wolfpackpublishing.com

Paperback ISBN 978-1-64734-505-1
eBook ISBN 978-1-64734-504-4

YOUNG GUNS GONE BAD

CHAPTER ONE

Summer mornings break early in the mountains of central Nevada and the air heats quickly, often leading the day into booming thunder storms. Terrence Corcoran was doing his best to stay in his bedroll until the sun was fully above the horizon before rousting himself out. "I really don't wanta," he muttered. He unrolled his pants and shirt that he used for a pillow, and got dressed, strapping on a heavy Colt revolver before checking on his prisoner. Getting the fire started wasn't a priority this time of year. However, coffee was.

"Good morning, Mr. Evans. Sleep good, did you? Looks to be a scorcher today. Be worse when we drop out of these mountains and hit the valley floor. How's that jaw feel this morning? Bet you never take another swing at me." He was smiling, prodding the miserable outlaw, having a good time of it.

"Go to hell, Corcoran," Evans snarled. He couldn't help rubbing a manacled hand over a sore jaw. One eye was puffed up and a dark purple.

Eureka County Deputy Sheriff Terrence Corcoran was laughing and joshing all the time making a nice fire and getting a pot of coffee going. Corcoran was tall and strong, and was dedicated to the task of being a good lawman. He had most people believing he was from Ireland, but he was born on a boat four days out of his mother's home country, the family on its way to America. His long, wavy, reddish hair picked up all the sun's highlights as he busied himself in camp.

Corcoran wore a massive mustache, had bushy eyebrows, and flashing green eyes. When happy, that face sparkled, but when angry, danger was palpable. After tracking his man and taking him down in just two days, his morning was delightful. "Mr. Evans there are people that love to come to these mountains to hunt. They hunt deer, elk, even big horn sheep. Not me, Mr. Evans. No sir. I love to hunt stupid criminals, outlaws what ain't smart enough to get away from me. That's what I love, Mr. Evans."

"Why don't you just shut the hell up, Corcoran." Evans wrestled with his handcuffs, tried to shake the ankle braces, and growled.

"What do you want for breakfast, Mr. Evans? Sidemeat and eggs? Sourdough pancakes? Well you ain't gettin' any. We're having hard biscuits and coffee. Don't like it? Tell the sheriff how mistreated you've been."

Evans growled some more but didn't say anything this time. Corcoran had chased him down, high in the Diamond Mountains after he'd tried to strong arm a man who had won a few dollars at the Bonanza Club two nights before. "Old Zack will be glad to get his little purse of gold back and I'll be glad to sleep in my own bed tonight, Mr. Evans. You'll be sleeping on a slab of split wood in the jail. Yup, that's where you'll be."

"Why don't you go to hell, Corcoran." Evans snapped when it seemed the deputy would never shut up.

"That is a possibility, Mr. Evans. Not today, though." He put two hard tack biscuits on a tin plate, filled a cup with boiling coffee, and handed it to the cuffed and tied prisoner.

"How do you expect me to eat this?" Evans balanced the plate on his outstretched legs and held the cup in one hand. He was sitting, tied to a sapling aspen tree.

"I'd suggest quickly, Mr. Evans. We're leaving as soon as I get the animals saddled."

Evans was known to pilfer from time to time, was thought to steal from businesses, but this was his first arrest for a serious and violent crime. The man was forty something, skinny, mostly bald, and generally filthy in appearance. "You need a bath, Mr. Evans."

"It took you two days to catch him, Corcoran. You're getting slow in your old age." Eureka County Sheriff Ed Connors enjoyed joshing his senior deputy. Connors was in his second term and was the second Eureka County sheriff having Corcoran as a deputy.

"Thirty-two ain't old, Ed. It's comfortable. Besides, it's summer, the mountains are beautiful this time of the year. I knew where old Ezra Evans was, just wanted another day in the mountains. He's a grouchy old guy. I didn't have time to check on Zack Bennett. Was he hurt bad in the assault?"

"No. His head hurt for a day and Doc Sanford got him sewed up tight. He'll be glad to get this little leather pouch." Connors walked to the pot belly stove and poured the two of them some hot coffee. "Had another fire last night, Terrence, and just like before, a house was robbed several blocks away during the fire."

"Same as before?" Connors nodded and Corcoran sat down with his coffee. "Third time. Coincidence just went out the window, Ed. Whose house was lost and whose house got robbed?"

"Fire boys saved the Avery house, but Jack Hopkins lost several guns, a strong box of bills, gold, and some jewelry. You need to talk to him. I'm sure he's involved somehow."

"How would that be. Robbed himself?"

"Sounds cockeyed, I know, but he simply won't talk to me."

"Like some of the others, Ed. They're being intimidated. I'd be willing to bet he knows who robbed him and is too terrified to talk about it. I've seen this before and it's ugly. I've known Jack for a long time. I'll have a chat with him." Corcoran stood up, finished his coffee, feigned a punch at the sheriff and danced back from a return punch.

"Right now, my dear and skinflint of an employer, I'm heading for the Bonanza Club and a cold beer along with a steak this big." He laughed, holding his arms outstretched. "Maybe a dozen cold beers and two steaks."

CHAPTER TWO

"Hello, Jimmy Henderson. I'm trail tired and in dire need of cold beer," Corcoran said. He stood at the long bar in the Bonanza where Henderson was the owner, and a long-time friend. "Ezra Evans is behind bars, again, and Zack Bennett has his winnings back in his pocket."

Henderson was taking a turn behind his own bar, something he did from time to time, and poured Corcoran a full flagon. "Had another fire while you were gone."

"Connors just told me. What's the word around town? I'm seeing a definite pattern on the one hand, and with a lack of willing witnesses, some dangerous witness intimidation."

"I think that spells it out. Hopkins lost a couple of those pretty rifles he loves and is unwilling to discuss the theft at all." Henderson watched Corcoran empty his beer mug in one long drink and filled the mug for him. "Townsfolk seem to think the Cannon boys are behind it."

"They've been in mischief all their lives, but this would be a big step. Arson and theft. Big step, indeed. Maybe I'll have a word with their father. Emil Cannon's been in the county almost since you opened your first tent saloon, Jimmy." Corcoran was referring to Henderson arriving in Eureka days after the first gold strike and opening a tent saloon called the Bonanza Club. He calls it his bonanza just as the miners refer to their big strikes.

"Emil Cannon was a fair miner, Terrence, but not much of a father. Those boys are protected by their mother, Rose. She don't believe those boys can do anything wrong. Hah!"

Henderson was interrupted by a body flying through the air, wrapped in gingham skirts and flowing blond hair, screaming Corcoran's name. Little Cindy Cook had her arms wrapped around the big deputy and was covering his face with kisses. "My goodness," he said. "Maybe I should leave town for a day or two more often."

"Oh, Terrence, I missed you. I have an elk stew going. You need to keep your strength up. Do you want one or two bowls?'

"How about one bowl, some sour-dough biscuits, and you for company." He set her back on the floor, patted her cute little bottom and watched her almost run for the kitchen. "My goodness," he said again. Henderson just walked down the long bar, smiling.

"We'll talk about the Cannon boys when I get my mind back on being a deputy. Right now, I'm just a lonely and hungry man."

"Evening, Jack." Corcoran finished his early supper and some time with Cindy, and was standing on the front porch of Jack Hopkins' cabin, down in the canyon, east of town. "Ed Connors told me what happened while I was out of town. Sorry about your loss. Got a couple of minutes to talk about how it came about?"

"I'll tell you the same thing I told the sheriff. Don't want to talk about it. It's my loss, let it go." Hopkins was an outdoorsman, near fifty, made his money selling a fine claim that was picked up by one of the large mining ventures. He received a piece of the action every quarter. He spent great amounts of time roving the mountains of central Nevada, drawing and painting pictures of the beauty of the land.

Many of his drawings were published in eastern newspapers, in particular the ones that featured some of the majestic elk that thrive in central Nevada's highlands. He not only painted them, he hunted them as well. More than one family, down on its luck, had survived a winter by way of Hopkins' elk hunting.

"Not like you, Jack," Corcoran said. "You provide for more than one family here, with your hunting. Those rifles were special for you and someone took them. Is that someone threatening you? If so, that's a serious crime, also. These fires are being set to draw people to them so robberies and thefts can take place in relative safety. The people doing this must be stopped, Jack." Corcoran was scolding but gently, and with a smile on his rugged face.

"If you know who they are, tell me. They can't hurt you if they're behind bars. You're too good a man to be intimidated this way."

"Probably just some stupid kids, Corcoran. Let it go," Hopkins said. He turned and stepped back into his cabin, closing the door. Corcoran stood on the porch for a couple more minutes, hoping the man would come back out, but he didn't.

"Just let it go, he said. Just a couple of stupid kids, he said. No, Jack Hopkins, I won't let it go." He rubbed his hand over his chin, thinking. "Yes, he said just a 'couple' of kids. Two kids. I was right, one to set the fires, then two to rob, steal, and intimidate." Corcoran was muttering as he rode his big stud horse, Dude, back up the main street. "Ed Connors mentioned the Cannon brothers. It's best that I have a little talk with Emil Cannon in the morning. Those boys of his have been in trouble since the day they were born."

He saw a light on at Doctor Sanford's house and stopped to say hello. Sanford had been in town for several years and was looked on as a philosopher as much as a physician. "Evening, Doc. Hope I'm not interrupting something."

"Not at all, Terrence. Come in. I was about to have a wee bit of brandy, it you'd care to join me."

"Delighted," Corcoran said. "Thought I'd pick your brain on the fires we've had recently. Three of them and all taking place at the same time as break-ins and robberies."

"A nasty business," Doc Sanford said. "Certainly looks like a pattern, eh? Well thought out, though."

"How's that?"

"Fire, Terrence. The most dangerous thing in little communities like ours. All these buildings built of wood, sitting high in the mountains where the wood dries out fast. Fire will flash right through a town, and everyone knows it. When the alarm goes off, the town responds, and a criminal mind will know there's easy pickings."

"That's exactly what I'm seeing, Doc," Corcoran said. "There's a secondary problem, though. None of the victims will talk about the fires or the robberies. They're scared, Doc. It would take more than one person to make this work. One or two to complete the robbery after at least one person set the fires. The robberies have netted enough money and merchandise to make the operation worthwhile."

"Worthwhile enough to threaten people?" Doc Sanford asked.

"I think so. Jack Hopkins' European rifles would bring a nice sum if they were sold, and he had a box full of cash, gold, and jewelry. Added up, that robbery brought in a tidy sum."

"You have ideas, Terrence, on who might be doing this? Must be local, to know where and when to set the fires."

"For sure," Corcoran said. "My mind keeps going back to the Cannon boys but I have absolutely nothing to base that on except prior behavior."

"Theirs or their mother's?" Sanford sat back, took a taste of his brandy and continued. "She took it personal when Emil got hurt. Wonders if maybe he did it on purpose."

"That ain't smart thinkin', Doc. Nobody wants a mine to collapse on himself."

"Rose isn't smart. She's the mine superintendents' sister and she was planning a life of luxury, with him makin' good wages, building a fine little ranch, and having a passel of boys to do the work. When Emil got hurt, well, the dream became a nightmare. She's never forgiven him for getting hurt."

Willy Cannon was nineteen and his brother, James, was seventeen. Both were tall and heavy, took after their mother, Rose, not their injured and weak father. Emil had been seriously injured in a mining accident when he first started working underground, and never fully recovered. Rose, on the other hand, was almost six feet tall and weighed close to two hundred, mostly fat-free, pounds. She showered her sons with love and protection.

"Spoiled little bastards," Doc Sanford said. "They've always been trouble makers."

"Right up to the point of committing a crime, Doc? That's why I question my thinking. They've never committed a crime that I know of, never even been accused of something as bad as burning down someone's home or strong arm robbery, more or less."

"They are capable of either, Terrence. Their mother provides them with more than motherly love. They can do no wrong, in her eyes. They were never forced to attend school, ran wild as youngsters, told their father to go to hell when he needed work done around the little place. If they could terrorize their father, they could surely intimidate someone like Jack Hopkins."

Doc Sanford got up, indicating their conversation was over. "Visit Emil Cannon but be careful of that wife of his."

"It's quite a match," Corcoran chuckled. "Weak Emil and strong Rose."

"Emil was a fine worker when he arrived, and met Rose through her brother, Clarence. Clarence Wilkinson is the superintendent at the mine Emil worked for, and introduced them. It was later that Emil was injured so badly. The boys take advantage of that at every opportunity."

"I'll see Mr. Cannon first thing in the morning, Doc. Thanks for the brandy." He stepped into the saddle for the short ride to his cabin. *I can't go see Emil Cannon. What am I thinking? What would I say? I think your boys are involved? Best to keep my thoughts to myself and my eyes wide open.*

CHAPTER THREE

The train pulled into the Eureka station on a bright summer morning and three young men stepped onto the platform. All three had a swagger, a challenge, as they stepped off the platform and into the dusty street. "We did good, boys. Far more than I expected. Let's meet tomorrow morning at my place and see if we can come up with another set-up. I have a couple of ideas."

Jacob Best was twenty, stood almost five feet ten inches and weighted two hundred pounds. He had a broad face, a flattened nose from too many fists making contact, and a distinctive scar on his chin. He didn't try to hide it with whiskers, seemed almost proud of how the knife created it. "That hardware store has some mighty fine merchandise waiting to be picked up." The other two boys let smiles cross their faces and gave knowing looks to each other.

"Sure something to think about," Willy Cannon said. Cannon had a natural sneer spread across a thin face. He eyes were shaded by heavy brows, his thin lips covered by a massive mustache. Long, thick, black hair blew in the wind. "We'll see you in the morning." He and his brother, James, walked to the corrals behind the station to pick up their horses.

Willy and James had broad, heavy shoulders and chests, thin hips and long legs, and when they swaggered toward the stables, men and women moved aside. The boys rarely smiled, had no social graces, and were not welcome in several of Eureka's bawdy houses.

The Eureka and Palisade Railroad Station was located directly next door to the Autry Livestock and Auction yards. Cattle, sheep, hogs, and horses could be loaded and off-loaded without the necessity of a spur line.

Autry maintained a set of stables as well. One could stable a horse, take the train to Elko, Reno, Salt Lake for shopping adventures, and have the horse at hand when returning. Visitors could rent horses and carriages. Jim Autry didn't miss a chance at this old life.

"What'll we tell Ma? We've been gone three days and she's sure to ask." James Cannon was a slightly smaller, slightly younger version of his brother, with one exception. James took great delight in hurting animals, people, feelings. He would hurt anything except his mother who doted on him as much as he did her.

"Tell her we were looking to buy some calves. Pa is always talking about gettin' some wieners. Let's run up Brookside Canyon, grab those steers we've been hiding, and bring 'em to the place." James may have been the younger, but he had the quickest mind of the entire family. "We've been wantin' to get them home some way. There's five steers and we've already got our brand worked into 'em."

The boys rode to the little canyon with the springs at its head and broke away the brush fence they had. Five fat steers with altered brands stood in deep summer grass. "As fat as they are, driving them to the home place will be easy," James laughed. "Right down the middle of the road, Willy. Let everyone see them. If they don't get out of the way, run 'em over."

The Cannon place was about five miles north of the train station on the road to Palisade. It was forty acres of rocks, stunted cedar, and more rocks. The property to the north had two natural springs, but there was no surface water on the Cannon place. Before his accident, Emil Cannon dug connecting irrigation ditches and was able to water, with a windmill driven pump, at least a few of his acres. The boys refused to keep the ditches open and they had fallen to disrepair.

"We'll have to sell these steers right away, James. Either that or dig out those irrigation ditches."

"Ain't gonna do that," James said. He got a nasty look on his face, spat some tobacco juice. "I'd never give Pa the satisfaction of seein' me dig them out. He built them, he can dig them out. It was him got hurt. Does that mean we have to do his work? To hell with that. Ma should have just left him. We'll bring the cattle down to the auction Saturday morning. They don't look like the same cattle we took just a few weeks ago."

Willy and James Cannon rode the open range of the Diamond Valley every spring and early summer, picking off calves before they were branded, or grabbing freshly branded calves if they weren't watched closely. They often would sell as many as twenty five calves over the course of a summer. Many in the cow county thought they knew how the boys got them, but they were never caught and nothing could be proved.

"Going down for the auction, Terrence?" Ed Connors went almost every week and Corcoran was often at his side. "Might see some interesting art work." That's what Sheriff Connors called how the brands were altered after cattle were stolen. It was high art making a running brand to turn a flying W into a rocking W. Some were more than just complicated and some were so obvious even Jimmy Autry refused to put the cattle on the auction block.

Corcoran had to laugh. "Some of those runnin' irons must look interesting when they use just a dash or bar to alter a brand. Artwork, I like that. What do you know about Jacob Best?"

"Best? He's been mighty close to the Cannon boys, stayed at their ranch when he first arrived in town. Says he does ranch work, but if he does, it's seldom. Seems to make enough to buy a drink and chase the tiger. I've had it in my mind that he spends more than he makes." He had to chuckle over that and Corcoran joined him.

"That boy has a nasty temper and I've seen him thrash his horse more than once. He's trouble but hasn't broke the law that I know of. Why?" Sheriff Ed Connors was leafing through wanted posters, looking to see if one mentioned Jacob Best.

"Been flashing some money at the Bonanza Club. Beat the hell out of a drunk that called him on a mis-play at the poker table last night. Serious over-reaction. Henderson told him to leave. Where did he come from?"

"Elko County, I think. Can't find any paper on him. He's maybe a year or two ahead of the Cannon boys. Willy's nineteen, and I think Best told me he was twenty when I talked to him. He's been seen at the auctions in the past. Maybe he'll be there this morning."

"Then I will go with you, Sheriff, but you're buyin' the coffee."

"Don't recollect mentioning that word, Corcoran," Sheriff Ed Connors chuckled.

Jacob Best was infuriated at being thrown out of the Bonanza Club. "You'll pay for this, Jimmy Henderson. You'll pay with everything you've got." Best stomped around the little cabin he had, nestled in a grove of pine trees, south of town. The road out of town narrowed to a single track trail that led past the cabin.

Best was angry most of the time, anyway, and usually because of other people. No one showed him the respect he felt he had coming. Why he felt that way couldn't be explained. The man never finished school, couldn't hold a job, and was not proficient in anything, at least according to most who knew him, and wasn't particularly good looking. The local working girls tended to shun him because he was sadistic and dangerous. More than one girl was beaten badly by the young Jacob Best, but the sheriff's office wasn't aware of that.

"Maybe it's time for the Bonanza Club to have an unfortunate accident with their oil lamps or cook stove. Maybe that fireplace in Henderson's office might just explode for some unknown reason." He was pacing around the two room cabin, cussing, talking loud, and getting more and more angry. He nursed a bottle of bad whiskey until it was empty and he found himself floundering around, unable to get up to get another, So he simply laid his head down and passed out.

Best's mother died giving birth to the boy. He was born in the hills of eastern Kentucky and raised by a sadistic father who spent more time drinking home brew than finding food for the table. The boy had an out of control appetite for young girls, was whipped by more than one angry father in those hills.

What drove him west, out of the hills of Kentucky, was lust for a fourteen-year-old girl. Her father found them in the corn crib and flailed Jacob Best with black leather harness straps out of the barn and across corn fields. Best was shirtless and bootless, and was never seen in the neighborhood again. He does show the scars, often, as proof of how tough he is.

The weekly stock auction was held at the Eureka County Stockyards, just a few hundred yards from the holding corrals at the Eureka and Palisade Railway station. It was a busy market with ranchers in the southern end of the Diamond Valley bringing their best. Most of the cattle, sheep, and hogs were shipped to the feed lots on the same day they were sold. "It's gonna be a scorcher, Ed," Corcoran said.

"Hope old Corky brought a barrel of beer and a cubic yard of ice," Ed Connors said. "Looks like some fine cattle gonna be sold today."

Dust from hundreds of head of stock, hundreds of stockmen arriving on horseback or by wagon, and a strong westerly breeze filled the morning air. "Look at those thunderheads boiling up already. You can almost feel the electricity in the air." Corcoran led the two into Autry's auction barn, nodding to many as they threaded their way toward the show ring. "Want to go in on a steer, Ed? Give us plenty of meat for the winter."

Connors just shook his head and continued walking through the crowd. "Let's take a walk through the pens, check out that art work."

Buckaroos were moving several hundred head of cattle around, getting them lined up for the proceedings, dust was blowing thick, and Corcoran held up as they passed the third set of pens. "Look at that sloppy work, Ed. Nice looking cattle but the original brands were from different ranches. Might be interesting to see who the owner claims to be."

"That's Emil Cannon's brand," Connors said. "At least that's what it is supposed to look like. Can't make a case on sloppy branding, though, unless someone complains. Let's just watch."

"Don't have to. We're being watched right now. Willy and James Cannon are off to your right, almost glaring at us. Looks like Jacob Best is moving toward them now, too. It might be a good time to say howdy. If they're the ones doing the intimidation, let's just see if they like being intimidated." He couldn't hold back the snicker.

Connors had to laugh as the they moved through the pens and throng of buyers and sellers, toward the three young men watching them.

"What the hell are they doing here?" Jacob Best asked. "That Corcoran needs to be put under some six feet of hard rock. Were those your cattle they were looking at? Ain't the right time to start a fight with that big bastard, with all these fine upstanding folk around. Sure would like to see that bastard taken out."

"They can't say or do anything," Willy Cannon snickered. "Me and James have bills of sale for each of those head, and that's the reason for the altered brands. Learned that from an old hand up in Elko. He'd line out a hundred calves every spring and then make up the bills of sale."

CHAPTER FOUR

"I don't want to hear another word about this, Emil. You're wrong and you know it. Why, for heaven's sake, what makes you think those boys would do something awful like stealing cattle? Those boys are hard-working, trying to build a herd for us, buying, trading, working hard to get young steers and heifers. I don't want to hear another word about this."

Rose Cannon strode from the porch, back into the large kitchen of their slowly decaying home, grouching about how her husband was always finding fault with their children. *Me and the boys will move out of the God-forsaken country one day, Emil Cannon. Then what will you do, with you gimpy leg and bad back. Knocked down by a couple of rocks and you've become useless. My boys as rustlers? Why, they wouldn't steal if they was starving.*

Emil limped out toward the barn, cussing softly, almost whimpering from the pain in his legs
and back. He recognized those messed up brands,
burned on with thrown together running irons,
crudely applied. "Damn fool boys are gonna end up
in prison sure as hell. Rose thinks they're cute little
angels. Those kids weren't cute little angels when
they were born."

His dreams were shattered years ago, along with
his legs and back, when a part of the mine he was
working in collapsed. He had dreams of this little
ranch supporting a growing family. In those early
years he dug irrigation lines, built fences, and bought
and bred a small herd. He was thrilled with son
number one, Willy, and even more so with number
two, James.

He saw them working hand in glove with cattle,
growing winter feed, protecting their water supply.
But it wasn't to be. After the injury, the boys mocked
him, refused to do their chores, and Rose always
took their side. They could do no wrong. They were
little angels, she said.

He always believed that somewhere in her background, Rose Cannon must have an outlaw or close
to one in the family. He knew better of course. It
was her brother, Clarence Wilkinson, the mining

engineer where he worked, who introduced them, almost twenty years ago. "My whole life ruined by a small pile of rocks falling on me," he muttered. He couldn't do any of the heavy work around the small ranch and the boys quit helping years ago. A gnarled up knee, twisted back, and one useless arm kept him from doing what he knew needed to be done.

The doc told him it might all end someday, but when was that day? It's been years, Emil almost cried out, and it hadn't gotten one bit better. Why would he say something like that? He was ready to give it up, move to town, take a cripple's job somewhere. *Cripple's job? What, sweeping sidewalks in the morning? Bah.*

It was a slow process, this thing called rot, and it was making good headway. Fences wouldn't hold a tumbleweed, irrigation ditches were in ruin, grass quit growing years ago, and the roof leaked until Rose climbed up and patched it. "All because of a load of heavy rocks that picked that instant to fall on me," he muttered.

As badly as the boys treated him, as often as Rose berated him and cajoled the boys, Emil Cannon knew he had to do something to keep his boys out of prison. There might not be any mutual love, he reasoned, but they were his boys, he had a responsibility, even if neither boy understood the meaning of the word. He tried to teach the boys responsibility, but when they wouldn't work, Rose came down on their side, saying they were too young, they needed their freedom to run and play, that ranch work was too much for young boys.

She was saying things like that even when they were twelve and fourteen years old, and Emil finally gave up. He was fuming as he paced around the barn. This thing with rustling cattle, altering brands, and parading the animals into their corrals was the last straw. Emil had to do something and didn't have the slightest idea of what to do.

"I can't go to the sheriff," he muttered, kicking at a clump of horse apples. "Not turn in my own boys. Rose won't listen for a second." He was frustrated, angry, and hurt all at the same time.

The more riled he got the more his injured leg hurt and Emil finally had to limp up to the house. A good mid-day nap might ease the pains in his leg, he knew, but nothing would cure the ache in his heart. "I'm going to lie down, Rose," he said. He started through the kitchen toward their bedroom.

"Clarence and his family are coming for supper, Emil. Don't embarrass me in front of my brother."

"I've never embarrassed you in your life, Rose. I

worked for your brother if you remember. He and I have been good friends all these years. What are you talking about?"

"I'm talking about how Clarence always says such wonderful things about that daughter of theirs and you never say anything about Willy or James. You always leave it up to me to say what wonderful boys they are."

Emil didn't say anything as he walked into his bedroom, but he did smile as he thought to himself. *I don't lie, Rose.*

"Good morning, Willy," Corcoran said. "Those your cattle in pen there? Looks like a fair representation of your father's brand."

"They're ours," Willy Cannon said. "You buying today?" His snicker and cocked head said a lot more than the words. He grinned at his brother and turned to saunter off toward the sale barn.

"Maybe not buying, Cannon. Maybe just talking. Then again, maybe just looking." He smiled, tipped his head and turned to walk back toward the corrals. He took three or four steps, turned, and looked squarely at Jacob Best.

"Tim McCracken will be in later this afternoon to talk to me about how to file a complaint, Mr. Best. Mean anything to you?" Corcoran turned to walk off.

"Who the hell's Tim McCracken?" Best asked.

"The man you beat the crap out of the other night. The man who's a better poker player than you," Corcoran laughed. "Remember, Mr. Best? Zack Bennett and Tim McCracken? Well, if charges are filed, I'm sure your memory will be restored." Corcoran turned and walked off, chuckling more than loud enough for Jacob Best to hear.

"What's he talking about?" Willy Cannon asked. "You get in a fight? And we weren't there? Shame we missed it, eh James?"

All the anger of the other night flooded through Jacob Best and he almost went for his sidearm. James Cannon reached out and held his arm. "No, Jacob. This ain't the time or the place. What happened to make Corcoran act like that and make you so angry?" Best might not ever know it or recognize what happened, but James's little gesture probably saved his life.

"Guy cheating at poker and I kicked the crap out of him. Other guy stepped in and I thumped him hard, too. Bastard Henderson threw me out of the Bonanza Club. I'm gonna burn him out. I swear, I'm gonna burn him out."

"Take the money out of his safe first," Willy Cannon laughed.

"Ain't funny," Best snarled. "You funnin' me, Willy? You lookin' for trouble, boy?"

Cannon had his Colt in hand that fast, shoved the barrel right into James Best's nose. "Don't never talk to me like that, Jacob Best. You got a bad temper and a bad mouth, and we all got a good thing goin'. You lookin' to break up what we've got goin'?" His quick moves, his quick anger surprised both Best and his brother, James.

"No, Willy, no." Best almost whimpered, feeling the tip of the big gun nudging his nose, hearing the angry and threatening words. "I'm just upset at Henderson, not you. I want his blood, not yours."

James was far more surprised at Jacob Best's reaction than Willy. Best always swaggered about, seemed always ready for a fight, and it was at that moment that James Cannon realized that Jacob Best was a coward. He was a bully when he had the chance, but a coward when called out. Best was the oldest of the three and James was the youngest, but in James' mind, he, James Cannon, just became the leader of the little gang.

"Put the gun away, Willy. Watch your bad mouth, Jacob." James Cannon stepped between the two, kept a close eye on the sheriff and Corcoran, and tried to calm a building storm. "The whole damn county is here and the law with them. Let's watch our cows get sold and go somewhere to talk about our next project. Let's remember we're together for the money." For many years, Willy had been following James' lead, and now, learning that Best would back down fast when met head on, gave James a tremendous feeling of power.

Willy Cannon was slow pulling the gun down, but did, and Best relaxed his stance some, before the three walked toward the sale barn. It was Ed Connors who saw the action and told Corcoran about it as they found Corky and his barrel of beer.

"So maybe they're not as tight as we thought they were," Corcoran mused. "The Cannon boys have been trouble makers from day one, Ed. Sneaky, surly, and back stabbers. Best has been getting a reputation around town, too. It would be a big step for the Cannon boys to become arsonists, thieves, and thugs, but I wonder about Best. I'm gonna keep a close eye on all three of 'em."

"I'll send a wire to Elko, Terrence. See what we can learn about Jacob Best." They were standing at Corky's Beer Barrel watching the sale's progress. "This is the Cannon cows coming in now," Connor said. "I wonder if Emil knows about it?" Corcoran spit some beer, laughing right out.

"You got a way about you, Sheriff."

CHAPTER FIVE

"Evening, Clarence. Hello, Amelia. Glad you could come. Rose is in the kitchen now. Hello, Cynthia, my, but you've grown up. Quite the young lady."

"Hello, Uncle Emil," Cynthia said. Her smile lit up the front porch of the Cannon home. "I'm thirteen now, and mama says that means I'm almost a woman." She giggled and bowed to Emil Cannon, before walking into the big house. *What a contrast between her and my boys,* Emil thought. His smile of welcome turned sour.

Emil stood quiet for a moment, watching the girl sashay in. *I wonder what my life would be like if I had a daughter instead of sons. It isn't the sons' fault, it's my accident that changed things. A daughter would have been nice, though.*

"Gonna cost me a fortune in clothes," Clarence Wilkinson chuckled. "How are the boys?" Wilkinson had run-ins with the Cannon brothers since the day they were born. "Willy was over the other day, said he needed some dynamite. Still trying to move those rocks, eh Emil?"

Emil stood quiet, a frown slowly coming across his face. He just nodded to his wife's brother. *We ain't blowing rocks or cleaning ditches. What in hell would Willy want with dynamite? Whatever it is, I'll wager what little money I have left that it's illegal.*

Amelia Wilkinson was thirty but looked more like sixty. She had been ill and frail most of her life and giving birth to Cynthia thirteen years ago almost caused her death. She had not recovered from the ordeal. "Wish I could be more help, Rose. I'm really tired of being sick all the time."

"Don't give it a thought, dear, Cynthia is a big help. Just sit at the table while we put the finishing touches to our supper. Let me get you a cup of tea." Rose and Amelia had a strong relationship, far stronger than Rose had with her brother, and helped the lady at every opportunity.

"Where are the boys? They will be here for supper, won't they?" Amelia asked. "They are so big and strong. Clarence always wanted a boy, but after so much trouble with Cynthia, I couldn't go through another pregnancy."

"They should be coming along soon," Rose said. At least she hoped they would. They needed to spend more time with their uncle Clarence, develop some skills for their future lives. They haven't been able to learn anything from Emil since his accident. She wasn't aware that Clarence had offered the boys good jobs at the mine and they almost told him right out to go to hell.

Emil and Clarence were having a glass of whiskey, sitting on the porch watching the sun dive toward the far horizon. "Been a good year at the mine, Emil. That stock of yours will have a nice dividend this year."

"That's my entire income, now," Emil Cannon said. "Boys don't do any work around the place, there's no water or grass, no crops. Rose won't even try to grow a kitchen garden, more or less something to sell. It's not a nice thing to say, but I hope I die young."

"Bah!" Clarence said. "Rose never made those boys do a lick of work, Emil, and they scorned you. It isn't nice to say, but I'm afraid they'll never amount to anything. I tried to get them on at the mine and they refused to even listen. That's good money, and several trades to learn. Steam engines, heavy machinery, carpentry. My God, Emil, they flat out turned me down."

"I don't doubt it for a second, Clarence. Not a second. I'm sure they're involved in shady dealings. They showed up with several fat steers wearing a bad example of my brand and took them to the sale yard today. Wouldn't even talk about where they got them. They always have money to spend, but not on the family. Haven't given Rose a half eagle ever that I know of, but have plenty to spend in town."

"Looks like them riding in now, Emil. There's three of them." Clarence stood up, shading his eyes from the last rays of the sun.

"Probably bringing that foul mouthed friend, Jacob, with them. That boy's got a mean streak in him half a mile wide. Has the manners of a hungry badger."

James and Willy Cannon, along with Jacob Best reined their horses in and tied them off at the front of the house. "Hello, Uncle Clarence," James said, jumping onto the porch and offering his hand. Willy ignored the two men and led Best into the house. "Did you bring that pretty little cousin of mine with you?"

"You bet I did, James. She's inside helping your mother with supper. Have you given any more thought to my offer of a job at the mine? We're always short-handed, and there are some good positions open right now." Clarence Wilkinson started off as the chief mining engineer and wwas now the Mine Superintendent.

"Not interested, Uncle Clarence. Got other things going for me." James answered. Emil thought he was rather short in his response.

"How did the sale go, James?" Emil wondered if the family would see even a dime from the sale of those steers, even if they weren't Cannon stock.

"All right, I guess." James said and he turned sharply and walked into the house.

"Interesting," Clarence said.

"Hi, Ma," Willy said. He gathered Rose in his strong arms and gave her a big hug. "Little Cynthia, got someone here for you to meet. This is my friend, Jacob. Jake, this is my cousin, Cynthia. Mighty pretty little girl, isn't she?"

Jacob Best looked Cynthia up and down to her mother's horror. Cynthia actually backed up a step. "She'd do if you weren't particular," Best said.

"That's not a very nice thing to say to a young girl," Amelia said. She put her arms around her daughter and held her tight. "You're not a very nice man." She looked at her host. "Rose, who is this unmannered oaf?"

"Jacob Best, you should be ashamed. I think it's best you leave. Willy, don't bring him back and I think maybe you should think twice about your friendship with such as he." Rose hadn't spoken that way to one of her sons for years, and it took Willy back a step, too.

"We're goin'. We don't need this kind of crap," Willy said and pushed Best toward the door just as Clarence and Emil came in. They didn't say a word, just shoved their way past and headed for their horses.

"What was that all about?" Emil Cannon saw Cynthia, crying in Amelia's arms, and Rose standing with her hands on her hips, scowling.

"Willy's friend insulted Cynthia," Rose said. She gave a quick look to her brother and dropped her gaze when she found him frowning. "I told him to leave and Willy got upset, too." As she finished talking they heard the three horses galloping off.

"That Best boy is a trouble maker," Emil said.

"He's a little more than that," Clarence said. "He beat Zack Bennett bad the other night. So bad that Jimmy Henderson threw him out of the Bonanza Club. There might yet be charges filed. Your boys are running with bad company, Rose." Rose didn't say anything, just turned and walked toward the hot stove.

Emil wondered if it wasn't the other way around. Maybe it was Best running with a couple of bad boys. "What brought that on, Clarence? Ezra Bennett drinks too much but he's not much for fighting."

"He's a fine poker player, Emil. You remember that. He wiped you out more than once," he laughed. "This Best feller called Ezra a cheat and beat the dickens out of him. Hurt him bad. Those at the card table said Best didn't know enough about poker to even be at the table, and Bennett cleaned him out."

"He's good at that," Emil laughed. "I haven't liked that boy since Willy and James started bringing him around. Even you didn't much care for him, Rose. Always feared for those boys getting in with a wrong crowd."

"Willy and James are too smart to be led astray, Emil, and you know it," Rose said. She wasn't going to listen to any more. "Jacob Best was wrong, but that doesn't mean my boys are wrong. They've been brought up with good manners and know right from wrong. I won't hear anymore about them running with the wrong crowd. They would never do that."

Both men stood quiet when Rose turned back to the stove. She was muttering, just loud enough for them to know she was angry at them, not her boys. Cynthia moved from her mother's arms to her father's, still quietly crying. "Don't pay any mind to a man who's only intent was to insult you. It means he has doubts about his own manhood. Real men don't insult beautiful women, my dear."

Clarence wanted to tell his sister just how wrong she was, but felt better of it, particularly since Emil didn't say anything. He wondered just how different things would be if Emil hadn't been hit so hard by that rock fall. Life had peculiar ways of lining out our lives, he thought. Clarence had spent the greater part of his life working underground and never got a scratch, and Emil never made the first year.

"Let's have supper and talk about something more pleasant," Rose said. She took Cynthia out of her father's arms and walked her to the stove to help. She pulled a Dutch oven full of pork shoulder from the wood stove while Cynthia filled one bowl with mashed potatoes and another with thick brown gravy.

"That wasn't a very nice thing to say to my cousin, Jacob. Cynthia's a beautiful girl and you know it." Willy still had fingers of anger kneading at his nerve ends from earlier in the day and wasn't going to let this get away from him.

"She's a fine looking girl, Willy. Just fine. I'd like to have some of that, but you sure shouldn't ever let a woman think you're interested. They think that and they'll take you for everything you've got. They're more fun to take when they're angry at you, anyway. A woman that's all soft and gentle like ain't much fun. A lot more fun when they're kickin' and scratchin'. You get 'em to screamin' in fear and it's even better."

Jacob Best was laughing, almost clapping his hands as he talked. "Hell, Willy, she'll be beggin' me to take her next time I see her. She'll have my back raked bloody by the time I'm through with her."

"I don't want to hear that kind of talk, Jacob," Willy said. Anger welled to the surface, he wanted to smash Jacob's face, but at the same time, what he was saying intrigued him. Fear, terror, gets a woman excited? "That's my cousin you're talkin' about."

Willy Cannon was surprised by his own anger, his own feelings about Cynthia, about how his mother had raised him to respect women, to treat them fairly. Terrorize a woman? Willy would open doors for women, always walked on the outside of his mother when in town, never used foul language. Willy Cannon was conflated and simply kept his mouth shut.

"Oh, hell, Willy, I've heard you almost say the same things about Cynthia," James said. "She might be our cousin, but she's one fine looking girl. No man in his right mind would turn it down and you know it."

"Well," Willy said, "I ain't gonna talk about it." Willy had secret thoughts about his cousin, thoughts that included some of what Jacob said, but more. Much more. And now the concept of terror has entered the picture.

The rest of the ride into town was fast and quiet until they reached Jacob's cabin. "Let's work on getting our hands on what's in the hardware store. There's a lot of stuff that can be sold quick and that old skinflint, Harry Martin, probably has money hidden away, too." James led the group into the cabin. "I know he has a safe in the back office. I've seen it."

"I want to get my hands on money right away," Jacob Best said. "Before we hit another place where we have to run off to sell things, we need some runnin' money." He laughed along with the Cannon boys. "When the sale was over I saw several of the sellers leave on the stage coach going west. They were carryin' thousands of dollars boys."

"Yeah," Willy said. "Some of the older men, the ones that bring their wives to the sales, ride the coaches and let their hands make it home on horseback."

"That's a long lonely road to the Monitor Valley, Big Smoky Valley, and Austin, and those ranchers would be carrying their purse," James said. "There's a sale every Saturday, and those ranchers are there with their cattle every week."

"Martin's Supply and Hardware can wait a week or two, eh?" Willy was chuckling, thinking about it. "I'll get the schedules for the coach runs, and James, you and Jacob find us a good place to stop the coaches.

"There's more than coaches, too," Willy continued. "Many of those men don't ride home in a coach. A few do, sure, and we can sure stop a coach any tine we want, but most ride home with their buckaroos. That would be a little tougher, taking on a crew. If they send the crew home and ride out with their family, they'd be easy pickin's." Willy was snickering, thinking about scaring a rancher's family while he took all the money the old man had.

"I'm lookin' forward to whuppin' on an old man as I count the money I took from him," he laughed. He found his calling, this idea of intimidation and terror, fascinating after using it on Jack Hopkins during their robbery. To watch a man twitch in fear, to see tears in a man's eyes when threatened, brought a surge of power to Willy Cannon. He'd seen that in James and didn't recognize its power.

"What I want is a pocket full of money. You can beat on anyone you want, Willy. I want the money," James said.

"You find us some good places to hit those coaches, James, I've got some business to take care of," Jacob said. "Zack Bennett needs a good talking to, and so does Tim McCracken. I'm gonna put the fear of Jacob Best in both of them." He didn't mention it, but he also planned to spend some time hoping to get to know little Cynthia Wilkinson better. *I liked it when she started crying and ran to her mother. I know how to make her cry even more.* "That sale next week's gonna bring us some big money," he said. "Big enough for me to take a woman for my own."

CHAPTER SIX

"What do you want?" Jack Hopkins opened the door to a loud knock and came face to face with Jacob Best. Best was carrying a shotgun and aimed it at Hopkins mid-section.

"I hear you've been talking to that deputy, Mr. Hopkins. Don't you remember what I told you? What I'd do to you and your home if you did?" He used the heavy scattergun to push his way into the house and slammed Hopkins across the side of the head with it. The edge of the barrel opened a gash several inches long and blood flowed freely. "Don't want to hear about that again, Mr. Hopkins."

Jacob Best stepped into the living room of the small cabin, and simply swung the shotgun, breaking an attractive lamp, then pulling his knife and slashing at a sofa. "I don't like it when I tell you not to do something and you do it anyway. You need to be punished, Mr. Hopkins." Hopkins was cowering and the brought Best to his full bully persona.

"I didn't tell Corcoran nothing. I told you I wouldn't." He was wiping blood from his head, almost crying from the pain. Best was standing in front of the older man, threatening him with that heavy shotgun.

"As long as we understand each other, Mr. Hopkins. I don't enjoy this and I know you don't either." He was snickering, holding the gun as if ready to swipe it at him again, and scowling. Instead, he turned, spotted another attractive Victorian style oil lamp and lashed at it.

"No! That was my mother's." Jack Hopkins cried out, but Jacob wasn't in a mood to listen. He lashed out again, and this time made contact. The lamp shattered, spilling coal oil, broken glass, and memories all over the floor. Best was laughing, Hopkins was crying, and intimidation was working.

"Those rifles brought some good money, Mr. Hopkins. Thank you," he said. He was laughing as he walked out of the house.

Hopkins was not a large man, an outdoorsman, yes, but a fighter against a man twenty years or more his junior and twice his size? No. He went to the basin and washed the blood away, cleaned the deep cut the shotgun made, and put a plaster on. "Maybe I was wrong, not telling Corcoran. I can't go up against a man that size." He spent the next half hour cleaning up the mess.

Jacob Best rode out of town and toward the Richmond Mine. Wilkinson, as superintendent had a company provided home on the mine property. It was a compound that doubled as the mining offices and super's home, with the house sitting next to the offices. Best settled into a copse of trees and underbrush a couple of hundred yards back, and watched the site for the next hour, wondering just why the Cannon boys hadn't already had their fun with that delightful cousin.

Best was twelve when he attacked his cousin and got caught. His father beat him black and blue, made bloody welts that didn't heal for weeks, and threatened the boy with the law. Best hadn't been home since, but always remembered the thrill of the attack, how the girl screamed when he ripped her dress.

He saw Cynthia helping hang out the laundry, watched her work in a little kitchen garden, and had nasty thoughts about her. Finally, she took a long walk across a meadow and into a grove of cottonwood trees to sit in the shade and have a glass of something, maybe water, maybe lemonade. Best rode down out of the trees and across the grassy side hill. He boldly rode right up to the girl, sitting in the shade of the trees.

"Well, hello there," he said. He stepped off his horse. "Cynthia, isn't it? Remember me?" He had a nasty little smile on his face and enjoyed seeing the fright come across her face. "You actually are a rather attractive girl."

"You!" She yelped, jumping to her feet. "Leave me alone. Go away, you horrible man."

"Now, now. Here I came all the way out here just to see you and you treat me this way. That's not very nice." He took several quick steps toward the girl, holding the reins in one hand and holding the other out for her to take.

"You stay away from me," she shouted. She turned to run back to the house and he reached out and grabbed her. He pulled her up close, wanted to kiss her, but she struggled, bit him and kicked herself free.

She didn't hesitate, and screamed louder than Jacob Best had ever heard a woman scream. He saw Mrs. Wilkinson step out onto the porch, but worse, he saw Clarence Wilkinson come out of the mine office carrying a rifle. Jacob Best let the girl go, jumped on his horse and sank the spurs deep.

Wilkinson didn't recognize him but he saw Cynthia sink to the ground, he brought the rifle up and got two quick shots off. He missed with both.

Between the scream and the two shots being fired, everyone in the mine office and those in the house, were outside, rushing toward Cynthia, Clarence leading the charge. "Are you all right?" He had his arms around his daughter. She was clinging to him, crying, sobbing. "Who was he? Who?" Clarence Wilkinson demanded.

"It was that horrible man at Uncle Emil's house. He tried to grab me. I bit him, papa."

"Good," Wilkinson chuckled. "Let's get you back to the house. Your mother must be frightened out of her mind. You're sure it was Jacob Best?"

"Yes. I'm sure, Papa. He even said so. I'm scared."

"Amelia, take care of her," Wilkinson said. He ran back to the compound's barn and corral, got his horse saddled, and was racing for town. He was debating whether to find young Jacob Best and kill him on sight, or make a formal complaint with the sheriff. "Mess with my daughter, Mr. Best, and you're gonna die."

It was his background of making good business decisions that allowed him to make this one, and he rode straight for the sheriff's office. He was still shaking with anger when he stepped off his horse and strode up to Ed Connors' desk. "Need your help, Ed. Got some coffee, or something stronger?" Anger and fear were spread across his broad face.

"Jack, it's good to see you. What the hell happened to you?" Corcoran was sitting at a table in the Bonanza Club having a plate of their free lunch and a flagon of cold beer. "Get in a fight with a big old bear?"

"Fell off the damn porch, Terrence." Jack Hopkins had every intent of telling Terrence Corcoran exactly what happened, but couldn't do it. He rubbed a finger across the now bloody dressing on his head. The memory of that rifle barrel slicing across the side of his head was just too strong, the pain strikingly real. "Getting old, I guess."

He sat down and nodded to the barman to bring a cold beer. How could he tell Corcoran that Jacob Best stole everything that meant anything to him, gave him a good beating, and whipped him with that rifle? How could he tell Corcoran that he did nothing when Best broke his mother's favorite lamp?

"I saw Jacob Best hanging out with the Cannon boys at the sale yard the other day, Jack. Seems they had some steers to sell, but seemed to have some money to spend. Are you sure you don't have something to tell me?" Corcoran sat back, a smile on his face. He wasn't going to threaten or intimidate the man. Seems as though someone else had already done that.

"I don't know what you mean," Hopkins said. His voice soft, his eyes averted. He didn't stutter, but Corcoran knew he was holding back something. "Just came down for a cold beer, maybe a cold slab of meat or cheese. That Jacob Best is a real bastard but he doesn't mean anything to me. Little Louise Larsen, works at Mandy's House of Pleasure might want to talk to you about the man. She can't see out of one eye right now." There, he thought, at least Corcoran knows something.

"That so? Corcoran nodded his thanks. "Maybe I'll pay that darling little lady a visit." *The man's got a nasty wound across the side of his head and says he fell off the porch? Nuts. He was hit hard with something and he's scared quiet. If Best is doing this, he's really got this man scared. He tells me one of the working girls got beat up but won't talk about him getting beat up.*

"I talked with Zack Bennett yesterday, Corcoran. He said Jacob Best threatened him."

"He beat the hell out of the man, Jack. He whipped on Tim McCracken, too. Sure would like to hear your story."

"No, Corcoran. This is different. Best went to Bennett's cabin and told him that if he talked with you or the sheriff, he'd kill him."

Corcoran just shook his head. "Listen, Jack, you've got to understand that unless you talk to me about what happened to you, I can't do anything. Jack Bennett has to tell me about his problem, not you. Louise Larsen has to talk to me, not you. You have to talk to me about your problem."

"But, Terrence, I don't have anything to say to you. They do." He wouldn't look at Corcoran, kept his eyes on the table. The man had a strong grip on the table, and was shaking with fear and Corcoran shook his head slowly, back and forth. *I'm so ashamed. I'm a better man than this, but that man has me scared stupid. He's the meaning of terror.*

"You don't need to be afraid, Hopkins, if you tell me what happened and I take the bad guy out. The whole town can see you sitting here talking to me. If Jacob Best is threatening you, he'll get word of this."

Hopkins didn't say anything, didn't look up, just sat at the table, staring at the floor. "It's up to you, Jack, if you want these threats to end." Hopkins didn't say anything and Corcoran got up, slowly, looked down at the man and shook his head. "I'll be there when you need me, Jack, but I can't help if you won't help me."

Corcoran walked down the street toward Mandy's little palace, for a talk with Louise. "He said Zack Bennett had a visit, too." Corcoran was muttering as he made his way up the hill toward the usually busy whore house. "Zack's tougher than Hopkins. Bigger too. That's one of the things Best has going for him. His size and youth." It was a busy one-way conversation for the two blocks to Mandy's.

Mandy told him Louise had a bad night and was sleeping in. "Wake her up, Mandy. This is important. I don't have time to be nice about this." He tried not to smile, but that didn't work. Corcoran, after all, was Corcoran and Mandy LeFevre was lovely and charming. She was no more French than he was, but the way she mangled the language told everyone that she was from somewhere else.

Mandy was nearing thirty, stood an impressive six feet tall, and had the measurements that made that stature just right. Her black hair was gleaming, and her deep brown eyes seemed to be offering something. She fluttered those eyes at the deputy sheriff, gave him a wonderful smile. "You be better off with me, big man. I teach you things little girls don't know. We leave Louise to sleep, eh?"

"No, sweetheart, we wake the little girl up." He gave her an equally inviting smile that might have said, 'Maybe later, dear lady'. "You wake her or I do," he said. This time there was no smile and Mandy cussed under her breath as she led Corcoran down a long hallway. There were closed, numbered doors, every several feet, on both sides of the hall.

"She works in number seven, big man. She says, men get lucky in number seven." There was a delightful tinkle of laughter from the madam. It took several strong knocks on the door to get the pretty little dove out of the rack.

"Corcoran," she cooed. "This is a pleasant surprise. Come in, come in." The bruises on her face told a terrible tale and Corcoran bowed Mandy goodbye and stepped into Louise's room.

"I was told a nasty little story half an hour ago, Louise, and I think I'm looking at that problem right now. I fully understand that you and the other girls don't want to talk about some of the problems you have with your visitors, but this is different, isn't it?"

"He'll kill me," she whimpered. The bruises were evidence of a beating, but there was more, Corcoran knew. "He marked me, Terrence. I'll be scarred for life." She let her nightgown fall to the floor and Corcoran couldn't hold back the gasp.

"My God, Louise." The still bleeding knife wound was the letter B, badly carved in the middle of her stomach. "Jacob Best did this? And beat you, too?"

Louise was whimpering as Corcoran led her back to her bed. She let him doctor the terrible wound with ointment and cover it with a bandage. She slipped under the covers and Corcoran sat down on the edge of the bed. "Start at the beginning, Louise. I need to know everything. That young Turk has stepped over the line and I'm gonna get him."

"He was laughing, Terrence." The tears flowed in blubbering sobs as she spent the next hour telling Corcoran about the horrible things Jacob Best was capable of. The fear flowed from her, she cringed with every question Corcoran asked, and as he got up to leave, she reached out and grabbed his hand. Her fingers wouldn't let go and she dragged him back down.

"He'll kill me, Terrence. Don't let him know I told you all this. Please." Her pleading eyes were almost more than Corcoran could take. He wrapped her in his arms, kissed the top of her head, and stood back up.

"He will never hurt you again, Louise. Never." He bent down and kissed her again, gently, on the top of her head, pulled the covers up tight, and walked out the door. He put together what she told him, what he thought happened to Jack Hopkins, and knew it was way past time to bring Jacob Best in. "Not a hanging offense, damn it," he muttered. He slipped into the Bonanza Club for a cold beer and a talk with Jimmy Henderson. Henderson had some girls who did some on-the-side business, too, and might have a story to tell.

"Jimmy, I'm about to put the clamps on that Jacob Best feller. Beat the hell out of one of the working girls at Mandy's. Any of your girls come up with lumps and bruises they shouldn't have? He's got a bad habit of whuppin' on defenseless girls and old men who don't or can't fight back."

"You better get the irons on him damn soon, Corcoran. Zack Bennett has sworn to kill him the next time he sees him." Henderson was chuckling but Corcoran could see he was also being serious. "Bennett isn't the kind to take the beating he took with favor. When he's sober, he's tough and mean. Worked underground for a long time, Terrence. He can still swing a four-pound single-jack for hours and not raise a sweat."

"I've seen him in the drilling contests," Corcoran said. "I've seen him clean out a bar, too, but those were in days gone by. He's a drunk, and Best tried to beat him half to death. Afraid he wouldn't be much of a threat to Best right now. That's Best's game, Jimmy. Go for those who can't fight back."

CHAPTER SEVEN

"I need to file whatever papers are necessary, Sheriff," Clarence Wilkinson said. "My daughter was just attacked by Jacob Best. I'm only giving you a short time to do your job, Ed, then I'm doing my job." Wilkinson and Connors had been friends for years, had ridden in more than one posse together, and held each other in high regard.

"Sit down, Clarence. Let me get you a cup of coffee. Best, eh? Sounds mighty serious. Tell me, and don't leave anything out."

Wilkinson took the offered cup of coffee, well laced with fine bourbon, and sat down, almost glaring at Ed Connors. "Rode right on to our place and put his hands on my Cynthia, Ed. No man is allowed to do that. She's just thirteen years old, Sheriff."

"Give me all the details, Clarence. I'd like to say,

take it easy, but I won't bother. I will ask that you let us do our job. Don't make things worse for us." Sheriff Ed Connors did what he could to calm the man but wondered what his position would be if some guy tried to manhandle his wife or daughter.

"We've had other complaints about this Jacob Best, Clarence. I'll get a warrant out immediately. Corcoran is working on his case, as well. We think he's behind some of these fires and strong arm robberies. I don't want to say this, but your nephews might also be involved."

"Willy and James?" Wilkinson finished the coffee and Ed Connors re-filled the cup. "The Best boy was with Willy and James the other night at Emil's house. It's because of that, that I recognized him. Best was rude to Cynthia that night and Rose threw him out. Willy and James running with a bastard like Best? Damn, Ed. That would kill my sister. She thinks those two little angels can do no wrong." His eyes were downcast and he just shook his head.

Connors handed Wilkinson a form to fill out. "Put it all down, Clarence. Everything. We'll put that fool away for a long time. Has he threatened you or Amelia? He threatens and then follows through with beatings, is what we're being told."

"That little snot-nosed bastard threatens me and

I'll skin him alive." Wilkinson took his time and filled out the paperwork for Connors and decided to have a beer at the Bonanza Club. As Mine Superintendent, he didn't spend much time in the saloons. Some of the workers get a snoot full and they'd forget their manners. It was a quick walk across the street.

"Corcoran," he said, walking to the table where Henderson and Corcoran were talking. "Mind if I join you?"

"Must be a slow day at the mine to get you into town," Corcoran said. "Sit a spell." Wilkinson sat down, nodded to the barman for a glass of beer, and lit a cigar.

"Just filed a complaint with Ed against a man named Jacob Best. He said you're working on something dealing with him, too."

"They're piling up," Corcoran muttered. "What did he do to bring you to town. Surely didn't have the guts to threaten you." Corcoran wanted to chuckle but the angry look on Wilkinson's face told him no, don't do that.

"No, not me. He made improper advances on my daughter, Cynthia. Put his hands on her, Corcoran. He ran like the coward he is when I came out after him. Catch him or I will."

"Don't do anything rash, Clarence. It's our job and we good at our work. How old is Cynthia?"

"Just thirteen," he said.

"Oh, my. I don't really have to ask this, but with Best's intimidation tactics, I have to. Would you testify in court to what you just said? It's important."

"Damn right I will," Wilkinson said. "You didn't have to ask."

"Best has whipped on people, Clarence. Threatened them if they file a complaint or testify. He hasn't killed yet, but he is capable. He has come close. He'll come after you in some way, to keep you from testifying."

"My God, Amelia," Wilkinson said, jumping to his feet. "She and Cynthia are alone. I've got to get home." He shook hands with Corcoran, nodded to Henderson, and almost ran from the saloon. They heard his horse move out at a brisk lope.

"That's one man who won't back down from Jacob Best. Is Best still living in that wretched cabin up in the trees on the south side?" Henderson nodded and Corcoran finished his beer in one swallow. "Guess I better pay that boy a visit."

"Better bring that shotgun Ed Connors likes so much," Henderson said.

"Think I'll swing by Zack Bennett's place on the way out. He's fit to be tied about the whipping he took, but if he's drinking, he'd be no match for Best."

Bennett was strong as a mule but wasn't able to hold his liquor.

"If he gets falling down drunk, Best'll beat him to a pulp, Corcoran," Henderson said.

"You gotta hide me, Willy. I can't go back to my place." Jacob Best rode hard into the canyon where Willy and James kept their stolen cattle. He had blood stains on his shirt and pants, bruises on his face, and his knife scabbard was empty. When he jumped from his horse, he went flat on his face in the dirt. He was holding one leg tight, sitting in the dirt.

"What the hell happened to you? You hurt bad?" Willy ran from the brush corral and knelt down to look at the injured leg. "That's a bullet wound, Jake. What happened?"

"Bastard attacked me, Willy. That drunk that cheated me at cards shot me." Willy remembered the story, remembered that big deputy telling Jake that charges might be filed. "I went to that bastard's house to set him straight about filing charges against me, and he attacked me." Jacob Best seemed surprised that someone would fight back. He always thought he was the dominant one.

"He won't never cheat nobody again at the poker table. He won't never attack nobody, either. You gotta protect me, Willy. They'll be lookin' for me."

"Let's get that leg looked at first," Willy Cannon said. "We'll ride out tonight for the cabin me and James got. Way up in the Diamond Mountains. Won't never find you there." He helped Jacob to his feet and acted as a crutch, leading him to a stand of trees near the spring.

"I got a bottle in my saddlebags, Willy. I'm gonna need that when you dig for the bullet. Damn, it really hurts. Ain't never been shot before. Pa whupped on me bad, but never been shot."

Willy laid Best down in the grass and went for his horse, got it tied off and unsaddled. He grabbed the half empty bottle and came back to where Best was, in the shade of the tree. "Must be over ninety degrees, Jake. That wound's gonna fester up fast. I ain't never dug a bullet out. Wish Ma was here. She'd know how."

"Ain't got time for that, Willy." Best grabbed the bottle and started drinking big gulps of hot, raw, whiskey. Willy ripped the pants-leg open and looked at a ragged hole in the man's upper leg.

"What the hell'd he shoot you with, a shotgun? That's nasty, Jake." Jacob didn't answer, just kept drinking hot whiskey. Willy pulled his knife out, took the bottle and poured whiskey in the wound and across the knife. Jacob Best howled out his pain, thrashed about, and grabbed the bottle back. "Gonna hurt worse than that in a minute, Jake. Better hang on to something."

Corcoran pounded again on Zack Bennett's door. "Come on, old man, get your drunken butt over to the door." He pounded once more and this time he used the handle of his Colt. Still no answer and Corcoran was about to turn and leave.

"No, I better not, damn fool might be hurt" he muttered. He tried the door and found it unlocked. The single room was in complete disarray, the big table on its side, chairs broken and upended, and over in the corner, not moving, Zack Bennett's mangled body. Corcoran also found an ancient, single shot, flintlock pistol, recently fired, still in the old man's hand.

"My God, Zack. Oh, damn. Just damn," Corcoran said. He knelt down to examine the body and found a knife stuck deep in Bennett's chest, knife wounds in several areas of the body, and indications that someone had been shot but able to get out of the cabin. The trail of blood led to the back door and outside.

Corcoran ran for his horse and rode hard for Doc Sanford's. "He's dead, Doc, but tell me everything you can from what's left." Corcoran rode to the office to bring Ed Connors to the cabin. "Bennett put up one hell of fight, Ed. The bad guy is shot and probably beat up some."

"You figure it's Jacob Best?"

"Fits the frame, don't he? Threat's been made. Bennett preparing to file charges on the previous beating. Jacob Best beat the hell out of Louise Larsen sometime yesterday, and Jack Hopkins is walkin' around more scared than anyone I've seen in a long time. Need to find that boy and fast, Ed. Along with a natural meanness, he's paranoid, thinkin' everyone's out to get him. We got to get him fast."

"Head up to his cabin, Terrence. I'll work with Doc Sanford. Got your shotgun?" Corcoran had to smile. Connors was the second person to remind him of the shotgun that Connors like so much.

"You bet." He chuckled, turning his horse east and riding toward the other end of the canyon that is home to Eureka. Jacob Best's small cabin, mostly falling apart, sat in a grove of cottonwood trees, weeds, brush, and rocks. He bragged he got it and the acre it sat on for five bucks and a cold beer. "Man got taken," Corcoran murmured, kicking the door open. It took less than ten seconds to determine there was no one home.

There was a lean to shed near a makeshift corral and that was the extent of buildings on the property. "Man lives lean," Corcoran said, mounting Dude for the ride back to town.

CHAPTER EIGHT

Willy Cannon was covered in blood, holding three small round pieces of lead. The initial wound to Best's leg was twice its size now and the patch job Cannon did was sloppy and crude. He used the last of the whiskey to clean the wound and let the young outlaw sleep. The plan was to leave late at night for the Cannon brother's high mountain cabin but Willy wasn't sure Jacob would be able to make such a trip.

Willy didn't take much interest in ranching, knew little about animals but was alert enough to understand a large loss of blood, and if he knew anything, it was that Jacob Best had a large loss of blood. "Mama would have him fixed up and on his feet in a flash," he murmured. He stumbled over to the creek and did what he could to wash most of the blood off, even wrung out his shirt and pants.

Willy was twenty years old and his first thoughts were of mama. Mama always did everything for her boys. He had never been required to do anything, learn anything of any consequence. "Mama would know what to do," were his first thoughts as he stood over a good friend who might just die because Willy never learned a thing.

Willy shuddered when he remembered that James left that morning to scout the road between Eureka and the Big Smoky Valley and wouldn't be back for days. He would have to make all the decisions, take full responsibility for everything. Willy Cannon hadn't taken responsibility for anything, ever. What's worse, he always let James make the big decisions.

"I got no business doing any of this. He got himself shot, he can damn well take care of himself," Willy muttered. He walked to the cabin and hung his shirt and pants to dry. "James'll be back in a day or two, I'm just gonna ride on home and be with mama." He looked at the unconscious body and something changed.

He found himself thinking twice about running off and leaving Jacob Best to die. For the first time in his young life, Willy Cannon felt compassion for another human being. "I gotta help him," he finally murmured. His plan was simple, ride out late at night, hope nobody would see them, and make his way to the high mountain shack.

"I'm gonna have to tie him to his horse to get him up to that cabin. There is some food there, always, but no medicines or anything. He's gonna die on me, sure as all hell." He kept up a lively conversation as he tried to get both horses ready for the trek. Willy wrote a short note for James, not giving many details, just that Jake was hurt and the two of them would be at the mountain cabin.

The midnight hour was fast approaching and Willy had to manhandle the still drunk, half-awake Best into the saddle. The wound was more open to the night air than bandaged, and blood flowed down the bare leg. "This is gonna be a rough ride, Jake. You gotta hold on tight. Don't make me have to tie you down."

Jacob mumbled something, tried to giggle, and weaved back and forth in the saddle. Willy took the lead rope and led off through the canyon and onto the main road into Eureka. He took the north fork and rode at a walk for almost five miles before turning onto a trail that led deep into the Diamond Mountains. He had to stop often and get Best straightened out in the saddle. "No company so far, Jake. Make this turn and we're free." The main road from Eureka to Palisade ran alongside the railroad tracks and was busy most of the time. Not late that night.

It was a hard climb on a dark night into rugged mountain country. They were on a trail that followed a stream for several miles. He wanted to stop and build a fire, have some coffee, even thought once of simply leaving the wounded Best. Willy parted company with that first trail for another, still climbing steadily, and rode more north. There were many switchbacks, steep and rocky terrain that the horses had trouble with.

Willy Cannon was a good rider, but he was leading another horse carrying a wounded man who wasn't doing much to stay in the saddle. Storm felled trees littered the path and had to be gone around or moved, tumbled rocks had to be avoided, and there was little moon but the blanket of bright stars gave him enough light.

"There it is," he said as they came to a deep gash in the rocks and rode straight into the defile. "The first time James led me through here I thought he was nuts." The trail was narrow and steep, rocky enough that few prints were left if anyone was following.

It broadened some after a twisting half mile, and finally opened into a meadow at about the eight thousand foot level. Sitting in a copse of tall pines and aspen was the crude cabin along with a small corral. A natural spring bubbled up in the middle of the set of trees. It took all his energy to get Jacob off the horse and into the cabin. There were two bunks, a wood stove, table, and two chairs. Just enough for the brothers.

He found it easier with the early morning light. Willy figured they had spent at least six hours making the climb. The Cannon brothers had never really committed major crimes, other than cattle rustling, but called the cabin their hideout. They spent many days and nights there, shot deer and elk often, and pretended to be real outlaws. They were cattle rustlers and would be hung or shot if caught, but there was no paper hung on walls featuring their names. They justified their rustling by saying that even the ranchers put their brands on calves they found on the prairie.

Picking off young calves late at night, the ones that hadn't been tagged or branded yet, was their specialty. For a rancher to lose a calf or two to predators in that country was normal, so the Cannon boys were never suspected of being the predators. They were young wolves practicing for their future lives. And telling grandiose stories to each other in their high mountain cabin.

Willy laid Best on a bunk and went to tend to the horses. Even though it was mid summer, nearing ninety degrees on the valley floor each day, at this altitude, it was cold in the early morning hours. Willy got a fire started and a pot of coffee boiling.

In all his almost twenty years, Willy Cannon had gone out of his way not to take responsibility for anything, shirked whatever came his way, dodged work, and defied authority. And, now, he was responsible for a man's life. He almost cried it out several times, trying to get the wound cleaned out, thinking about what might happen in the next few hours or days. Willy Cannon wanted his mama. He shrank back and cried out when he took what was left of the bandage from Jacob's leg wound.

"I don't know what to do," he muttered. The creek, back in the trees, might still be running but it was late in the year. He found a basin and walked out of the cabin. He wanted to throw the basin away and get on his horse and ride off. Run away. He was good at that. Why did he stay? Why did he fill that basin with icy spring water?

He knew enough to put a pan of the water on the stove to heat, found a bottle of whiskey in a cupboard, ripped Jacob's shirt into strips, and cleaned the wound. Best moaned several times when the whiskey was applied, and seemed to be coming to. "You're hurt bad, Jake. Lie still while I wrap this up." It was a little better job than he had done in the meadow.

"What the hell are we gonna do, Jake?" He didn't expect an answer. "We gotta get some food, more whiskey, and some real bandages. Ma's gonna have a million questions, too. You gotta get well, Jake, so's we can rob those coaches."

The thought actually brought a hint of a chuckle to the big boy. "Old James is out there stalking, Jake, so's we can." He finished the coffee and watched the sun brighten the surrounding forest. "I'll ride down to our place later and get what I can." He fell into the other bunk, exhausted.

"What do you see, Doc?" Ed Connors was sitting at Zack Bennett's table nursing a cup of coffee.

"This would have been the fight of the century, Ed. Zack has multiple knife wounds, some deep and painful, and the other man must be well bruised, not to mention, shot."

"He wasn't shot with a bullet, either," Connors said. He held a powder flask and nodded at a leather pouch on the table. "This is like buck shot that he had in that old pistola. That thing must date back into the seventeen hundreds. Maybe even earlier.

Has to be a nasty wound."

"I've seen those in California, Ed. They're what the Conquistadores carried. They call them horse pistols, I think. Monster load of powder and multiple lead balls or whatever was handy. Some used stone, I was told. Whoever got shot with this is hurt bad."

"You pretty sure it was just one person?"

"Just one, Ed, and he's got a bunch of lead in him."

"I'm gonna check around outside," Connors said. He followed the trail of blood out the back door of the tiny cabin, found where Jacob Best had his horse tied off. Best had been dragging one leg and Connors noticed that he had a hard time mounting. "Shot in the leg, eh? That'll slow him down some. Leg wounds are usually heavy bleeders," he mused. "Might want to look for a body." He had to chuckle and followed horse prints that led around the cabin and onto the street. Connors lost them in the mess of other traffic. "God knows where he went from here."

Connors walked back in the cabin. "Don't know if old Zack had any relatives. I guess you'll have to hold the body for a day or two until we find out, Doc."

They were interrupted by Corcoran coming back. "The Best cabin's empty but not stripped. Best was not planning on running away. Find anything that will help us, Doc?"

"Only the fact your outlaw is hurt bad, Terrence. He took a round of buck shot to the leg. Old Zack Bennett died hard but put up one hell of a fight."

"I know an outlaw who's gonna die hard, too," Corcoran snarled. "He's upped the ante, Ed. From beating on people to murder. Send a bunch of wires out, will you? I'm gonna move around town and see if anyone saw him ride out. Leg wound, eh? Might stand out in someone's mind."

"Speaking of that, Elko sheriff answered my wire. Jacob Best was picked up for attempting to fondle a young girl up there. Let go because of his age, it was few years ago, and the fact there were no witnesses. Suggestions of other encounters, but no further charges."

"He's got further charges now, Ed. I'm gonna get that fool and he ain't gonna like it."

Connors led him out the back door and showed him where Best's prints ended in a jumble and Corcoran rode down that lane and into the downtown area. "A wounded man ain't gonna be making stops," Corcoran muttered. Corcoran stopped at the dry goods store with no results, a stop at a small shop near the Bonanza Club with the same answer. Everyone he asked said, "Nope. Ain't seen no injured man."

"Well, I know he didn't go back to his cabin and that means he rode west or north. I wonder how far?

He was friends with the Cannon boys, but Wilkinson said Rose threw him off the place a while back. Would he go there?" Corcoran made up his mind to head to the Cannon place first thing in the morning. He rode down out of the Eureka Canyon and checked around the train station and holding pens to see if anyone had seen him.

"The man's a ghost," he chuckled. "How can you ride out of town, wounded and bleeding, and not be seen?" Corcoran even glanced down, from time to time, to see if he could spot blood on the busy road, knowing he wouldn't. "Gettin' dark," he said to his horse, Dude, and rode back into town. "Talk with Emil Cannon in the morning."

Ed Connors flagged him down. "Find anything?"

"Nobody saw him, Ed. I'm gonna ride out to the Cannon place in the morning. If he's hurt as bad as we think, we're more likely to come up with a bled out body than a living breathing murderer."

"That would be best," Connors snickered. "Meet me at the Bonanza for a cold one."

"You're buyin'."

CHAPTER NINE

"Howdy, Emil. How you feeling?"

"Tired and worn out, Terrence." Emil Cannon was cleaning one of the stalls in the barn and put the rake down. "What brings you out here on a blistering hot day?" They could see the heat waves as they looked out the barn doors and across the Diamond Valley. Grasses shimmered from the heat, not cooling breezes.

"Wondering if a man called Jacob Best might be around. Understand he and your boys are tight."

"He ain't welcome here, Corcoran. No sir. Was mighty rude to our niece, Cynthia Wilkinson. Rose ran him off." He wiped the sweat from his face. "Willy was here earlier, said something about spending the next few weeks at a cabin he and James built in the Diamonds." He spat some juice, kicked some dirt, and scowled. "Those boys have been mollycoddled by Rose from the day of their birth. Not a shred of worth to either one. Sorry, Terrence, you don't need to hear all that. I'm just really fed up with the whole bunch of them."

"Did Willy say anything else?"

"Not to me. He don't talk to me much. Got a sack of food from Rose and lit out. Wasn't here half an hour. Took most of our smoked meat and a full sack of coffee. Sold stolen cows and can't buy his own food. Worthless," the crippled old man snarled.

"Do you know where that cabin you spoke of, is? If Jacob Best is with your boys, they could be in serious trouble. Best is wanted for murder, Emil."

"Murder," he said. "My God, Terrence. Murder. Who?"

"Zack Bennett's dead and Best was shot in the fracas."

"That's why Willy was here." He was very quiet for a few seconds. "He got supplies and lied again to his mother. Zack Bennett murdered? You get that boy, Corcoran. You get him."

"Sorry about all this, Emil. Thanks for your help." Corcoran rode back to Eureka with a head full of problems. Corcoran now had Willy pegged as an associate, but didn't mention that to Emil. "At least I think I know where Jacob Best is. Biggest problem is, I don't know where where is," he laughed. "Diamond Mountains are almost a hundred miles long, ten thousand feet high, and there's a man in that long string of rocks I want bad."

James Cannon rode up to the little shack where they kept their rustled beef and found the note that Willy left him. "Jake Best ain't quite the man he wants to be," he snickered. "Got himself all shot up, eh?" He cussed when he found the empty whiskey bottle and rode out of the canyon toward their high mountain cabin. "Me and Willy have got some serious talk ahead of us, I think."

It was dark when he rode into the little pasture. He could see smoke from the chimney and two horses in the make-shift corral. "Hello, the camp," he hollered out. "It's James Cannon here."

"Glad you're here, brother. Ride on in," Willy yelled back. He stepped out of the shack with a shotgun in hand. "We got us a little problem."

"I read your note."

"It don't tell the story, James. Jake's about half dead. Let's put your horse up and we can tell our stories. What have you found out?"

"Gonna be easy stoppin' coaches in several places, with plenty of room to get away, but if Jake is all shot-up, is that gonna change everything? Is he really in that bad a shape?"

"I pulled three pieces of lead from his leg, James. He can't have much blood left in him, either. I got food from Ma but didn't tell her nothin'. If Jake hadn't been so nasty to Cynthia we coulda brought him there. Ma would know what to do."

James and Willy spent the next several days nursing Jacob Best and talking about what they looked on as their future. "It really don't matter much whether Jake lives or not," James concluded one morning over coffee. They were walking through grass and brush toward the springs, which they did when they spoke just among themselves, now that Jacob was conscious most of the time.

"We got us our hideout, we know where the coaches run and where to stop them. We don't need him. He would need us, but we don't need him." James snickered some. "Ain't like we're all partnered up. It was all of us come up with this plan but it was him got hisself all shot up."

"He tried to get out of bed last night but couldn't. That leg ain't infected but it's sure a mess." He shook his head as they wandered through the trees. He was tired of Jacob Best taking up all his time, all his effort, and now, all his talking time with his brother. He changed the subject. "There's a big sale this week, James," Willy said. "We'll leave Jake here, ride out and hit a wagon filled with rich ranchers, and ride right back here."

"We can make our decision about him after," James said. "I'm damn excited about robbing a stage coach or a wagon with a rich rancher in it." He was almost dancing, he was so primed. "Let that big time gangster in there die, Willy. We are gonna be rich."

"What if we have to shoot somebody?" Willy asked.

"They they'll die, too." James was laughing as they walked into the cabin.

"I ain't really big on shootin' somebody. I could if they was tryin' to kill me, but just to shoot a man? I won't let you down, Brother. I won't."

They spent the next few hours making their plans, James drew maps and Willy worried about shooting someone.

"You about healed enough to take care of yourself for a day or two?" Willy sat down on the side of the bed. "Me and James got some things that need to be taken care of."

"What things?" Best asked. "You runnin' off and leavin' me to die?"

"You ain't gonna die," James scoffed. More and more, James saw just how weak their friend was. Not from the wound, just weak and maybe even a coward. "There's plenty of food, even half a bottle of whiskey. Gonna move some cattle is all. We'll be back as soon as we can. You're a big boy. You can take care of yourself for a day or two." It was almost a challenge and James hoped Best would take him up on it.

Jacob Best had been a loner most of his life and wasn't the least bit worried about the boys leaving out. He was feeling a lot better than he let on. "I'll manage," he said. It never crossed his mind that the Cannon boys were about to rob a rich rancher.

James and Willy spent most of the day riding down out of the mountains and made their first stop at the sale yard holding pens near the railroad. "If we find out who's selling we'll know where best to hit 'em," James said. They scanned the yards, talked to a couple of buckaroos about the cattle already there, and rode on into Eureka.

"Best we stay at Jacob's place tonight, eat his food and drink his liquor," James snickered. "Kinkaid's got a lot of cattle in those pens, Willy. He's out of the Big Smoky Valley and has a fancy coach he and his wife ride in. He'd be an easy hit. Big old fat man. Don't think he's throwed a rope or broke a bronc in years. Let's buy some food and ride out to make ourselves ready."

"Instead of spending the night at Jake's cabin?" Willy asked and James nodded back.

James was just stepping down from his horse in front of Charley Stone's Supply and Feed store when Terrence Corcoran stepped out. "Just the boys I've been wantin' to talk to," he said. "Where would I find Jacob Best?"

"Ain't seen him in a week or more. I'd check his cabin if it was me," James said. "Excuse me," and he tried to step around the big deputy.

"Not yet, Cannon. Best murdered a man and I'm gonna get him. If I find you aren't telling me the truth, I'll include you in the charges. Now, I'll ask again. Where would I find Jacob Best?"

"I'll answer the same way, Corcoran." James Cannon stiffened at Corcoran's comments, saw fear in Willy's eyes. "Ain't seen him in more than a week. Now let me pass."

Corcoran smiled, bowed deep, and stepped aside. Cannon shrugged and stepped into Stone's shop. Corcoran's smile disappeared and he followed the boys into the large supply store. He watched them buy some things men would want on a long trail ride, things that could be easily tucked in saddlebags, like coffee, flour, sugar, and dried meat. *I think I might just want to follow those two where ever they're head-*

ing. *Too early to be meat hunting, they ain't prepared to be on a rustling adventure. Interesting.*

"Where you boys headin' for?" Charley Stone was a scrappy old guy who bought the store after being mashed up during a cattle drive a few years before. He limped bad, complained loud, and drank much. "Looks like a long ride."

"Headin' for Austin, Mr. Stone. Got some cattle to look at and there's a turquoise mine that's mighty interesting, too." James was open and friendly with the storekeeper and Corcoran was just close enough to hear. Corcoran walked back outside, almost scoffing at what he heard.

"Those fools can't fix a fence, more or less buy cattle. They sure as hell can't mine turquoise," he chuckled. He walked down the street to the sheriff's corrals and saddled Dude. "Goin' for a little ride, old man. Bet you a silver dollar it ain't gonna be Austin." He was on speaking terms with his horse, had been for years.

CHAPTER TEN

"I'll be damned," Corcoran murmured after trailing the Cannon boys for most of the day. "Maybe they are heading to Austin. Maybe Jacob Best is waiting for them in Austin." That idea made more sense than anything to do with a turquoise mine. He turned around and headed back for Eureka. "Think I'll send a wire to the Lander County Sheriff to watch for the boys and see if they lead him to Best."

"Good idea," Sheriff Connors said. "Nobody in town saw Best anywhere. He moves like a shadow, Terrence. We've got to put the clamps on him soon. If that was his first killing, those that follow get easier and easier, I've heard."

"How much further, James? We're twenty five miles or more out of town. Ain't seen no dust behind us."

"I thought that dumb deputy would follow us but I don't think he did. Kinkaid's ranch is in the Big Smoky Valley, Willy, and we'll jump him well this side of the turn off. There's some big rock formations and hills that come right down to the roadway, some miles in front of us where we can jump him. After the hit, we'll ride north for a day, then head back east to the Diamond Mountains and our hideout."

Willy had to chuckle at the comment. "Think Kinkaid will head out right after the sale?"

"Don't matter. Whenever, as long as he's rolling in money, is fine with me," James laughed. "I want to take his money and make him feel the pain of losin' it. Ain't nobody got a right to have that much money, anyway. Pa says you gotta work hard to make good money. That fat old Kinkaid couldn't work hard if you had a cattle prod workin' on him. We'll just take our share, thank you," he said.

They made up a fair camp a mile or so off the old emigrant road and worked on their plan. "Best if we come from either side of the road, Willy. That cut through those rocks is perfect for us. That way the driver would have to make a decision on which one of us to shoot, and the other one can then shoot him first."

"I still don't much care for this idea of killing someone," Willy said. "Point the gun should be enough."

"It won't be," James almost laughed at him. "One of them on or around that coach is gonna want to shoot you, so you better get it in your head to shoot first. This ain't little boy stuff, Willy. We gonna be rich and to get rich, somebody else is gonna have to die. Bet on it, brother."

Willy went under the bedroll blanket thinking about whether he would even be able to shoot someone while James was worrying the same thing. James knew he could kill, knew without a doubt, but worried about whether his big brother would let him down. James had the same worry at sunrise.

"Leg hurts but not that bad," Jacob Best murmured. He stood on the wounded leg for the first time just minutes after the boys rode out. "They better not have left me high and dry up here." He found his rifle and used it as a walking stick, and found he could move around fairly well. He limped his way to the door to make sure his horse was still in the corral, found some downed cottonwood limbs and started to work on a real walking stick.

"Maybe they aren't runnin' out on me," he muttered. Jacob spent the next two days doing as much walking as he could. He changed his bandages, used small amounts of whiskey to keep the wound clean, and watched it slowly crust over. It was during the long cold nights that he put together a new plan, one that would make him happier than he had been in years. "That little girl is gonna be mine. Her loving daddy is gonna die and so's the Cannon's mama. She called me some ugly names and he tried to shoot me. Gonna die."

He had other thoughts as well, remembering the terrible beatings he took from his father, his uncles, even some of the other boys when he tried to go to school. He wanted girls and somewhere in a dark corner of his stunted mind, believed every girl he saw wanted him to physically take them. It was when he tried that the beatings happened, and that was often. It was later he discovered that working girls didn't always complain.

His pathetic little mind was filled with the terrible things that would happen to Cynthia, particularly since she fought him off. For two days, that's all he could think of, and worked hard to make himself strong enough to ride. "I'll bring her right up here. This will be our love nest." He was laughing loud and wildly, his eyes bright, dancing, as he looked around at everything in the cabin.

"What did the Lander Sheriff say?" Ed Connor and Corcoran were standing at the bar at the Bonanza Club, late in the day.

"Said he hasn't seen the Cannon boys and there's no one in Austin that fits Best's description. I suppose they could have turned south somewhere, but they told Charley Stone they were headed for Austin. If they're up to something criminal, it's out of our jurisdiction. Going to the sale tomorrow?"

"Yeah, I am." Ed Connors drank down a glass of beer. "Heat's killing me, Terrence. Been thinkin' about what you said. You and me go in on a good lookin' steer and hang the meat in Jimmy Henderson's ice house. We'd have fresh beef for more than a year."

"Let's do that," Corcoran said. He motioned Henderson over and told him their plans.

"Well, I got a carcass fee, you know." Henderson said.

"And I got a Colt and a badge." Ed Connors tried to snarl. Several men at the bar turned when the laughter rang out.

"All right, fine," Henderson said. "Gonna be a lot of money changing hands at that sale tomorrow. Big boys are bringing cattle in from everywhere. Kinkaid from Smoky, the boys up north in the Diamond Valley. Heard they even got a herd come in from the Monitor Valley. Hope they spend some of their sale money here."

"That's just about a given," Corcoran laughed. Cindy Cook came flying out of the kitchen and threw herself at Corcoran.

"I got an elk steak this thick waiting for you, Terrence. Want beans with it?" He took her by the hand and let her lead him to a table, all set for two. "I like elk, too," she whispered. "And you, big boy." Corcoran just grinned, thinking how nice dessert would be.

"My cabin 's bigger than yours," she said. "When we get hitched up, we'll live in mine." Corcoran just smiled, didn't say a word.

Saturday arrived in sweltering heat, even at Eureka's altitude, and there wasn't a breeze of any kind to moderate things. Dust and humidity hung thick in the mountain air as buyers and sellers mingled in the sale barn, along with hundreds of head of fine Nevada beef, stirring in their pens.

"They all look mighty tasty, Corcoran," Ed Connors said. "You know more about this than I do, so you pick, but don't spend all my money."

"We'll pick one about a thousand pounds, still young and tender, Ed. I keep looking for the Cannon boys or Jacob Best. Haven't seen any of them."

"There's Emil and Rose Cannon, with Clarence Wilkinson. Let's go have a chat, shall we? They just might know something." They moved through the crowd, nodding and smiling to friends. "Morning, Emil. Rose. Nice to see you here. Adding to your herd, Emil?"

"Ain't got no herd, Ed," Emil smiled. "Three feisty heifers ain't a herd, but I might find a couple to add on."

"Hoped we might run into the Jacob Best boy while we were here," Corcoran said. "Seen him around anywhere?"

"I'll shoot him if I do," Rose Cannon said. "Said some ugly things to my pretty little niece. Vile man. Don't know why Willy and James like him. He's just the opposite of my boys. My boys would never say or do what that boy does."

"He'd already be dead if I saw him before you," Clarence Wilkinson said.

"Along with your charges, he's now wanted for murder," Ed Connors said. "Killed Zack Bennett."

Corcoran saw Emil scowl slightly at the comment. "Where are the boys? This is one of the biggest sales of the year."

"They have a camp up in the Diamond Mountains, Mr. Corcoran. They like to spend some of their summer up there." Rose smiled but Corcoran noticed it wasn't one of her energetic smiles, and her eyes certainly weren't looking at him, either.

She knows something. Maybe something that even Emil doesn't. Best is wounded bad and her boys haven't been seen for some time. Corcoran couldn't get it out of his head that the Cannon boys were tied tight to Jacob Best.

"Enjoy the sale," Connors said and steered Corcoran over to the beer bar. "Second time I've heard that."

"I wonder if that's where they do their brand altering?" Corcoran said. They watched the sale, saw fat steers sell for more than they wanted to spend, saw some ranchers leave the sale barn, smiling all the time, with fists full of money, and others, smiling for sure, spending those dollars on fine cattle. "We're in the wrong business, Ed."

"I've never in my life thought of spending that much money all at the same time." The sheriff was standing straight, slowly shaking his head. They had a couple more beers and walked back to their horses. "Looks like Sonny Kinkaid made out okay. Look at that carriage he rides in. Let's say hello." Ed Connors said.

"Somebody said he had it shipped in from New York, driver and all. Four up and all that silver work. Between his weight and all that silver, he needs four horses," Corcoran chuckled.

Sonny Kinkaid didn't ride horses because he couldn't get on one, even with a mounting block. The wealthy rancher weighed well over three hundred pounds and only stood about five feet and eight inches tall. He was a jovial man, lost his wife in a terrible accident several years ago, and devoted all his energy to making more money, which he flashed about at every opportunity.

The Eureka chapter of E Clampus Vitus, a miner's organization, held a turkey shoot every year during the county fair and Kinkaid was always one of the winners. He shot pistol, rifle, and shotgun, and was considered an expert in all of them. He had a Henry Rifle that had been hand engraved and inlaid in silver and gold. That Yellow Boy really was yelloiw.

"Get good prices, Sonny?" Ed Connors asked. "Looked like some fine stock you brought over."

"Hello, Sheriff. Nice to see you. Corcoran," he smiled. "I haven't seen you in the Smoky Valley for some time."

"Your shootin' keeps the bad guys out of there, Sonny. Nice to see you. How's Tails McGee?"

"Just as nasty as the last time you saw him. I'll tell him you asked about him. He and the crew left out about ten minutes ago."

Tails McGee was the Kinkaid Ranch cow boss and a meaner man you wouldn't want to meet. On the other hand, you couldn't have had a better man standing behind you. He and Corcoran had tried many times to drink each other under the table and there never had been a distinct winner.

"You must be working him hard if he isn't coming to town for a cold one before riding out."

"Last time you two got together I didn't see him for a week, Corcoran," Kinkaid laughed. "Looks like my man is waving me on. Once he gets those chargers in harness, all he can think of is making dust. Probably be home by dark the way he drives 'em. Tell Jimmy Henderson he ain't gettin' none of my hard earned money this time."

"I don't care how good he thinks those horses are, he ain't gettin' home until late sometime tomorrow." Corcoran shook his head. "Man's a good judge of cattle but can't tell a mile from a yard." He and Connors watched the big carriage and four pacers move quickly down the road. "Mighty pretty," Corcoran said.

"Sale should be over, Willy. Let's get up in them rocks and see who's coming by. Wouldn't it be nice if fat old Kinkaid came without his crew."

"If he does come, we got to kill him right away. He's the best shot in Central Nevada. How's best to stop 'em? Shoot the lead horses and then the driver? Ain't never robbed a coach," Willy Cannon said.

"Just like we talked," James said. Those doubts

jumped out at him. *Will he freeze up and get me killed? Willy ain't no coward, we've been in too many fights, so I know that. This ain't the time.* James's mind was in overdrive with worry. "Listen, Willy, if the driver don't stop, shoot a lead horse and then the driver. That's all you need to think about. Don't let them horses run off. Hope Kinkaid sends his crew home first. That Tails McGee is one mean bastard. We gotta kill him on sight, if he's along."

"If the whole Kinkaid crew is with the coach, we should just let it pass on by," Willy said, and James nodded his agreement. "There'd be others."

They had their horses tied close by and scrambled into the rocks to watch the trail. They could see east and west from their spot. James looked east and Willy, west. "Dust will tell us if it's a cow crew or a single coach and we'll have plenty of time to get to the horses," James said.

It was less than half an hour later that James spotted dust coming their way. "Looks to be a coach, Willy. Let's move. You get on the other side of the road. We ride out giving the driver plenty of time to see us and pull his team up. No witnesses, Willy. Pull your kerchief up and talk all growly." The anticipation of so much money coming his way made him almost giddy.

CHAPTER ELEVEN

"You sure you want to ride up here in the dust, Mr. Kinkaid. Be nicer in the coach." Seamus O'Reilly had been driving Sonny Kinkaid for more than five years and knew all the talk in the world wouldn't change the man's mind. He reached down and gave the large man a help stepping up into the driver's seat. "Suppose you want to drive, some," Seamus chuckled.

Kinkaid was huffing hard when he took the reins and urged the four big horses out of the sale pens and yards. "I've always loved to drive, Seamus. Feeling the power of those wheelers when they move out, and the cadence once they hit their stride." Sonny Kinkaid had a broad smile across his red face, and urged the horses on. "We'll make thirty miles before we stop for the night, Seamus."

Seamus chuckled, thinking they'd be lucky to make twenty, as late as they were starting out. "We'll use water and grass to guide us, Sonny, not distance. There's an outcrop, a pass, we have to go through and a springs just beyond that. Good water and grass for the horses, Mr. Kinkaid."

Sonny Kinkaid was good for about an hour on the reins, maybe a little more, and he pulled the teams to a halt. "Time for my nap, Seamus," he laughed. He never admitted he didn't have the energy for any more, but his nap was most important. O'Reilly helped him down and got him into the carriage.

Sonny opened a bottle of whiskey and took a deep draught. He smiled at his long-time driver. "Let's go home, Seamus. Let's go home." O'Reilly knew the old man would be fast asleep in minutes and found his seat, gathered the reins, and urged the four-up into a solid trot.

It was several hours later when Seamus saw the road through the outcrop of rocks. "Good," he muttered. "We'll have a good camp with fair grass and cold water."

He had the horses in a comfortable trot as he neared the rocks. Two men wearing masks rode out, one on each side of the road, and motioned him to stop. Seamus made an instant decision and whipped the horses into a hard gallop. He fumbled under the seat for his shotgun. The man on Seamus's left pulled his rifle up and shot one of the lead horses, causing the other horses to stumble, one falling, the others getting tangled in their tack.

A second rifle shot killed O'Reilly. Sonny Kinkaid was thrown to the floor of the carriage by the wreck and slowly pulled himself back to the seat. James Cannon threw the door open and shot Kinkaid as the man tried to get seated. Cannon jumped from his horse and struggled to get Kinkaid's body out of the carriage. It took three tries before the rotund rancher tumbled out and onto the ground.

Willy grabbed the reins from James' horse while James worked his way through Kinkaid's pockets. "Lots of cash here, Willy. Must be more inside." He jumped in the carriage and opened Kinkaid's valise and one other case. "More cash here. We did it, Willy." He stuffed everything in the valise and jumped onto his horse. It was a mess in the middle of a well-used road and they needed to leave at once.

"Let's ride north, cross-country, until dark before we make camp. Somebody could come along on this road at any time." James led out and Willy was right with him. "Probably at least two hours before dark." The summer sun stayed up a long time and there was always a lingering sunset. They rode at a strong lope until their horses tired and walked them before resuming the lope. A stand of locust trees stood out on the valley floor and James led them toward the trees.

Most of the mountain ranges in Nevada run north and south with valleys in between, often featuring streams fed by snowmelt or natural springs. Springs in the middle of the valleys could be spotted because of cottonwood and other big green trees.

"Looks like old holding corrals and a shack, Willy." They rode up on a run-down cabin, all but turning to dust, sitting in the grove of locust trees. "Ain't nobody been here for a long time. Let's get a fire going. I'm hungry enough to eat a bear." There was nothing in what was left of the rotting cabin, but others passing by had built up a nice fire ring. It was obvious that more than one buckaroo had slept under the inviting trees.

Willy was a little slow getting the horses taken care of, even slower gathering wood for the fire. "What's the matter with you?" James asked.

"You just pulled that rifle up and shot those two men, James. I ain't never seen anybody killed before. I'm kinda sick, I think." He walked slowly over behind one of the large trees, holding his stomach. James could hear him retching, and went to get firewood himself.

"Better get used to it, brother. We've never seen

this kind of money in all our lives, and it took us less than ten minutes to get it." He had a small fire going and a pot of coffee simmering in a matter of minutes.

"We gotta leave out of here well before dawn, Willy. We'll ride more north in the morning, swing east through Coyote Canyon in the Cortez Range, and then across the valley and into the Diamonds. It'll be hard for anyone to follow and we can ride on south, high in the mountains, to our cabin."

Willy wrapped himself in a blanket, despite the summer heat, and settled in by the fire. "You're supposed to be my big brother," James scoffed. "You're acting like a little girl. How many hogs have you slaughtered? How many steers and lambs? Ain't no different. Hell, Willy, you didn't have to clean 'em or skin 'em." He was laughing as he added more wood to the fire. "Let's eat and get some shut-eye."

"You eat, James. I'm gonna stare at the fire and then sleep." He wondered if James was right. Sure, he'd put many animals down, cleaned the carcass and cut it for curing, but this was different. He knew what the difference was. They killed two living, breathing, human beings. Rose saw to it the boys had at least seen a bible, and Willy knew he had committed the most serious crime he knew about.

My God, what have we done.

Riders from Jim Baker's Sleepy P ranch in the Monitor Valley spotted the wreckage in the middle of the roadway from half a mile out. "Somebody's in trouble," Miles Jackson said. "Let's help," he called out. The four buckaroos spurred their horses into a solid run and were on the scene quickly.

"That's Sonny Kinkaid's rig," Jackson hollered. They found the horses still tangled and the one horse, dead. Sonny Kinkaid's body was sprawled in the dirt at the side of the road while Seamus's body was still in the driver's boot. "Jason," Jackson called out. "Ride as hard as you can for Eureka and bring the sheriff. Antonio, look for sign."

Jackson, foreman at the Sleepy P was off his horse and going through Kinkaid's pockets. "They cleaned old fatso to the bone," he chuckled. "Wonder why that fool didn't have at least some of his crew with him?" He stuck his head inside the carriage and found the empty wallet and strong box. "That fancy hand-tooled leather valise of his is gone."

"Damn fool, if you ask me," Francisco Almeida said. "I think Antonio found some fresh prints leading off north. Looks like two horses going straight up the valley. He's following and we can catch up as soon as the sheriff gets here."

"No," Miles Jackson said. "No. Old man Peterson's gonna need us back at the ranch. Let Castro follow and the sheriff can catch up with him. We need to get back to the ranch and then send someone to let Tails McGee know he doesn't have a boss anymore. Let's get the road cleared, get the horses loose from their harness. We'll bring 'em with us. We better get these two buried. They'll sour fast in this heat."

It was a hard, fast ride back to Eureka for Jason Whipple. The older buckaroo spent most of his time around the barns anymore, not chasing young, feisty steers, or breaking strong colts. He was in more of a sweat than his horse when he jumped from the saddle in front of the sheriff's office.

"Sheriff," he yowled, rushing into the office. "Old Kinkaid's been kilt and robbed. You gotta come."

"Easy now, Jason. Here, sit down." Ed Connors poured the man a solid glass of whiskey and motioned for Corcoran, working on some reports, to join them. "Nice and slow, now, Mr. Whipple. What happened?"

Whipple drank the glass of whiskey in two long swallows and got himself settled some. "We was ridin' back to the Sleepy P when we come on the Kinkaid's carriage. Old Sonny was shot up and dead along with Seamus O'Reilly, too. One of their horses was shot up, too. About twenty miles out, maybe."

"Corcoran, ride out. I'll send out wires and me and Mr. Whipple will follow."

"On my way," Corcoran said. He kept his horse, Dude, in the corrals out back and was saddled and on the road in minutes. Dude was a big strong ranch horse and Corcoran set him in a hard trot, eating those miles with ease.

"Never could understand that man," Corcoran muttered. "Riding out with pockets full of cash money, and nobody to ride guard. Damn fool in my mind. Tails McGee ain't gonna like this."

It was late in the day when Corcoran rode up to the wreck. Jackson and Almeida had the bodies buried, the horses untangled, and the carriage moved off to the side of the road. "Nice to see you again, Corcoran," Jackson said. "Kinkaid took two rounds and O'Reilly got hit twice, too. Not a piece of eight left, either."

"Antonio found some prints leading north," Almeida said. "I'll show you. He's following now." Corcoran followed him to where the Cannon brothers and Antonio Castro rode north.

"Can you wait for Sheriff Connors?" Corcoran asked Miles Jackson. "I know you want to get back to the ranch, but I want to get a good start on this chase before the dark stops me."

"We'll wait," Jackson said. "We'll get word to Tails McGee, too. Chase 'em down and kill 'em hard, Corcoran. Never did like Sonny and all his talking about money, but I don't like what happened, either."

"Thanks, Miles. Hope Tails will catch up, too." Corcoran mounted Dude and set off cross-country, following the well-marked trail. "Shouldn't be hard to follow these tracks," he murmured. It was twilight and Corcoran knew he would run out of light soon. "Get a handle on where these jaspers are heading, anyway. If it were me, I'd run like the devil for Palisade."

Castro had been chasing cows through the great Nevada range lands for years and put his horse in a hard trot, following an easy trail. The Cannon brothers hadn't tried to hide their trail in any way, and Castro finally had to give up because of darkness. He dug a little hole, filled it with ripped up sage and sat by a small fire, letting some dried meat and hard biscuits soften up in hot coffee.

"They can't go, either, in this dark." He chuckled. The stars were bright on a hot summer night, but there was no moon to help. "I'll catch up in the morning." He was asleep in minutes and up before the eastern sky started to lighten. Cold water, cold biscuits, and Antonio Castro was in the saddle. He hadn't ridden five miles when he saw the flickering light of a campfire in the distance.

"Damn fools," he muttered. "That looks like an invite to me." He rode as close as he dared and dismounted to carefully move in on the killers. He scrambled quietly from sage to sage, from stunted cedar to piñon pine, sometimes on his belly, mostly at a crouch. He watched James Cannon put some more wood on the fire. "There should be two," Castro said. He looked around and couldn't see Willy. "Both horses are there, where is number two?"

He was too far out for his sidearm to be that effective, and crawled, ever so quiet, to within thirty yards of so of the fire. He pulled his revolver and slowly pulled down on James Cannon, who was filling his coffee cup.

Castro probably never heard the shot nor felt the bullet that ripped through his head. Willy stood ten yards to his side, his pants still down around his ankles. "There's a sight I hope I never see again," James Cannon laughed right out. "Thank you, big brother. I owe you big time on this one. Let's get moving. If there's one, there might be more. Let's ride, brother."

"Why was he here?" Willy asked. "I looked up and there he was, looking to shoot you dead. Who is he?"

"Probably with a crew and they rode up on Kinkaids's wreck. Let's hustle, big brother, there's sure to be more."

They saddled and rode off, leaving the fire burning but bringing the coffee pot and tin cups. "We gotta change our plans and make tracks for the Cortez Range, James. We can cut across that range and into the Diamond Valley quick. You wanted to use Coyote Canyon, but we'd be best to go cross country. It's too easy for them to follow us down here in the valley."

"Hard not to leave good tracks for someone to follow. Wish we were in rocks. Well, we will be," James said. They turned east and made a straight line run for the towering Cortez Range and were in the rolling foothills in a couple of hours. The foothills became steep rocky mountains fast.

"Let's find that south mine road, Willy. Remember where it is?"

"Yeah, but we gotta climb clear to the top and over to find it. That mine is high but on the east face. It's a good road as I remember it." Willy had tears running down his face as they rode.

"Enough traffic on that trail that we can shake anyone following," James said. He saw the tears coursing through dust and dirt and wondered just what his brother was thinking. "Use the mine road into the valley, and jump into the Diamond Mountains. We can dodge our way along the high country to our cabin. Are you crying?"

"I just killed a man, James. I saw him crawl through the dirt while I was doing my business, saw him take a bead on you, and killed him."

They were riding at a steady climb, making switchbacks, wending their way through standing groves of tall trees. Around felled timber. Willy was sitting straight in the saddle, but his head was lowered.

"You saved my life, Willy. Don't never forget that. I know I won't."

"I ain't never gonna forget that, James. But I ain't gonna be able to forget what I did, neither. Gonna haunt me, some."

"Think of the money that's in our pockets, brother. That'll cure your haunts," James chuckled. Willy didn't. Willy knew he had to shoot the man or watch his brother die, and, he knew that it was because they killed those two at the coach that was why the man was there in the first place.

"I'm trying, James. Where will we go? Can't stick around here. Not after what we done."

"Ain't no way anyone would know it was us killed old Kinkaid, Willy. We get back to our little cabin and talk about this. Gotta keep movin'." He said.

There were several mining operations in the Cortez Range, a big one north toward Palisade, and another, lesser mine, to the south. It was that mine they were heading for. The South Mine had a well-graded road they used to bring their ore to the railroad in the valley. It was steep, had terrible switchbacks, but was kept up by the mine. There would be enough traffic that the two riders' prints would probably be hidden in a matter of hours.

"You think there was someone with that Mexican?" Willy asked.

"Hope we never know," James said. "You made a mess of yourself last night over me killing those men and taking their money. And this morning, big brother, you simply dropped your trousers and killed a man. You all right? You got nothin' to cry about." He was laughing as they rode hard into the steep slopes of the Cortez Mountains.

"I was doing my business, James. He just showed up and was gonna shoot you. I didn't even think, just shot him."

"Shot him dead, you did. When we cross the ridge up there, the mine road should be about twenty miles to our southeast. Maybe another two ridges and then the crest of the range. Let's ease off on the horses. This is steep country and I ain't walkin'."

CHAPTER TWELVE

"Gotta give it up for tonight, Dude. Can't see the trail. There's good grass for you, old boy. We'll start off in the morning." He hobbled the big stud and had some water and cold biscuits before crawling in his bedroll. He was up as light filtered through morning clouds, and had the same meal to start the day.

"A little easier to see when it's light, eh old man?" He chuckled as he mounted the horse and continued following the three distinct horse prints. Nothing had moved through this valley except wild animals for a long time. It was a cold morning and Corcoran was thankful for no wind. As the day blossomed, he could see threats of thunder heads building over the ranges, east and west. "Might get wet later today, big boy. Gotta catch these bastards before the rains come." Corcoran was well aware that rain would wash out the fresh tracks.

The trail moved through undulating desert floor, peppered with stands of pine and stunted cedar, acres of sage, and deep arroyos created by flash floods. "Looks like an old cabin or line shack out there," he muttered. The prints led right up to the cabin and the already rotting body of Antonio Castro.

Corcoran took the necessary time to bury Castro, found his horse and checked the saddle bags, taking the dried meat, biscuits, and coffee for himself. He unsaddled the horse so he could bring it along. It never hurts, on what might be a long chase, to have a second mount. "These boys ain't afraid of killing," Corcoran muttered. "And they've got one damn billfold full of cash money. They just don't know how close to meeting that old fire-tending bastard down below they are," he chuckled.

He noticed the change in direction immediately. "They're going to cross the Cortez," he muttered. "I expected them to ride north toward Palisade. Maybe they aren't road agents. Maybe they're local boys gone bad. If they know that range, know where the South Mine is, they could get on that road and get lost fast. Damn," he said. "First the rain, now a well-used road. Gotta catch 'em before either of them. Can't be that far in front of me."

Sheriff Ed Connors and Jason Whipple rode up to the robbery scene well after dark and were flagged down by Miles Jackson. "Glad you made it, Sheriff. Nasty business. We buried Kinkaid and his driver over there and will take his horses back with us."

"Corcoran on the trail? Which way?"

"Rode out north, Sheriff. My man, Antonio Castro was already on their trail. Just two men did this. All Kinkaid had to do was have a couple of hands riding with him. Damn old fool, if you ask me."

Ed Connors just shook his head. He agreed with what Jackson said but didn't want to come right out and say so. "You're headin' back to the Sleepy P?"

"Yup. We'll get word to Tails McGee. Let's get rollin' boys," Jackson hollered out. "Keep us informed, will you? I'm sure old man Peterson will want to know."

"Sure will, Mike. Ride easy, it's a dark night."

"Open road like this ain't hard to ride on at night, Sheriff."

Ed Connors agreed with that as he stood in the middle of the old emigrant trail, watching the three buckaroos trotting off. "No sense in trying to catch up with Corcoran and that Sleepy P rider," he mused. He stepped into the saddle and rode slowly back toward Eureka. "North, eh? Probably heading for Palisade. I'll send more wires when I get back."

"Old Willy must be a pretty good doctor," Jacob Best chuckled, putting more weight on his wounded leg. "Oh, that does hurt," he said, leaning heavy on his walking stick. "Wonder if I can even get on a horse?" Best had been able to hold in the anger but it wouldn't hold for much longer. Every step he managed hurt like hell and he blamed everyone and everything around him for that pain.

His leg went out from under him and he crashed into the table and onto the floor, cussing loud and long. He broke a chair trying to get back on his feet, and in his anger smashed it over and over onto the table. He all but fell into the other chair, breathing hard, sweat pouring from his face. "That old man shot me and I'm glad he's dead."

The Cannon brothers had been gone for three days and Best had changed the dressing, used the walking stick, and done everything he could to be fit. There were times he could limp and stumble all the way to the corral. There were other times he couldn't make it across the cabin floor.

There was plenty of food in the cabin, water close by, and at that altitude, little summer heat. The heat

Best felt had nothing to do with seasons. "I'm gonna get that little girl. I'm gonna kill her big old tough daddy and take her for mine."

Using the walking stick he hobbled out to the corral and brought his gelding out. Getting the saddle on and cinched down wasn't as difficult as he thought it would be, but Jacob knew getting on the horse would be painful and hard. To put his foot in the stirrup meant putting all his weight and then some, on the wounded leg. His first try brought a cry of pain and he almost fell down.

"Gotta do this. Can't get that gal otherwise. Gotta," he cried, trying again. He spent every night having fantasies about little Cynthia Wilkinson, to the point he knew he had to be able to ride. He had to ride to the Wilkinson home and get that girl. She was his, she just didn't know it yet. "I gotta get on the horse." This time he held tight to the saddle horn, not putting all his weight on the wounded leg. Holding tight he lifted his good foot into the stirrup and swung himself into the saddle, just fine.

"I knew I could do it," he muttered. "I can do anything. I killed that man who cheated me, I'll kill that whore if she gets mouthy, too. But, I can ride a horse and that's the only thing that's important right now."

He rode around the corral for a few turns, trotted the horse, loped him gently, and reached down and opened the gate. "This is the real test," he said, touching heels to the horse, and rode off through the trees for an hour. Coming back, his leg ached but the bandages held, there was no bleeding, and he stepped down the same way he mounted, using the saddle to hold him. "A couple of days to get my strength, and Cynthia, baby girl, you'll be all mine." He had a horrible leer spread across his face.

"We cross that ridge up there, Willy, and we should see the South Mine road. I keep looking behind us and haven't seen a speck of dust."

"Me, too," Willy said. "What I do see is thunder heads building in. It's gonna unload on us, James. Think we should hole up somewhere?"

"Hell no," James said. "Best thing that could happen. We make for the road and let it pour, Brother, let it pour. Wipe out any trace we were within a hunnert miles of here. No, Willy, we ride for that ridge and get on that road."

It was a steep three mile climb to the ridge, switchback after switchback, great stands of stunted trees, boulders the size of barns, and when they reached the summit and looked out across the top of the Cortez Range, the first few drops of rain began to spatter their dusty clothes. They untied their dusters and were laughing as they got them on.

"Road should be just a few miles that way," James said. The ride down from the sawtooth ridge was steep for the first mile and then leveled out some. "Be glad to ride on a real road, Willy. This cross country riding takes it out of me."

"Being as rich as you are, you're just gettin' soft, is all," Willy laughed. They rode through a stand of tall pines and fir and saw the mine two miles down from where they were. Threading through trees, outcrops of huge rocks, and a gully or two, the men rode their horses onto the mine road. The wind was howling and the rain came in sheets within minutes. As they passed the gates to the mine property, a train of three large ore wagons, each with six up, made its way toward the road.

"My God, we are the lucky one's today, Willy. Let's make sure they are behind us. They'll wipe out our prints in nothing flat." They rode at a solid trot for the next several hours, only slowing to a walk to let their horses catch their breath. The long day was coming to an end when they made the final descent into the Diamond Valley and trotted out onto the Eureka-Palisade highway. Thunder and lightning were their constant companions along with heavy, cold summer rain.

"Let's camp at Wolf Creek, James. There's a good outcrop of rocks we can get under and good grass for the horses." They followed the main north-south road for three miles before turning onto the trail that led them to Wolf Creek. "We'll be dry and warm, and this trail will lead up high up in the morning."

"I like the dry part," James laughed. "Do you think Jake will be alive when we get back to the hideout?"

"In a way, I hope not," Willy said. "Sometimes he scares me. Don't much like sayin' that, but he does. Will he want a share of what we took?"

"He can want all he wants, Willy. He ain't gettin' any. The way I see it, he might have helped thinking up the idea of holding up wagons but we did it. He can suck hind tit if he thinks I'm giving him any of mine."

"He won't like that but I'll back your play all the way," Willy said.

Corcoran was hours behind the Cannon boys and didn't seem to be getting closer. He was pushing Dude, but climbing up through the rugged Cortez Range was difficult at best, and riding cross country, trying to stay on their trail, made it more difficult. "Whoever it is I'm following, knows this country well. They're working their way toward the South Mine, and sure as hell if they hit that main road before I catch up, I'll lose 'em for sure."

He was making a tough climb toward a sawtooth ridge when the storm let loose. Hurricane strength wind ripped through rock outcrops, and cold rain came in torrents. Corcoran got into his duster quickly and continued the chase. Over the ridge and down through rocky outcrops and stands of trees, and the deputy saw the mine, off a few miles.

"Damn, damn," he cursed, knowing the killers were probably moving at a fast trot on a well graded roadway. "With all the mine traffic, I'll lose 'em for sure." He saw muddy remnants of their tracks move out onto the roadway and as he passed the entrance to the mine property, he saw the tracks of multiple horses and wagons.

"Well, Dude, this chase is over. Let's go home." He stayed on the mine road all the way down to the valley floor and looked for a spot to camp. He found an outcrop off the road half a mile or so, and made camp. "Sheriff won't like this report," he said. He had a good fire going under a rock overhang, and felt the storm begin to ease up. "I wonder where those killers are from? They knew enough to hit old man Kinkaid when his pockets were full, so does that mean they are from Eureka? Or discovered the fact because they were at the sale?"

Corcoran struggled with too many questions and not enough answers until it was seriously dark. The rain had stopped, thunder and lightning moved off, and he finished his supper of smoked elk warmed in hot coffee. "I was thinking of looking for horse prints leading into the Diamond Mountains in the morning, but with the rain we had, that would be foolish. I don't like to be outfoxed like this."

Corcoran rode hard, spent too much time berating himself, but watched the sides of the road all the way. The rain the day before wiped out all traces of men and animals and the only prints he was able to pick out were either from late the night before or early that morning.

"Amazing how much timing plays in one's life, isn't it Mr. Dude? We ran out of daylight the night of the robbery and that put us well behind in our chase yesterday, which gave the thunderstorm a chance to end our chase." The thoughts wouldn't go away and it wasn't a pleasant ride.

He moved at a brisk trot through the day. "It's pretty clear to me that whoever those killers are, I probably know them. They almost have to be local. Jacob Best? I don't think so, with that shot up leg of his. My intuition tells me it's the Cannon boys but that's such a big step for them to take."

The idea of the boys being rowdy trouble makers one day and outright killers the next was more than Corcoran would accept. "Of course, if it was them and Best doing the fires and robbing people," he murmured, and let the thought just hang in the air. "Emil's the one that will hurt the most if it is them. Rose will blame everyone but them, but Emil will think because of his injury he was never the father he could have been."

CHAPTER THIRTEEN

"Afternoon, Ed," Corcoran said, stepping into the office. Corcoran's normal blustery self wasn't evident in his greeting. "Hope you have more to report than I do. One of Peterson's crew was killed when he chased the killers down, and they managed to get across the Cortez Range before I could catch up. Damn rain washed out any chance of following a trail."

"Afraid you've got more than I," the sheriff said. "Just the two men? Planned out well, I'd say. Do you think they specifically pinpointed Kinkaid? According to Jimmy D, he had a lot of money from the sale."

"I don't know, Ed. That cut in the mountain where they hit the carriage is a perfect spot, and it has been well known for some time that Kinkaid carries a lot of money. My mind keeps leading me back to Jacob Best and the Cannon brothers. Can't get them out of my mind. The Cannon boys have never been anything more than trouble makers, but Best? That's a whole new story. He's a killer and he's wounded. My mind keeps telling me there should have been three men to attack Kinkaid, too. Maybe the third man couldn't because he was wounded."

"Interesting theory, Terrence, except for a couple of things. You said the Cannon boys are just trouble makers. The two you were chasing are cold blooded killers. The auction yard manager said that Kinkaid might have had as much as five thousand dollars on him when he rode out in that fine carriage. We'll have to watch for some high spenders."

"I'm gonna clean up and make my rounds. Since you haven't said anything, I assume there's been no sightings of Jacob Best."

"Nary a one," Sheriff Connors said. "Or of the Cannon brothers. Fits into your theory, eh?" Connors shook his head, poured another coffee and settled down at the desk. "Haven't heard back from the Elko County Sheriff, either, since his first wire. Think I'll send him a reminder."

"Tough riding, Willy. We'll make the cabin by dark, though." The boys were riding along close to the peaks of the Diamond Range, on no kind of a trail.

They followed game trails when they went the same way, but other than that, they were wending their way cross-country through extremely difficult terrain. Groves of trees so thick they had to go around, broken and felled trees littering open spaces, and magnificent stands of solid granite standing in their way.

"It would suit me fine if we just keep riding, James. I ain't as good with numbers as you are, but when you counted all that cash money out, there's enough for us to just move on out of this territory. Go to a big city. Ain't never seen nothing bigger than Elko, myself."

James was laughing as they maneuvered their way around a great outcrop of rocks, working to cross over a busted up ridge. "There's two or three more big sales this year, Willy. If we get one more hit like this one, we can buy Elko. You're right, though. Traveling just might be in our future." They rode in silence, working their way through the tumbled rocks and over the ridge.

"I ain't thinking about a three way split with Jake," Willy said. "Even though it was partly his plan. I don't trust him, either. He said he knifed that old drunk, but he didn't kill him right away since he got hisself all shot up. Maybe his idea of robbing a rancher after the auctions, but it was us that did it."

"We'll just see how it plays out, Willy. Don't get all riled about something that might not even come up. Besides, as badly wounded as he is, we'd just shoot him and get it over with."

"Still get a bad stomach thinking about that," Willy murmured. "You killed two men and I've killed one. I don't like it, James. I don't."

"Had to be done, Willy. Sure couldn't leave one of those men alive to tell the sheriff who we were. And, big brother, if you hadn't killed that feller, I'd be dead. Had to be done." Willy didn't say anything as they pressed on.

The day would have been a hot one if they had been down in the valley, but riding well above seven thousand feet, it was comfortable. They took a break about mid-day, watched thunder clouds build to their west and north, and decided to make as much of the good weather as they could.

"Might be another night out, James. Doesn't bother me at all. I could spend the rest of my life like this."

"And you'd welcome the winter, I suppose," James laughed. "No, I want some of the better things I've heard about. Big old beds, somebody serving me food and drink, silks and wools. You can have your mountains, Willy. I want a big city and more gold than I can carry. You're not having second thoughts on all this, are you?"

"Not about the gold, no, but I don't want to be known as a killer. Robbing some rich old guy doesn't bother me at all. I don't like the killin'."

Jacob Best floundered around in the mud after he rode back up to the cabin late in the afternoon. He still had a hard time mounting and dismounting his horse, and in a torrential downpour, the saddle leather was slick and the mud was too. His hand slipped while getting off the horse, the walking stick skidded out from under him in the mud, and down he went.

The words that echoed through the copse of trees surrounding the little cabin were as ferocious as the thunder and lightning. Jacob tried to get back on his feet, the rain pounded, thunder rattled anything that would move, and the lightning made him cringe. With help from the walking stick and a stirrup hanging down, he managed to get back on his feet. He was covered in mud that was slowly being washed off by the pounding rain.

"Better be some whiskey left," he said. There was anger, for sure, but what flooded his thoughts even more was the humiliation of falling on his face, even if no one was there to see it. He stumbled into the cabin and got a fire lit, put some coffee on, and found a bottle in the cupboard. Dressed in clean pants and shirt, wet ones hanging near the fire, Best calmed himself with a glass of whiskey. His leg ached from falling in the mud but he was pleased with the ride he made. "Just another few days and I'll be fine." While he had his pants off, he sat near the stove and cleaned the wound again. There was no sign of infection and it didn't hurt that much when he poured some whiskey on the wound.

For several days, his only thoughts had been on capturing Cynthia Wilkinson and the pleasures he would enjoy, but with the rain pounding the cabin's roof and the wood stove showing red in its iron, thoughts of Willy and James crept in. "Wonder if those two young idiots pulled it off? Willy ain't got a piece of smart in him and James thinks he's smarter than anyone. It would be a wonder if they made the attack even," he said.

"If I'm gonna have that girl, I gotta have money and that means working with those two for a few jobs, if they're still alive." He had to snicker. "Still alive? Yeah, there's that. We'll have to play those cards as they're dealt, I think. It's been several days since the sale, so if they ain't dead or in jail, they should show up soon."

Morning came as bright and warm as spring at that high altitude, instead of the blazing summer in the valley. Jacob was outside trying his best to chop wood. He couldn't put as much weight on his bad leg as was needed, and the job was slow and sloppy. He got a couple of arm loads inside and was taking a break, sitting in the sun, when he heard riders approaching.

He hobbled as fast as he could to the cabin and grabbed his shotgun when the two men rode in. "Far enough," Jacob yelled out. "What do you want"

"Just passing through," one of the men yelled out. "Looking for elk or deer, didn't know the camp was here. We'll circle wide. Didn't mean to bother you, none," the man said. Best watched the two move out and around the camp and continue on up the side of the mountain.

He cradled the scattergun in the crook of one arm, and using the walking stick, limped out of the cabin. He realized just how dangerous his situation was. "I can't stand without that stick. I gotta lean on something. I can't shoot this damn gun without using both hands." He hobbled to his log chair and sat down, humiliated again and cussing softly.

"I ain't as ready as I thought I was," he mumbled. He spent the next few hours trying to stand without the walking stick, and trying to manipulate the shotgun with just one hand. "Sure as hell ain't gonna let anyone know about this problem."

It was late in the day, more thunder storms threatening the evening skies, when James and Willy rode in. Jacob heard them coming and scuttled into the cabin and stood at the open door, his handgun at the ready. "Hold up, there," he hollered. "What do you want?"

"It's James and Willy," James hollered back. "Don't shoot."

"Come on in," Jacob yelled out. "Been expecting you. Bring money, did you?"

Willy and James looked at each other, knowing the argument they feared would definitely be taking place a little later. "Some," James said. "Hope you got some food in that old cabin better than dried bull meat."

CHAPTER FOURTEEN

"I know that's the way Sonny Kinkaid handled his money, the way he flaunted it about, made him a natural target, Sheriff, but I also know that the ranchers, the buyers and sellers, who come to my auctions, need to feel safe. Just what are you doing to catch those killers?" The stockyards owner, James D. Autry, called Jimmy D by his friends, was worried about the next sale, scheduled for Saturday.

"Kinkaid and old Seamus being murdered, right out there on the road, has the ranching community plenty worried, Sheriff. I gotta tell 'em something."

Ed Cannon knew this was coming and knew that he had nothing to tell Autry. "We're working hard on this, Jimmy D. My best answer to the ranchers when they come to the sale is to not travel alone. Ride with their crews, if they have a crew, or create a crew. Kinkaid made himself a target and the outlaws took advantage of it."

Cannon and Autry were sitting at a table in the Bonanza Club, enjoying Jimmy Henderson's free lunch. Cold meats and cheeses, warm fresh bread, and cold beer. Buy the beer, get the lunch. "Just like they do in New York City," Henderson told people when he began the practice. He read about free lunches somewhere and loved the idea. He said it works well in Denver, too.

"Corcoran has a couple of ideas he's working on, we have our eyes and ears open, Jimmy D, but that was a well-planned operation. Those ranchers need to know they are targets when they carry large sums of money around without protection."

"I know you're right," Autry said, "I just don't like it." Autry spotted Corcoran coming in the swinging bat wings and called him over. "Good to see you," he said.

"Hello, Jimmy D. You expecting to get those really good prices this week, again? Priced old Ed and me right out of the market."

"Always hopin' for that," Autry said. "We're talking about the buyers and sellers bein' worried because of Kinkaid's killing. Got any leads on the killers?"

"Just ideas right now," Corcoran said. "Did you tell him what we discussed, Ed?"

Connors nodded. "Yup. They need to ride with protection. These are long lonely roads out here and it ain't hard to hijack a coach or single rider. The railroad stopped stage coach robberies, for the most part, on the road north, but the east-west road is wide open to attacks. I'd have to have a hundred deputies and it wouldn't be enough."

"I'll put notices up," Autry said, "and spread the word about protection. Catch those bastards, Sheriff. Catch 'em and hang 'em high. Three good people in the ranching community are dead because of them."

Autry left for the stockyards and Corcoran stayed at the table with Sheriff Connors. "He's right and the ranchers have every right to be frightened. We can't do a damn thing more than what we're doing. Hasn't been a single sighting of the Cannon brothers or of Jacob Best. Sale's tomorrow, Ed. We better be there."

"Planned to be, Corcoran. Sent another wire to Elko yesterday. Interesting that we're not getting any response. Sheriff up there's usually helpful."

He was about to say something more when two big, burly ranchers and a half-dozen buckaroos came into the saloon. "Sheriff Connors," the largest of the two said, "just the man we want to see. I'm Fred Garrett from the Rockin' M and this here's Ornery Pike, my foreman. I'm head of the Diamond Valley Cattlemen, and I've got a poke of five hundred dollars as a reward for the capture of the men what busted up old man Kinkaid." He flipped a buckskin pouch, apparently filled with double eagles, onto the table. The thud could be heard throughout the saloon.

"We're puttin' up posters all over town and we'll put 'em up at the stockyards, too. Thieving cowards need to be hung, Sheriff. This might make someone talk a bit, eh?"

"It just might, Garrett. It just might," Connors said. Corcoran hefted the pouch and needed two hands to do it.

"We need to talk about another job, boys," Jacob Best said. They were in the cabin sharing the last of the bottle. "You did good on that job, but we need to make another couple of hits, make enough money to get the hell out of this dump of a town. Go somewhere that's got lots of money and women."

"You might want to tell me more about this we stuff, Jake," James said. "You can't walk across the floor. How you gonna rob a stage coach or stop a rancher with a few buckaroos to back him up? Ain't no we, Jake. It's us, me and Willy." James was standing near the stove, Willy was sitting on a chair that was pulled back from the table, and Jake was sitting at the table, such that he was off to the side but at an angle between the boys. Jake saw determination in James' eyes, and saw his predicament of being in the middle of a crossfire.

"Thought we was partners," Jake said. His voice was low and slow, and his hand was easing close to his sidearm. "Planned all this together. Thought we were a crew."

"Talked some, we did," Willy said. He got to his feet and walked over to stand near James. "Talk ain't doin'. Me and James did, Jake. You got yourself all shot up on a personal problem and didn't do nothin'."

"You can't just walk in here and cut me out." He almost pleaded. The anger rose, coupled with humiliation, but he also fully understood that those two Cannon boys could gun him down in an instant. "I can ride," he cried out. "I can shoot. It is our plan, not just yours. We can hit that weekly stage coach that runs to Austin, we can hit the ranchers leaving the auctions. We're a crew."

Jacob Best needed money and would grovel to get these boys to help him. He would drop them in an instant if circumstances were different, but right at that moment, he needed them. How could he run off with little Cynthia Wilkinson if he didn't have money? How could he get money if he didn't have them?

"I'm a big part of this and you know it," he said.

He wanted to pull that hog leg and shoot both boys three times each, but saw their hands touching their guns, saw determination in their eyes, and reverted to being the coward he was. Intimidation is the weapon of bullies and cowards. If they don't have the advantage, they sink into the slime they're from. "We're supposed to be a crew," he almost begged.

Willy looked over to James for guidance. It was always that way. Willy might be the older but James was the leader, the smarter one. He shrugged, looked over to Jacob, back to James, but never said a word. James had just a hint of a smile working its way across his young face and stepped over to Jacob.

"Not this time, Jake. Pack your gear and get out. It's just me and Willy from now on." He had his hand on the handle of his Colt, his legs were slightly spread, and an angry look was in his eyes. "If you're too crippled to pack, just ride on out without packin', then. We don't need you, Jake."

The silence in the small cabin lasted for many moments. Jacob Best sat at the table and knew he didn't have a play. They had him between them again, he was mostly crippled, and he wanted to kill those boys bad. He wanted Cynthia, needed money, and could feel all of that slipping away. Was it always going to be this way? Every time he thought he was on the road to gold and riches, somebody would jerk the chair out from under him.

Raging anger flowed in one direction and the bile of cowardice had a nasty ebb to it as Jacob Best sat glaring at the two smug young outlaws. "I'll leave, boys, but don't put yourselves in my sights. Ever," he wasn't the intimidating outlaw he thought he was and caught the snicker from James.

Once again it was somebody else running his life. That drunk that cheated him at cards found out what that meant. Jacob Best knew he had to leave, but also knew these boys had to die. He slowly got to his feet, used his walking stick to hobble to the door, took up his shotgun, but not menacingly, and walked out of the cabin. James and Willy waited, and after a long period of time, heard Jake ride off into the gathering gloom of night.

"Didn't think he'd do it," Willy said. He let a long breath out and sat down at the table. "I was sure he'd draw on us."

"Not me," James said. He snickered. "Kinda wanted him to. I found him out at the stockyards, Willy. He's a coward." He headed for the door. "I'm gonna check on the horses. Don't trust him to just ride off. When I get back let's talk about a stage coach that needs stopping." He was chuckling softly as he headed for the corral, but he had his eyes wide open. Best was the kind of man who would shoot you in the back.

Jacob Best rode out from the cabin knowing it would be pitch dark within the hour, knowing he only had a bedroll tied to the saddle, some dry meat, and a canteen of water in his saddlebags. He also had desire, and he hoped that would get him by, at least for a while. He rode down through the canyon and into a wide meadow with a spring, and made up camp in some aspen and pine trees. Which would come first, he wondered, the Cannon boys' death or the capture of Cynthia Wilkinson?

Try as he might, Jacob Best couldn't bring the lovely pictures oh he and Cynthia into a dream. There was always someone there, keeping her from him, keeping him from the gold. It was a cold and hungry night, and the morning only offered a bite of dried meat and drink of cold water. He needed food, needed money, and needed help.

The first two items he could find when he got back to Eureka. The third wouldn't be available to a man like Jacob Best. He had no friends. A friend was someone to be used, and he used anyone who might, otherwise, have become a friend.

The morning dawned bright and clear in the high Diamond Mountains, and Jacob Best fought off anger and humiliation just getting a fire going. Picking up wood for the fire, managing a walking stick, and fighting off the pain of a serious gunshot wound, had him winded before his first cup of coffee. Pictures of James and Willy Cannon lying dead were vivid in the man's mind, along with more enticing pictures of the lovely Cynthia, standing just out of reach.

I can make my way back into town, but not until late at night. I've still got a few dollars from what we sold, but that Hopkins fool has money. Probably has food. What's best is, he's afraid of me. He smiled remembering how nice the man's house was, how many things he had that could be sold, which meant the man had money. His plan was set and he knew that it would take him most of the day to work his way out of the mountains, and even then, he couldn't ride into town until dark. It would be a long, hurting, and hungry day.

As he made his way off the mountain he never let his mind rest. He knew there were line camps in the hills around the big mine, and that would put him near Cynthia. *Get enough food from old man*

Hopkins, he could hide out in a shack and make his plans for abducting the girl.

"One thing at a time," he murmured. "First, old man Hopkins for food and supplies, then a place to live." His wounded leg ached from the long hours in the saddle. He stopped once late in the afternoon and tended to the wound. No infection, but because of having to use his legs in the stirrups, his leg was much stronger.

He was working his way cross country along the foothills, up one rise, across the top, down the other side, and when it was dark, he saw the lights of Eureka just a couple of miles in front. He got his bearings, knew where he was in relation to Jack Hopkins' home, and continued.

"Be eatin' hot meat and drinkin' good whiskey in a couple of hours," he chuckled.

CHAPTER FIFTEEN

"I'm gonna make my rounds, Ed, and call it a night." Corcoran didn't have to do that, but enjoyed it. The night deputies could handle the door rattling chores, but Corcoran liked to say howdy to anyone out and about and make sure all the businesses were safely locked up for the night. He'd spend a few minutes trading tall tales with anyone out on the streets. Some of the stories would be exciting, some a bit ribald, but always well worth hearing.

"Long day, Terrence," Ed Connors said. "See you at the stockyards in the morning. Those posters might just bring us some information. Five hundred bucks is a nice reward."

Thunder heads built up but never released their fury on Eureka that day and Corcoran enjoyed the cool evening breeze as he walked the main street of the mining/ranching town. "Been here a long time," he mumbled. Many times over the years he had been approached to run for the office of sheriff and turned it down every time. There was always someone he respected running for the office and he backed them.

"Seen this place grow," he muttered. Like so many little mining camps across Nevada, Eureka came into existence because of gold and silver, which seemed to be plentiful. It was the Diamond Valley that had made it a town. Ranching, with good water, plentiful grass, and transportation, turned the mining camp into a flourishing community.

Piano music and the hum of voices filtered from the Bonanza Club and he wandered across the street and through the doors. Day shift miners, a few buckaroos, and some businessmen were scattered between the long bar and the tables, Three Fingered Jack was at the piano, and Spike Turner was behind the bar.

"How about a cold one, Spike. Everyone behavin'?"

"Nice as all get out, Terrence. Anything more on Sonny Kinkaid? That was a nasty thing done to him."

"Cattlemen put up a five hundred dollar bounty on the killers." Corcoran liked saying that. "That's a lot of money for someone with information. You heard anything?"

"Wish I had. I could use five hundred." He was laughing as he poured Corcoran's beer. "Everybody's talking but nobody's saying anything. You noticed we haven't had any fires or robberies since?"

"The thought's been there, Spike. Haven't seen those Cannon brothers or their trouble makin' friend Jacob Best, either. I can't tie them to any of this, either. Best, he's wanted for Zack Bennett's murder, but the Cannons are off the map."

"Willy ain't really a bad boy, Terrence. He's dumb as a dead tree. It's his brother James that stirs the mud. He's got a mean streak in him. Old man Henderson put out the word that Jacob Best isn't welcome in here, and now we hear he killed that old guy."

"He's a mean killer, too, Spike. You see him, you let me know. Might put some money on his head, too."

Corcoran finished his beer and continued his rounds of the businesses, eventually heading down into the north canyon and his cabin. "I like quiet nights like this," he murmured.

Jacob Best came into town from the north, stayed as far to the east as he could, and slowly made his way through quiet neighborhoods to Jack Hopkins' house. "Damn this leg," he said, having trouble dismounting. He tied his horse to a fence post. He still needed that walking stick and it kept him from being able to use the shotgun.

There was light coming from several windows as Best made his way to the back door. He would have been seen from the front, he thought, and banged on the kitchen door with the walking stick. He held his revolver at the ready. Hopkins had just stoked the fire in the kitchen stove and opened the door immediately. The welcoming smile on his face disappeared immediately.

"You! What do you want?" Hopkins snarled, but stepped back quickly when Best shoved the gun in his face and pushed his way in. Best waved him over to the table and Hopkins sank into a chair. He was still hurting from his last encounter with the vicious outlaw. "You already stole everything I had. They ain't no more."

"Pack me a sack of food and I want all your money. You do that and you might live," Best said. "Hurry it up. I got one short fuse, mister, and its lit." The gun was waved about, aimed at Hopkins' head, and the man stood up slowly.

"Food? I don't understand." His voice quavered, his legs were unsteady, and he was certain he was about to die. "I have a few dollars in a tin," he said. "I'll get it." He started to walk toward the living room and Best motioned he would follow. Hopkins also had a shotgun, fully loaded after Best's last visit, near the front door.

Hopkins noticed immediately that Best was half crippled as they moved into the living room. Victorian styling prevailed, with some beautiful Tiffany lamps, lace curtains over the windows, and ornate furniture. "Ah," Hopkins said. "Here it is." He was standing in front of a secretary and opened the front to get the tin box.

He handed the box to Best who could not get the box open, hold the Colt on Hopkins, and still use the walking stick. Best fumbled with the mess and Hopkins lunged for the shotgun, grabbing it just as the Colt slammed into his head. He, Jacob Best, the tin box, and the walking stick all crashed to the floor.

"Damn fool," Best said. Hopkins was bleeding heavily from the gash on his head, but was still fighting. Blood was streaming from the head wound and Best had to fight to get untangled. He raised up on one knee and slammed the heavy pistol into Hopkins' head, over and over. Hopkins was laid out on the floor, unconscious and Best fought to get into a chair. He fumbled around and found the tin box, got it opened it, and was amazed to find several hundred dollars in folding bills along with some gold coins.

"Well, now, Mr. Hopkins," he said. He stuffed the money in his pocket. "Thank you." He hobbled into the kitchen, found some empty flour sacks and filled them with what he could find in the cupboards. "Coffee and that pot first," he chuckled. He had both sacks filled before he saw a large slice of smoked ham on the counter, and a pot of beans on the stove.

"Thank you, again," Best said. He filled a bowl with the beans and got a plate for the ham steak. It was almost a half hour later he managed to get the flour sacks tied onto his horse. One on each side, tied to the saddle horn. He mounted and rode slowly toward the south edge of town and then into the forest beyond. He rode south, into the steep side of the canyon and headed for the thick forest to the west. "Everything I needed," he muttered. "Food, money, and little Cynthia waiting for me. I don't need you, Willy and James Cannon. I don't need you."

Riding through heavy stands of trees in the middle of the night isn't easy and when Best thought he was clear enough of the town for a fire, he found a stand of aspen in which to sleep away the night. "I know a couple of hidden little line shacks west of here, and one of them is within a mile of Cynthia Wilkinson's pretty little self."

"It's gonna be a scorcher, Corcoran." Ed Connors was already sweating heavy as the two walked into the sale barn Saturday morning. Buyers and sellers were scattered about talking cattle, money, and the killing of Sonny Kinkaid. "Got them warnings up, I see," Connors said. There were one or two on each wall along with the wanted posters touting the five hundred dollar reward.

"If we're lucky those wanted posters will bring us some information, Ed. Cash money has a way of opening some mouths, I've heard." Corcoran wiped away some sweat and walked over to where Jimmy Autry was standing with a couple of cattlemen.

"Mornin', Jimmy. Got those posters up, I see. Thank you for that. Might very well save a life."

"It already has," one of the cattlemen said. Hank Taylor was from Lander County, near Austin, and in for the sale. "I've been pretty good at taking care of any problems," he said, "but that poster woke me up. I'm riding back with my crew, not in a pretty little carriage or the stage coach."

"That's good, Hank. Very good." Corcoran moved out of the barn to look through the pens, check out brands and see if there were any really mucked up runnin' iron brands. He was also checking the crowd for the Cannon brothers. *Nobody's seen them since well before the last sale. It's one hell of a big step from small time rustler to murderer, but I can't get that thought out of my head.*

He saw a couple of riders come at a gallop down the hill from town and walked back into the barn. Jimmy Henderson and another man came to a sliding stop at the barn's entrance. "Where's the sheriff?" Henderson barked as he jumped from his horse. "Old man Hopkins was killed last night."

Corcoran and Connors hit the door together and Henderson repeated what he said. "Got his head bashed in bad, Ed. Right in his own living room."

"Thanks, Jimmy. Come on Corcoran , let's ride." They ran to their horses and raced to Jack Hopkins place. There were lookers already gathered. Connors shooed them away and found Doc Sanford just inside the open front door.

"He's taken a hell of a beating, Sheriff. Probably died from a loss of blood overnight. Never regained consciousness. Wounds looks like a pistol barrel hit him hard, many more times than once."

Corcoran stepped around the body and into the house. He noticed a couple of chairs had been knocked around but nothing was broken. He walked into the kitchen and found most of the cupboard doors were standing open and a few items on the floor. "Somebody after food," he muttered. "Killed a man for food. All he had to do was ask old man Hopkins. Nicest man in the valley."

"Looks like whoever did this got Hopkin's tin box, too," Connors said. "Jack liked his cash and it probably cost him his life." He sat down at the kitchen table, fumbling to make a smoke. "Somebody needing food, meaning probably on the run, unable or unwilling to be seen, and willing to hurt or kill for it. Mean anything to you?"

"Whoever it was, Ed, was either invited in or pushed his way in. Neither the front nor the back door was forced open. Bastard might even have knocked first." Corcoran was looking at the empty bowl of beans and the plate where a ham steak had been. "A man similar to who attacked Zack Bennett comes to mind, Sheriff." He walked to the back door and stepped out, carefully.

"Might want to see this," Corcoran said. He pointed out Jacob Best's prints in the back yard mud. Prints showed someone coming in and leaving the house. "That boy's hurt bad, dragging that one leg as much as stepping out with it. These have to be Jacob Best's footprints." He found where Best had tied his horse and noticed which way the young outlaw had ridden off.

"Goin' into the wild-lands to our south," Ed Connors said. "Think you can follow?"

Corcoran didn't need any encouragement and ran to his horse, Dude, that fast. "I'll send Skitters to follow you," Connors called out, and walked back into Hopkins' house. "You go get that bastard, Corcoran," he muttered.

The trail out of town had been run over several times by passers-by, but Corcoran was able to stay on it, eventually joining a forest trail at the edge of town. It was a two-track that was used by wood cutters, hunters, and others moving into the wilderness. With all the thunderstorms, there hadn't been any traffic and Best's trail stood out.

Corcoran found where Best had nested up for the night and was able to see where the wounded outlaw had ridden after a good sleep. "Kill a man, eat his food, and still be able to sleep," Corcoran muttered. "I need to thump on that boy's head." He followed the trail for some time before losing it in a jumble of traffic when it neared the main road leading to the livestock pens and auction barn.

Deputy Sam Forget, most often called Skitters, rode up alongside. "You left plenty of trail, Terrence. Looks like this feller is on the smart side, getting his trail lost in the herd."

"He knew what he was doing, dropping out of the trees and onto this road. He was probably riding along here when Connors and I were in the barn." They rode along the roadway for a spell, hoping to see if Best turned off somewhere. "At least I've got a good look-see at his horse's prints. Nothing special but I think I'd recognize them. I'll find Connors and get a search posse organized. We'll scour these hills, all the way to and past the mine."

"The west-bound stage leaves Eureka at eight o'clock every Monday morning, Willy. We can stop that stage at the same place we stopped the rancher's carriage. It's a perfect place for a hold-up."

"We better leave now, then," Willy said. "Sure don't want to ride on the main road or be seen by anyone, either. There might even be a well-to-do rancher on board," he chuckled. "Hope there's cash from the sale."

They packed up quickly, just using their saddle-bags. "Don't want to take much, Willy," James said. "Got to leave room in the bags for all the loot." He grabbed four empty flour sacks and stuffed them under his tied off bed roll. "Just in case," he laughed.

The ride down off the mountain was tedious but the ride across the valley was quick. The day was hot, thunderstorms were flashing their presence well to the north and could make their way south if they wanted. "Hope we make that little rock overhang before the rains start," Willy said. "Don't like riding a horse in a lightning storm. Scares the hell out of me."

"Even if you got hit you wouldn't know it," James laughed.

"Ain't funny, brother. Saw a heifer got hit by lightning. She was a mess. And trees actually look like they were blown up by dynamite."

James noticed that Willy had nudged his horse into a little faster trot and had to chuckle. "Let's not wear these old boys out, Willy. We're gonna need everything they've got tomorrow. The coach is drawn by six-up, so we'll have to make sure at least one of the leaders is shot and down."

"I'll take care of that," Willy said. "You take care of the driver and whoever is up on the box with him. Hope it don't wreck. We'll want everyone out and emptying their pockets." He was laughing as they made their way across the broad valley, across a couple of rocky hills, through deep gullies, and toward the stone towers where they killed old man Kinkaid. The day was rapidly coming to an end and the first drops of summer rain were splashing the dust as they built their camp under the rock overhang.

Would Willy freeze up? James had that in his mind all day. Could he shoot someone just because that person was there? James knew he could, but Willy? *If he freezes, if he fails us, it could cost me my life. I won't die because of him, but will I sacrifice him if he fails us?*

CHAPTER SIXTEEN

Ed Connors led the seven men back toward town late on Sunday. "Whoever it was we were following gave us a nice weekend's ride, eh boys? Damn, he knew every trick in the book, using streams, rock strewn hillsides, even rock slides, to hide his trail. You did better than I could do, Corcoran, but he even tricked you."

Corcoran would have a hard time admitting that, but it was true and he had to live with it. Corcoran was known far and wide as the lawman who would bring his man in, and he wasn't living up to that. Jacob Best was either among the best at hiding his trail or one of the luckiest men in northern Nevada. "I'll get the bastard," Corcoran growled.

The posse never saw Jacob Best, might not have come within a quarter mile of the outlaw, as far as they knew. They ranged through rugged country south of the main immigrant road, through heavy timber, great stands of rocks and buttes, and rarely into open country.

Best was riding through a forest of pine, spruce, fir, and aspen, about a mile from Clarence Wilkinson's mine as the sheriff spoke to his posse, looking for an old line-shack he remembered.

"I'd like to come back tomorrow, Ed, and pick up the trail again. I have the idea he was looking for something as much as he was hiding his trail. I'd like to scour these hills."

"You need someone with you?"

"No, I work better alone. I'd like someone like Scotty but he's not able to ride anymore."

Corcoran was up and packed before sunrise and was ready to make his way to where the posse had quit the day before. "This is good summer range for the ranchers and that means there are line shacks scattered about. That's what I have to look for." He and Jimmy Henderson were talking, standing on the porch of the Bonanza Club, watching the sun make its way skyward.

"More than one buckaroo found shelter and food in the shacks, and more than one outlaw has done the same," Corcoran said. "If Best could find the one he wanted, it would probably be high in the mountains, probably in a small meadow or glade, and more than likely there would be a stream or springs close by. I'll be looking for the same thing," Corcoran said

He was at the Bonanza Club on the way out of town and found little Cindy Cook in the kitchen. She flung herself at him, showering the big man with kisses and hugs. "Now, now, darlin'," Corcoran said. "Later, sweetheart. I gotta go get a bad guy. Will you throw some food together for me? Enough for a couple of days."

"I could come with you, Terrence. We wouldn't need food. We'd have each other."

"Let's do that next week, Cindy," he laughed. He patted her on her cute little bottom and headed for the bar to pick up a bottle of brandy for the trail. It was just minutes and Cindy had a pack put together with meat, cheese, and bread. "Lot's of coffee?" He asked and she nodded. "Thanks, darlin'," he said. "Gotta go."

The Monday morning stage was standing in front of the Bonanza Club. Several passengers were waiting to board as Corcoran came out. "Looks like you got a full load, Mr. Simpson," Corcoran said. "Gonna be a hot ride today. Who's your messenger?"

"Mornin', Corcoran. Old man Dupree's riding with that monster shotgun of his. Them ten gauge barrels ain't twelve inches long," Simpson laughed.

"Puts a hell of a spray out there."

Clint Dupree was nearing fifty and had one of the best records of any of the men who rode shotgun for the stage line. Road agents in central Nevada shied away when they heard that Clinton Dupree was on board.

"He blew two of Humboldt Charley's men right out of their saddles, Corcoran."

"Keep your eyes open, Simpson. Had a carriage attacked on that road recently. Old Sonny Kinkaid and his driver were killed. Let Clint know that." Corcoran mounted Dude and rode out of town to, what he hoped would be the finish to his hunt for Jacob Best.

"I gotta keep it tucked away that Best is wounded. He might be, but he ain't moving around like a wounded man. I gotta think like he is not wounded." Corcoran kept a full conversation going all morning.

Best found the shack he was looking for. It was nestled in a stand of trees several hundred feet above the valley floor. He could see the mining operation a few miles out, built in the foothills. The mine featured a big drift into the mountains, a mill and reduction works a little further down the hillsides, using gravity to accomplish a lot of work, and the housing and offices were near the valley floor.

He had been there, but by looking down on the

complex, had a better idea of the lay-out. He saw the superintendent's home, remembered seeing Cynthia running about, and their brief encounter before Wilkinson chased him off with that shotgun. "That was the last time you'll ever do that," the killer grumbled.

Jacob Best's plan was simple. Spend the next few days learning Cynthia Wilkinson's routine, letting his leg wound heal more, and making off with his prize. "I'll take her to the Cannon boy's shack. It's even more hidden than this one. Bring her here until dark, then move north into the deep forest."

There was a small cook stove, rope bed with dirty straw mattress, table, and two chairs in the line shack. "No fires unless it's dark," he muttered. That meant no coffee and cold biscuits for morning meal. "Somebody would sure as hell see the smoke and come lookin'. I ain't too proud to drink cold water."

He saddled his horse, found it was much easier getting on board, and worked his way down the mountainside to where he could watch the Wilkinson's house in the compound area. He was well up the hill and to the east of the main mining works, hidden in a rock outcrop. He saw Cynthia hanging out wash as he settled in. "I got other things in mind for you, little girl," he snickered.

It was a lazy time and Best remembered an afternoon like this many years ago. He was eleven and the neighbor girl was twelve, blossoming into woman hood when he attacked her. Her father rushed into the barn and beat Jacob Best with an ax handle all the way off the property. When he got home, his father did the same thing. Best blamed the girl for the beating, still. "All she had to do was enjoy," he muttered, watching Cynthia, remembering.

"I can't figure out just what that fool is trying to do." Corcoran mused, following a trail that led up through heavy timber, then across a ridge, and down through a meadow, and again up through the trees. The big man spent the entire day tracing those prints and getting nowhere. "He has to be looking for something, and it has to be a line shack where he can hole up. There just isn't any other reason."

He had to chuckle some. "Of course, a wise man would already be in another county, miles from here. Best has killed two well-liked men in a small, close knit community, and he's still hanging around? He's after something and needs a place to hide."

Corcoran knew Best had been wounded in his first attack and wondered if that was why the fool hadn't simply run away. Maybe that wound was more serious than they thought, or maybe he had something else in mind. "Only thing we know about that boy is that he takes his frustrations out on women and that boils my blood," Corcoran murmured. In Corcoran's mind, all women were ladies until they proved themselves otherwise. Treat a lady wrong and suffer the consequences, and Corcoran provided those consequences at every opportunity.

Mid-day came and went, and Corcoran had followed Best west almost to the big mine on the hillside. Thunder heads were building all day and finally unleashed their fury with cyclonic winds and torrential rains. "And, thus my quest comes to an end," Corcoran muttered in anger. "All trace of horse prints just washed away. You're a lucky man, Mr. Best, but your luck isn't going to hold. I'll keep searching these mountains until I find you. Your killing days are over."

Even with a fine oilskin Corcoran was drenched by the time he got back to Eureka. He put Dude up at the sheriff's corral and hurried into the office. "Got washed out, Ed. He has to have found a line shack up there somewhere. Damn rain." He poured some coffee and stood as close to the stove as he could get. "Anything going on?"

"People are upset with the killings, Terrence. First Bennett, Hopkins, and now, Kinkaid and his driver. The fires and thefts. The Businessmen's Association, the Cattlemen's Association, my God, even the ladies social groups, are up in arms. Can't say I blame 'em since it appears we ain't done much about the situation."

"You work on keeping them under control, Sheriff, and I'll do my best to find the bad boys. Best must have some reason for wanting to be in a line shack in the mountains. Common sense would tell me to get the hell away from Eureka. He is wounded, but he can ride, and heading north would be my first choice. Not west and high in the mountains."

"The only thing we know for a fact is he wasn't involved in the Kinkaid killing. I'm not sure it was the Cannon boys, either. They don't strike me as killers." The sheriff shook his head, threw wood in the stove, and glared at the floor. "Damn."

"They don't strike me as killers, either, Ed, but you got to remember every killer had to have his first victim. Wasn't a killer before that first one. Those boys have never had boundaries, never had rules. They're young and wild, and might have seen a chance at getting more money than they had ever even thought of."

"The way some people in town are talking, if we do catch Best or the Cannon boys, it might get ugly. Bennett might have been a drunk, but many people enjoyed his company. Jack Hopkins was loved by almost everyone in town. We got to work fast before it gets out of hand."

CHAPTER SEVENTEEN

"Here they come, Willy," James yelled out. With no hesitation, he pulled his kerchief up, stepped out onto the road, and aimed his big Colt at the lead horses as Gerald Simpson drove his six-up around the rocky formation and through the cut. Willy Cannon, however, was slow to come out from the rocks on the other side, his rifle in hand, but not pointed at anyone.

In Willy's mind, James had everything under control and all he had to do was show that rifle. He got sick after James killed Kinkaid and his driver, even though he killed a man the next day. Killing another human being was wrong, was about the only thing his mother had taught him. Taking something from someone? Don't get caught. Shirking chores? Who cares. Rose Cannon even quoted the Bible about killing, but neglected the other stuff.

Clint Dupree saw the two outlaws immediately and leveled that monster shotgun at Willy. The blast blew Willy Cannon ten feet back into the rocks. James fired his pistol twice, the first shot dropping one of the leaders, and the second hitting Gerald Simpson in the knee. The horses fouled in their harnesses, Simpson fell from the high seat, and Dupree found himself holding on tight at the heavy coach was swinging about, wildly.

James fired a third time, knocking Dupree from the coach, with a shot through his leg. The fouled horses and coach came to a shuddering, dust-filled stop, and James ordered the passengers out. He gave one man an empty flour sack and told him to get it filled. He looked around and saw Willy's bloody body spread across a boulder at the side of the road. He simply shook his head.

"Hurry it up," he snarled. Passengers put their money and possessions into the sack and James grabbed it. One passenger, young, bearded, and mean looking went for his sidearm instead of his wallet, and James gunned him down with a shot to the head. He raced to his horse and fled north at a full gallop.

Two passengers, Gerald Simpson, and Clint Dupree, were all shooting at the fleeing outlaw, but he was already too far out for them to hit him. Both

Simpson and Dupree were wounded bad, but able to function to a degree. "Get him bandaged and get the bleeding stopped," Simpson said, nodding at Dupree. "Somebody grab that other horse and race like the wind back to Eureka."

"I'll go," Tom Harris yelled. He caught Willy Cannon's horse and rode off at a full gallop. Harris worked for Jimmy Autry at the stockyards. "That was the Cannon brothers," he muttered, putting the spurs to Willy's horse. "I'd know that voice anywhere. Were they the ones that killed Sonny Kinkaid? Bastards."

As the coach worked its way west Simpson and Dupree had watched large, almost impressive, thunderheads building to their north. As Harris rode hard back to Eureka, those bolts of lightning, massive blasts of thunder, and monsoon rains arrived in full force. Harris fought high wind, blinding rain, and the ever-present threat of lightning all the way into town.

Several of the passengers got busy tending Simpson and Dupree while others worked to unharness the teams and get them re-harnessed. "That man didn't have to die. Shouldn't have gone for his gun like that." Sean Morgan dragged the dead man off the road "The coach is fine, Mr. Simpson. Can you drive it with that busted up knee?" He was a gambler, the man named Morgan, and seemed to know what he was doing, directing the harnessing.

"If you can boost me up to that high seat, I can. Might want to ride up there with me in case I pass out or something. Damn me, but that hurts. How's Clint?"

"He's alive and cussing up a storm," Morgan laughed. "My name's Sean Morgan. Worked in a livery a while back. Your teams weren't hurt, except for that one leader the outlaw shot. The wheelers are fine, so we should make it back to town without much trouble."

"Good," Simpson said. "Get Dupree loaded and the rest of the passengers. Somebody will have to come back to bury those two, and we'll head back to Eureka. Did you see which way the bandit went? Sheriff's gonna want to know that."

"No hesitation," Morgan said. "He rode north as fast as that horse would go. The other one's dead as dead can be."

"Leave him be, then. That storm is here, damn it. Bundle up Mr. Morgan, we're gonna get wet as hell."

Simpson drove his now four-up out of the rocks, made a long wide turn around through the desert, and put the coach back on the road. The second leader was tied on and trailing. Dupree was getting lots of attention from two of the lady passengers in the coach. "You sure took care of that one outlaw," one of them said.

"Not the other, though," Dupree snarled "Dumb bastard didn't even ask for the strong box to be handed down." He chuckled through the pain. "Autry's livestock money was heading to the bank in Austin. That's why young Tom Harris was riding with us." He chuckled softly and winced at the same time as his wounded knee got bumped.

James Cannon didn't slow his horse down for half an hour, and then walked him to let him catch his breath. "Oh, Willy," he cried out. Willy tried to holler out to stop the coach instead of shooting the messenger, and paid for the mistake. "We talked about that Willy," James moaned. He rode cross country along the same general direction the boys took on their first robbery.

James Cannon rode straight into the teeth of the blinding storm, getting wrapped in his duster quickly. "Sloppy mud doesn't leave good prints in the ground," he muttered, "but that rain is cold. Gotta hole up somewhere when it gets dark. Hope that shack is still standing."

He put his horse in a solid trot and rode north until it turned too dark to see. "Won't be nobody trackin' me until sometime tomorrow. Got to make plans, got to sleep some." He saw his brother blown away so many times that night, that he was still groggy the next morning. It took some effort to get wet wood to light, but with a fire going he had coffee and biscuits as the first order of the day.

He wasn't worried about his morning fire being seen but he knew the remains of that fire would tell stories to those who were sure to be coming along. He warmed some dried meat in his coffee and tried to put together a real plan. Neither he nor Willy had thought much about what happens after a big robbery.

"That thunderstorm was a blessing," he murmured. He was sure that all that wind and rain would have washed out any tracks he might have made, but he didn't take into account the fact that he left on the same trail he had used in the previous robbery. Just one of many mistakes.

He was getting ready to saddle up and ride when he decided to take a look at his loot. He emptied the flour sack onto the ground near the fire. There was some jewelry that might bring some money, a wad of cash and quite a few gold and silver coins. A few watches were good, and a few were worthless. He just tossed them aside.

"Sure as hell not enough here to make this job worthwhile. Damn, Willy, there should be more. He threw everything back in the bag, saddled up, and was on the trail as the sun peeked over the Cortez Mountains. "I'll ride across the mountains and head straight for Elko, sell this junk and maybe not even come back." That had been in his mind all morning and he knew it was wrong but didn't know why.

That comment brought him back to reality. "I gotta go to the hideout cabin. All our money from the last job is there. I get it all now that Willy's gone. Gotta go there, first, then maybe all the way to Salt Lake City instead of Elko. Gotta move fast." That was the extent of his planning.

Tom Harris pulled the horse to a skidding stop in front of the sheriff's office, leaped from the saddle, and hit the door at a full run. "Sheriff," he howled, almost bowling Ed Connors out of the way. "Stage coach has been hit. Hurry, people hurt." Harris was trying to say everything at once and Connors and Corcoran grabbed him, got him under control and slowed down to a roar.

"Easy, Tom. You're safe," Corcoran said. "Slow it down and tell us what happened. Get out of your duster and sit down, there, next to fire, and tell us."

Harris sat down, shivering from the cold and wet. Connors handed him a cup of coffee, laced with whiskey, and he started talking, fast. The story spilled out in one, maybe two, long sentences, ending with, "Those Cannon boys were the ones, Sheriff. I'm sure of that. I'd know James's voice anywhere."

"The dead one, then would be Willy?" Corcoran asked. "Did anyone pull his mask down?"

"Not before I hightailed it back," Tom Harris said. "James was racing north when I left off. They didn't know that Mr. Autry had a strong box on that coach for the bank in Austin. James Cannon never once asked for the strong box, just what people were carrying. He should have known, since I was riding along."

"Stepped over the line with Kinkaid and that boy is a full-fledged murderer, stage coach robber, and just waiting to be hung, now," Ed Connors said.

"You sure he was heading north?" Corcoran asked.

"No doubt, Corcoran," Harris said. "He was going as fast as that horse would go, straight north. Must have run headlong into the storm that drenched me."

Corcoran walked back from the fire, paced around the small office for a minute or two, thinking, planning. "Ed, take a couple of deputies out to the scene and get on his trail. I'm gonna take a chance and take the main road north toward Palisade. If he's following his first trail, and I'm betting on it, I'll meet him at the south mine road. Let's ride."

Harris and Sheriff Connors rode west, at a lope, and Corcoran took the main road north to Palisade, following the rail line. "I"m gonna run out of daylight before I reach that mine road. Well, that's the way it's gonna be. If I can be near the intersection of that road shortly after sunup tomorrow, I've got a good chance of getting that boy. He's gonna run out of the same daylight," he chuckled.

Corcoran pushed old Dude hard, rode until he simply couldn't see anything, and finally pulled off the road and made a quick, cold, camp. "I gotta be moving fast before it gets really light," he said. He pulled the bedroll over his head and slept.

Connors, Harris, and two deputies met the coach coming back to town. "We left the other outlaw's body, and that of a man who tried to gun the outlaw down, out there, Sheriff," Dupree said. "Me and Simpson need help. Bleeding bad."

"Harris, you better ride back with them. You got to get Autry's money back. Simpson, take the coach right on up to Doc Sanfords. Me and the boys will get on Cannon's trail."

"Good luck, Sheriff. Get that boy and kill him

dead," Dupree shouted. Simpson already had his teams in a good run.

Connors had Skitters and Dean Berry with him and they rode to the scene of the robbery at a fast trot. "We'll run out of light soon, boys. Let's get Willy and the other in the ground and make as much distance as we can. That Cannon boy will probably stay on the same trail he used last time. I hope so, anyway. We'll ride until we can't see the trail."

"Hell, Sheriff, we can barely see the trail now," Skitters said. "if you know where he's going, it's best we just ride hard until we can't see. Ain't nothing to follow no ways."

Sheriff Connors spent some time going over the scene. "They were sure that it was just the two men. From the tracks leading off, I'd say they were right. We'll be chasing James Cannon, and he knows this country as well as anyone alive. He's cagey, and don't forget he's already killed. He won't be afraid of doing it again."

CHAPTER EIGHTEEN

Scattered clouds greeted the morning sun in gorgeous colors of red, orange, and yellow as a warm summer day got underway. Corcoran remembered tales of the sea from his youth and wondered if those beautiful clouds meant more thunderstorms for later in the day. "Uncle Patrick swore by that rhyme. Red skies in the mornin', sailor, take a warnin'." He chuckled getting saddled, with the understanding that he would again be drenched later in the day.

Corcoran was on the trail, figured he would be at the South Mine Road within the hour, and concentrated on how best to find his prey. He found the intersection well before any traffic to or from the mine was around. "Now, Mr. Cannon, you are mine."

Neither the gentle morning breeze, nor the thought of later storms, had an affect on Corcoran's desire to capture or kill the man who murdered Sonny Kinkaid and who robbed the westbound stage. "I wonder just how difficult that first step was for Mr. Cannon," he mused, walking Dude up the road. "From a two-bit trouble maker to a killer." He tried to remember the first time he had to kill a man, but, of course, the circumstances were considerably different.

"Hell, I carried a badge and he carried several hundred dollars he had stolen from the Village Emporium. Victoria, Pennsylvania, so many years ago." He remembered that first time in full color. "I sat down on a rock next to the body and cried like the baby I was. The outlaw was a killer, thief, evil man, but he was a living human being before he challenged me. I don't think he would have had those feelings, and I don't think James Cannon did either."

Was that difference what made outlaws? A lack of feeling for fellow man? From the day his father got hurt, James Cannon had no thoughts for anyone but himself, had no compassion for anyone, even his mother. If he wanted what someone else had, he took it. If he had to kill to get it, so be it.

Corcoran followed the well graded road about five miles into the mountains and took up a position at one of the terribly tight switch-backs. "I'll be able to see traffic coming from both directions and in plenty of time to make my moves on that bastard." He tucked Dude back into some pine trees where there was good grass, and made a nest in a scattering of rocks. "Might be a long morning," he muttered, and watched for someone coming down along the trail from the big mine. His mind played about some, letting him wonder about this decision of his.

"Won't I look like the fool if he rides north to Palisade, gets on a train, and disappears somewhere in Denver? No chance, Terrence, my boy, no chance. He's coming this way for sure."

On the other side of the mountain, a good twenty miles away, James Cannon was letting his horse work its way up through a jumble of rocks, patches of mud, climbing toward the crest of the Cortez Range, looming over their heads. He spent his early morning hours watching behind him for indications of a posse. "They'll be coming, I know that. I gotta get back to the cabin and get that money. I can go anywhere I want with that much money."

He saw most of the same terrain he climbed through last time, recognized an easier pathway in some places, and made fair time to the crest. Those heavy, black thunderheads were building to the northwest and the day was passing quickly. "Gotta be off this mountain before the storms hit," he muttered, "or find a good outcrop to get under."

He made the crest and was a few miles on the other side when he found the South Mine Road. He let his horse catch its breath before putting him in a strong trot. He hadn't run into any mine traffic going either way, and let his mind wander. Where would he go first? Salt Lake City didn't really interest him, but Denver did. He heard many stories about Denver. Uncle Clarence Wilkinson had told him about big mines, large ranches, the Rocky Mountains. James knew there would be money available for anyone willing to reach out and take it.

He and cousin Cynthia had even talked about running away once, but it was just talk. She was a pretty girl but too young for James. Still, Jacob Best thought she would be fine. "Maybe I'll just ride up to her place at the mine and see if she'd like to run away with me." His thoughts ranged through a wild incoherent list of ideas as he rode down through the mountains. The only constant was checking behind for approaching riders.

"He's doing exactly what Corcoran said he would do," Connors said. The three lawmen were starting the long climb through the Cortez Range. "After we cross that razor-back ridge, we'll work our way down toward the South Mine and connect with their road. That wends its way for miles down into the Diamond Valley. We won't be near that ridge for hours, boys, so take good care of your horses."

"Guess that means we'll be spending another night sleeping in the rocks, eh Sheriff?" Deputy Dean Berry was joking on the one hand, but was not looking forward to it. "I'm a bed and mattress man, myself."

"Find me some good hard rocks, lots of sharp edges to 'em, and I can sleep like a baby," Skitters said. "Yes sir, rocks, cold biscuits, and foul coffee for old Skitters." Berry just looked at him, shaking his head.

Connors was laughing as he led them up through the rough country. "Have your fun, boys, but keep in mind we're following a killer. You have to know he knows we are, too. Killed old Sonny Kinkaid, shot Dupree and Simpson, and would take a man with a star without a thought."

"They been talking around town that the Cannon boys were riding with that fool Jacob Best, Sheriff. It was just the Cannon brothers hit that stage coach yesterday. You think Best has run off from the county?" Skitters asked.

"No, I don't. He's wounded, might have some money he stole from Jack Hopkins, but that's all. No, he's hiding in those mountains south and west of town. We'll flush him out after we catch Cannon." Connors knew Best would flee the county as soon as that terrible leg wound was healed enough for him to ride hard for hours at a time. "He was shot with that ancient Spanish flintlock loaded with buckshot. He's hurtin'."

"We're gonna be mighty high in these mountains when those storms hit, Sheriff." Dean Berry was pointing at the huge thunderheads moving rapidly through the sky. "And they're gonna hit soon, I think."

"You just keep a good bead on them, Mr. Berry," Sheriff Connors chuckled.

They had been listening to rumbling thunder and seeing flashes of lightning for some time, but it was still on the other side of that wide valley. "We'll ride until it's just too dangerous, Berry. Start looking for an outcrop, though. Those storms are highballing their way here."

The wind had picked up and there was a chill to the summer air. "Day's getting short and the storm's getting close," Skitters said. "We're above the tree line and that makes us a target for them lightning bolts, Sheriff."

"It does that. Let's make for that rock pile over there and get under something." They found a large overhang, got their animals undressed and hobbled, and were settling in under the rocks when the first big splashes of rain fell. "Those first drops smell good," Ed Connors said. "After that, it's just rain and cold."

"I like it down in the valley," Skitters said. "There's a real perfume to rain in the sage and dust of the desert."

"I think you're both nuts," Dean Berry said. He flopped his bedroll out and sat down to watch the lightning show. "Probably last until dark and we'll be sleeping in the rocks."

"More'n likely," the sheriff said. "Let's get a fire going, get some wood tucked in and kept dry. We can snivel all we want after the chores are done."

"There she is," Jacob Best muttered. He was sitting on his haunches in a stand of aspen trees just a few hundred yards from the mining company headquarters compound. "I'll be with you in just a few minutes." He had his horse already packed and knew he would be able to make a quick get away if he could get her without making a big ruckus.

Cynthia Wilkinson was walking across the small meadow toward the trees, toward Jacob Best, on a beautiful summer morning. She had her morning chores done, the cow was milked and the eggs gathered, and had some time for herself. She loved sitting under the trees, watching the clouds scud through a wide open sky. She often brought books with her to read in the sunshine.

Summer was beautiful in central Nevada. She even enjoyed the cooling effects of late afternoon thunderstorms. She was daydreaming of a planned visit the family would be making to Elko sometime in the coming weeks when the lights went out. Best smashed her across the side of the head with the butt of his rifle, grabbed her up, and raced for his horse. Only the sound of a crushed skull broke the silence of the valley.

She was laid out across the front of the saddle as the outlaw's horse pounded through sage and grass for the main road north. He had a blanket over the girl's body and hoped that what few people he might run into would just think it was that, a blanket or bedroll. Once he reached the Eureka and Palisade rail line, he moved off the main road and into the foothills, believing he would be less likely to be seen.

It was an early morning and there would be little chance that someone would be out. He climbed up through great rock formations, stands of tall timber, and let his horse rest in a small meadow with a natural springs. It was already hot, the sunrise breezes ended hours ago, and he needed to get into the high country quick.

He stepped off into good summer grass and laid little Cynthia down near the springs. He pulled his kerchief off and soaked it in the cold water to clean her bleeding head wound. It didn't seem to bother him that she hadn't regained consciousness.

"All right, little girl, let's make you just as pretty as we can," he whispered. He saw a small gold bracelet and pulled it from her wrist. "Something of yours for me," he whispered. "I have something for you that you'll never forget."

His eyes were all over the girl as he wiped away dried blood and cleaned more from the open wound. She didn't respond to the cold water, to the cleaning, or to the jostling by Best. "Might have hit her too hard," he muttered. "ain't nobody gonna be hittin' me, though. Not this time. She's mine and will be until I need another."

He finished with the wound, wrapped her in that blanket and stepped back onto the horse. Cynthia laid across the front of the saddle again. He climbed into the Diamond Mountains, higher and higher, for another six hours before finding the Cannon boy's cabin. At least it was cool, but he heard the threat of a late thunderstorm in the distance. He carried her inside and laid her out on one of the beds and went back out to take care of the horse and bring in his supplies, the few he had.

There was food in the cabin and water at the springs, Best knew, and got a fire started. It was already getting dark, and he could hear great claps of thunder, not so many miles off, now. "Not a bad thing," he murmured. "Whatever tracks I might have left will be gone if it rains hard." He spent some time cleaning her wound again, and spent an equal amount of time making sure his leg wound was not going to give him problems.

The long ride into those massive mountains wore him out. His leg hurt, he was afraid he had hit the girl too hard, and he finally gave it up and stretched out on the second cot. He was fast asleep in moments, but the dreams weren't. He saw swarms of sheriff's posse's combing the mountains, he saw miners with picks and shovels chasing him, and worst, he saw pretty little Cynthia turning her back on him. It was a blinding flash of lightning and a thunder clap, right over the top of the cabin, that woke the outlaw.

The storm's fury descended on the little cabin late that night. Jacob Best sat up, groggy and looked about. He did as he promised, hadn't touched the girl. He told himself he wasn't going to until she was awake. She needed to know his pleasures. He lit a lamp, stoked the stove, and moved to her bedside to sit beside her. When he pulled the blanket back to see her pretty little face, he jumped up, almost screaming in terror.

Her face was almost gray, her body cold, her wound not bleeding. He was frightened, stormed around the cabin for a minute or two, cussing, slamming his fists into anything and everything, and finally slumped down at the table, his face in his hands. "Dead!" he screamed. "That pretty little girl of mine is dead." Thunder crashed, lightning lit the cabin as if it were daylight. "Gotta get rid of her. Gotta make it look like an accident."

Fear and panic drove him, half crazed, and Jacob Best spent the rest of the night working out one plan after another for getting rid of Cynthia Wilkinson's body. Rain pounded the cabin roof, Thunder rattled everything that would move, lightning blew more than one nearby tall pine tree to smithereens, and Jacob Best wasn't aware of any of it. "I can't have that stinkin' body around me."

Early summer sunrise blossomed in a clear sky but Best was sound asleep, his head on the table, the fire out, and the girl, still dead. It was bird calls that startled him awake, and the sight of little Cynthia's body that drove him from the cabin.

"What am I gonna do? Gotta get rid of that body."

He was aware enough to know her father would be organizing a search for the girl, knew he couldn't just bury her. "It has to look like she had an accident." That was the best he could come up with. He remembered a hunter's trail well down the mountainside from the cabin, that edged along a high canyon. "Hell's Canyon." He almost shouted it out.

"She could fall off that trail," he murmured. But reality stuck its ugly head in. "How did she get there?" He spoke it right out. "Still," he murmured, and went back into the cabin to wrap Cynthia's body in that bloody blanket. "Horses do have a way of gettin' crazy sometimes. I don't want to lose my horse, but they come easy late at night, from someone's barn."

They rode from the Cannon boys' cabin half an hour later. Jacob Best never noticed that because of the heavy rain the night before, he was making fresh tracks, the only tracks, as they moved through the trees and rocks, down the hillside. The canyon was a couple of hour's hard ride and a thousand feet below him. He would have to work through big trees, bigger rocks, and steep hillsides.

It was an arduous ride through deep forest and rocky ground. He intersected the trail and followed it to where it ran along the face of a cliff, with the deep canyon on the other side. He stepped from

his horse and pulled Cynthia's body down. He un-
wrapped the body from the blanket and wrestled her
back up on the horse. She slumped forward in the
saddle and he got her squared up some.

She was somewhat in the saddle when Jacob Best
let go of the reins, screamed at the top of his lungs
into the horse's face, then fired his pistol twice. The
horse panicked, tried to turn and run, the gunfire
added to the panic, and over the edge it and the girl
plunged. Best, covered in sweat, stood on the edge
of the canyon and watched as the two bounced off
rocks, falling hundreds of feet to the forested floor
of Hell's Canyon.

"What have I done?" He whispered, as he walked
along the narrow trail, dragging the bloody blanket
behind him. "Gotta hide this somewhere. Get into
town and find a horse. Gotta run," he murmured.
He saw the girl tumbling down the steep mountainside over and over as he made his way down off the
mountains, toward the valley floor miles in front of
him. It hadn't dawned on him yet, but it would soon.
He was alone, on foot, and almost fifty miles from
Eureka. Jacob Best was thousands of feet high in one
of the roughest mountain ranges in Nevada.

CHAPTER NINETEEN

"She's gone, Clarence." Amelia Wilkinson, out of breath, stormed into the mine superintendent's office, her face smudged from tears and perspiration. "I can't find her anywhere. I've called and called."

Clarence Wilkinson jumped to his feet when his wife barged in. It was still early morning, but the heat was rising fast. Wilkinson was doing a little catching up with paperwork. Normally this time of the morning would have found him deep underground directing the day's activities. Amelia was a sickly woman, had been since Cynthia's birth, and rarely paid her husband a visit in his office. "Slow down, Amelia. Tell me what's happened?" She was almost hysterical and Wilkinson stepped to her side and helped her sit.

"Cynthia," she gasped. "I can't find her. I've called," she said again. Clarence sat her down in a wingback chair and called for his assistant. Amelia was shaking in fear, tears rolled down her thin cheeks. She had her fingers locked on Clarence's wrists.

"Jeb, get some men mounted and bring them back here. Be quick." He turned to Amelia. "Start from the beginning and tell me everything." His voice, often at a deep rumble that could be heard a mile away, was soft, offering love and hope on the one hand but filled with fear. This was a father's worst fear, his daughter, abducted, abused, lost.

She tried to hold her sobs in, was shaking, but told her story. "Cynthia went down in the meadow to read and when I went to call her in she wasn't there. I called, Clarence, and called." She released her grip and almost fainted. "I can't find her." The sobs were deep, penetrating, and Wilkinson had to take deep breaths before he understood the full meaning of what she said.

"My, God," he said. He poured Amelia a glass of water, Poured a brandy for himself, and paced around the cluttered office, images of his daughter flashing through his mind. One kept coming back. The ugly scene of Jacob Best putting his hands on his daughter flashed over and over. "I'll have that sheriff's head for not catching that bastard," he said. He told Amelia to stay where she was and ran for the mine stables. Three men were saddling up when he raced in and grabbed tack for his stalled horse.

He could visualize Jacob Best saying something crude to Cynthia at Emil's house, and then, seeing the impudent little bastard putting his hands all over his daughter. Fear, intense anger, and a desire to kill flooded the man. He had to maintain his dignity, had to lead this search, not fold, not give up. He forced himself to be calm.

"I fear that Cynthia may have been abducted," he said to his men. "We'll ride to that stand of trees in the meadow where Cynthia likes to sit, and look for sign first. Everything else depends on what we find."

Clarence Wilkinson was a leader, the kind men followed. He never asked more than what he would or could do himself. The three men simply accepted what he said and would follow him no matter how long it took. There was a second motivation most of the men would blush about should it be brought up. Every man and boy at that mine loved Cynthia. She was a spark of sunshine, a bright star in the night.

They raced out of the company barn and down the hillside to the meadow. "We don't want to destroy any sign that might be here," he called out. They pulled up short of the rocks that the girl was often seen sitting on, and dismounted. It took just seconds to find Jacob Best's foot prints, Cynthia's blood stains, and where Best had his horse tied off.

"I'll kill that man," Wilkinson growled. His voice was low, quiet even, but his eyes were flashing wild anger, his mouth was set, and his fists were opening and closing. "Taylor, ride as hard as you've ever ridden for Eureka and bring the sheriff. Toby, you and Nils run back to the mine and pack enough for the three of us. Then follow my tracks. I'm leaving now. Catch up," he said.

Wilkinson mounted up and trotted off through the trees and rocks, easily following the tracks left by Jacob Best. No one but the outlaw had been on horseback in those hills in months. The trail led the big mine superintendent down to the main east-west road and then turned north following the railroad tracks for a couple of miles. The heavy rains the night before, and it still being morning, Best left definite hoof prints that were easy to follow. Wilkinson found where Best left the road for cross country travel, and stopped long enough to leave sign for the men who would be following him.

The more he thought about what might be happening, the more angry he became. He wanted to sink spurs deep, ride at a hard gallop into the majestic mountains, and had to fight to hold himself, stay calm, wait until he catches the man before letting his anger come out full force.

Rage may have been obvious but it was fear that drove the big hard-rock miner. He was more than aware that Amelia would never bring him another child and the fear of losing this precious little girl drove the man. In his mind, he would ride into hell, fight the devil himself to save her.

Sam Taylor leaped from his still sliding horse in front of the sheriff's office and raced in, yelling for the sheriff. Kenny Johnson, almost seventy-years-old, half deaf, and with a gimpy leg, was asleep at the sheriff's desk. Old man Johnson had been Connors' jailer, going on ten years. He never moved faster than a crawl and was startled into almost jumping to his feet.

"What in the name of hell is going on?" He held on to the desk with both hands, rheumy eyes searching for whatever it was making all the racket.

"Where's the sheriff?" Taylor demanded. "Cynthia Wilkinson's been kidnapped. Hurry, man, get the sheriff."

"Sheriff's leading a posse, chasing the stage coach robbers. He's got the deputies with him, all except for the night deputy, Shorty Rogers. He'd be home sleepin' about now. You say somebody got took?"

Taylor just shook his head at Johnson and knew Shorty Rogers couldn't help, either. Shorty lost a leg in the Indian wars and had a peg leg. Never rode a horse. He ran to the Bonanza Club to sound the alarm. Jimmy Autry and Jimmie Henderson were standing at the bar. "Need help," Sam Taylor said. He was out of breath and frustrated, fearful and anxious, all at the same time. "Clarence Wilkinson's daughter has been kidnapped. Can't find the sheriff."

"Slow down, Sam," Henderson said. He motioned for the barman to bring Taylor some whiskey. "Take it easy, catch your breath, and tell us what happened."

"Sheriff's chasing the men that robbed the stage. Corcoran's with him," Autry said. "Where's Wilkinson?"

"He's with Toby Erikson and Nils Oster, following what they think is the kidnapper. This is terrible. Poor Mrs. Wilkinson, so weak, so sick most of the time. Can you do something, Mr. Henderson?"

"Ride with us, Taylor. Let's go, Autry, we can pick up some men at the livestock corrals when we pass by."

After finding a couple of buckaroos at the stockyards, Henderson led his group out onto the main road leading to the mine just in time to meet up with Erikson and Oster. "We're following Wilkinson's trail," Erikson yelled out. "He's on the north road to Palisade."

The seven riders, with Erikson out front watching the prints, rode out at a good trot. "We have some food but not enough for all of us," he said. "Looks like the boss is following just one man. We're gonna get wet before long."

Erikson found the little mound of stones that Wilkinson left for him to see and, followed the trail off the highway. They rode through and into the brush and stunted trees of the foothills. "We'll be climbing fast, boys," Erikson said. The trail stood out, easy to follow, but hard riding because of the steep terrain, rocks, and heavy timber in places. Best was forced into many switchbacks as he climbed, following the terrain as it dictated.

The Diamond Mountains are a rugged, high, alpine like range and the men would be climbing well above eight thousand feet or more. The range was home to deer, antelope, elk, and desert bighorn sheep along with many smaller species. It was a hunter's paradise. The game animals shared space with summer feeding for the cattle ranchers in the Diamond Valley.

"The man seems to know where he's going, Mr. Henderson. Do you know this area of the mountains?" Erikson asked.

"I've hunted these mountains for years, Toby. There are trails to follow, but whoever ran off with the girl isn't using any of them. There are a few old line-shacks up higher. That might be where he's headed."

They followed Wilkinson's well marked trail for hours, climbing the whole time, all the time watching the thunderheads build. "We're gonna run out of daylight before long," Autry said. "Let's ride for another hour or so and then find a good spot to spend the night. Wish we knew how far in front of us Wilkinson is."

"That man's as strong as a bull, Autry. He'll follow this trail until he simply can't see for the dark." Sam Taylor had worked for Wilkinson from the time the mine opened, watched him win mining contests every year, and knew how much he loved his family. "His wife and daughter are his life. We won't catch up today. God help whoever he's following."

That should have brought some gentle chuckles, but fear for the child's life and dignity raged through every member of the posse. "Maybe we should just continue," Henderson suggested.

"What, then find out in the morning that we lost the trail hours before? No," Jimmy D said, "We're on a well marked trail, when we can't see we need to stop for the night." Henderson huffed a bit but understood that Autry was right.

Night fell fast in the timbered heights of the Diamond Mountains, and Clarence Wilkinson knew he had to give up the chase for the night. He'd sleep until early dawn, and chase that bastard down. "He has to stop, too. Can't run through these mountains in the dark." It was a warm camp, under a rock outcrop. He watched thunderclouds build high and come closer. He had a fire, had cold water, but had no food.

"Wish Erikson and Oster had caught up." He snickered at the thought. *How could they catch up. I was riding far harder and faster than I should have been. Horse will be glad for this night of rest.* He wrapped up in his bedroll, felt the overwhelming loss of his daughter, the extreme anxiety of an unknown end to all this, and was asleep fast, only to be awakened a few hours later when the storm opened up on the mountain. Rain fell in great curtains, driven by fierce winds. Wilkinson cowered as far back under the rocks as he could get. Lightning hit trees, thunder cracked so loud he thought his ears would be damaged.

He was far enough under the rocks that he could keep his fire going, and as the late night turned slowly to morning, he knew his chase was probably over. Heavy rain had fallen for hours and any prints that might have existed were washed clean away. "I'm going to move slowly around and see if I can find something," he said, but knew it would be in vain.

It was late in the morning that Erikson led the small posse up to where Wilkinson was sitting on a rock. "Washed us out, Toby. Would have had him today." Clarence Wilkinson looked like a beaten man as he gazed at his longtime friend. "My baby, Toby. I can't just turn back."

"Whoever did this seems to be moving in a definite direction, Clarence. That's what led us to you this morning. I think we should continue, staying in that same direction. He'll have to move this morning also, and that would give us fresh prints to follow."

"I think you just earned yourself a raise, Toby Erikson. I should have thought of that." He looked around at the expanded posse. "Any and all that want to continue, you're now on my personal payroll. We'll follow you, Toby. Lead on."

"You ain't payin' nobody, Wilkinson," Jimmy Henderson said. We're riding for Cynthia." Wilkinson nodded with a hint of a mile and motioned for Toby to lead the posse out.

"We're probably looking for a line shack or something similar, men. We need to spread out some but keeping in sight. Look for fresh prints or a cabin. Keep sharp and holler out if you see something."

Jimmy Henderson rode up alongside Toby Erikson. "Go on, Toby. You seem to have a feel for this."

"He's following the natural terrain but knows where he's going, Mr. Henderson. I sure hope I'm right. A man stealing a beautiful little girl like Cynthia needs to die hard, and I'm making plans as I ride."

CHAPTER TWENTY

The heavy rain and wind didn't let up until late that night, which frustrated Corcoran. "I wanted that fool to ride right up to me. I wanted to be looking in his eyes when I killed him. I hate outlaws and this one, the most." He had a fire going and made coffee before moving out where he could once again see the mine road. The morning was cold this high up, and Corcoran could see the road hadn't had a visitor since the rain stopped.

Just a few miles up the trail, James Cannon fought off the night, grabbed a quick cold biscuit to eat and saddled up. His only thought was to get back to his cabin, gather up all the money and whatever might be available, and head for Denver. He knew there were people chasing him and couldn't imagine just how close they were.

Less than three miles down the east side of the Cortez Range from where Cannon stood, Eureka County Sheriff, Ed Connors, stood in front of a small fire drinking coffee. "Let's get moving. Won't see any sign until that boy starts moving," he said. He quickly rinsed the tin cup and got his horse saddled. "We'll simply ride for the mine road and we'll intercept the murderer. Them rocks work out for you, Mr. Berry?"

"Comfy," Berry snarled, stepping up and into his saddle. "I'll never complain about my lumpy mattress again. You said last night that you thought we were getting close to our killer. What makes you think that?"

"That wind was blowing hard, just before the rains hit, Berry." The sheriff said. "If we were half an hour behind him, the wind would have altered his prints some. His prints stood out, if you remember. Now, let's move."

Connors led with Skitters off to the right some and Berry bringing up the rear. It was hard climbing on slippery rock, slimy mud, and cold air, and the posse made the best time they could. The sun was well up by the time they made the crest of the Cortez Range and dropped down through large rock formations to the trail that would lead them to the mine road. "He's on the road, boys," the sheriff yelled out. He was pointing at fresh horse prints on the trail. "Let's pick it up now." He put his horse in a trot and led the posse down toward the main road.

Cannon rode out from the rocks where he spent the night onto the trail knowing he had to shake the posse that was surely behind him. It was wet and muddy and as he rode he glanced down to see what a perfect trail he was leaving. He couldn't put his horse in a hard run down the hill in slick mud, they'd flounder for sure, and he couldn't just ride off the road, either. He'd be back in heavy trees and out-crops, and still leaving a strong trail to follow.

He was riding toward a steep switchback and just before the switchback he saw a large outcrop off to the side of the road. "Ambush time," he muttered, rode quickly to that rock, and around behind it, dismounting immediately. He had no idea he was being watched.

Corcoran spotted the movement at once and watched the outlaw jump from his horse, rifle in hand. "Somebody following that boy, eh?" He made sure his rifle was ready, checked his Colt for load, and hunkered down. Cannon was just out of range, the deputy thought, but if someone was coming, and he hoped it was Ed Connors, he could certainly help.

The switchback was a double and steep. Two switchbacks back to back made for steep country.

If he tried to get closer, he would be climbing up through jumbled rock and scattered trees, and about as visible as a man could be. The turns were wide enough for the heavily laden ore wagons to navigate, and that meant a lot of open space. "Gotta move up closer, but not scare that boy," he murmured. He stayed low, used every rock and tree around, and eased his way down to the next level.

Ed Connors motioned for Skitters to ride alongside. "He has to know that he's leaving a perfect trail for us to follow," Connors said. "What would you do?"

"Get behind a tree and shoot you," Skitters said. "I've been on this road a hunnert times, Ed. There's a bazillion places to set up an ambush. He's lived in these hills all his life. He knows that."

Connors motioned for them to stop and have a little chat. "Let's split up some. Dean, I want you to hold back several hundred yards and stay off the road if you can. It will mean hard riding but you might save our lives." He looked around at the rolling flanks of the mountains, and deep folds where they met and were the cause for switchbacks, and pointed up the hill.

"Skitters, keep your eyes wide open and ride on down the road. I'm going up there. Give me a little bit of a head start, and ride out. Each of us needs to remember where each of us is. Let's not shoot each other if get ourselves in a gunfight."

James Cannon caught a movement down the hill behind him and twisted to watch. He saw a man with a rifle move from sage brush to rock, slowly climbing up to where he was. He would disappear behind something, then move quickly. From Cannon's point, looking down the steep switchbacks, it wasn't hard to spot Corcoran's moves. If it had been level ground, he probably wouldn't have seen the big deputy.

Cannon slipped out from his little grotto on one of those moves. He slipped down to his horse and jumped in the saddle. "Where did that man come from?" Cannon muttered, riding into thick timber. "Did he come up the trail? Maybe there wasn't anyone behind me." Cannon rode at a slow walk through the forest and rocks, well off the mine road.

Cannon rode down, always down, always near but not on the mine road, and within half an hour had regained the well used highway, well below where he had been. He saw Corcoran's prints coming up and smiled. That was a big win for the young outlaw, and he urged his horse into a strong trot that would carry him for miles before that fool up there even knew he'd been given the slip.

Corcoran reached a point where he felt he would

be in good rifle range and settled behind some piled up rock. He hadn't gotten comfortable yet and saw a man, high on the side of the hill, working his horse toward the switchback. "That sure as hell looks like Ed Connors," Corcoran muttered. If he waved, Cannon would see him and if he did nothing, Cannon would see Connors.

Corcoran spent several minutes trying to locate the outlaw. He knew where he should be, but that spot was hidden now that Corcoran had moved. "Can't just sit here and watch Ed walk into an ambush. Damn it," he muttered, raised his rifle and put a shot into the rocks where Cannon should be. There was no answering shot, but Connors leaped from his horse and took cover in some stunted cedar.

Corcoran put his hat on the end of his rifle and waved it as high as he could reach, hoping to get Connors attention. If Cannon shot at the hat, he would give his position away as well. Connors spotted the waving flag and raised his rifle but didn't shoot.

"Somebody wants my attention," he muttered. There were no more shots fired and Connors slowly worked his way to his horse, and using it for protection, made his way down toward the mine road. He didn't draw any fire, either. "That's strange," Connors muttered. He saw Skitters come around the massive rock at the top of the switchback and waved him to a stop, pointing toward where Corcoran was.

Skitters was soon joined by Dean Berry and they watched Connors slowly descend through the maze of brush, trees, and rocks. It was apparent that if someone was hiding, they weren't going to shoot, and Corcoran stood up, again waving his rifle and hat. They all met in the middle of the road within minutes.

"Somebody was here, and very recently," Skitters said, pointing at Cannon's tracks that led off the road and into the forest. "Musta saw us or heard us."

"Probably spotted me," Corcoran said. He looked at the trail and then at the road. "I'd bet he made his way down the hill a mile or so and jumped back up on the road. He's making time right now, well in front of us."

"Just to make sure, Skitters, follow his trail through the trees." Sheriff Connors wasn't going to take any chances on losing this outlaw. "The rest of us, let's mount up and ride. If he doesn't get back on the road, Skitters, chase him down."

Skitters just nodded and left out. "I'll catch up." Corcoran said. "My horse is a mile down that way."

"Jump on," Dean Berry said. He offered a hand and Corcoran swung up behind the deputy. "You're too old to be walking." He got a stiff whack in the back for the comment and laughed, riding down the main road to where Corcoran had camped. "This Cannon boy seems to be pretty sure of himself."

"Too sure or just lucky, Mr. Berry. He knows his little trick will be found out and he'll be riding hard."

The posse was at a lope for the next many miles down off the high Cortez Range. James Cannon rode his horse at a lope, then a walk, then a lope and connected with the Eureka-Palisade highway much later in the day. He rode south for several miles before turning east and climbing into the Diamond Mountains toward his cabin and all that money.

"Won't be close before it gets dark," Cannon muttered. He rode up the little trail alongside a creek, looking for somewhere to camp that would be hidden and protected. He knew there were men following, knew also that they would be stopped by the dark. "I wonder who that was sneaking through the rocks. Sure glad I saw him."

CHAPTER TWENTY-ONE

"Do you really think we're gonna find something?" Nils Oster was tired, grumpy, and hungry. He was nearing fifty, spent most of his time in the office, always thought he would ride through hell's fires for Wilkinson, but had serious second thoughts on this cold morning. "There's been no indication that anyone has been anywhere near where we are."

"If we don't cut sign or find something by nightfall, we'll call it," Clarence Wilkinson said. He didn't say it in anger but he did give Nils a hard look. "We know he's in the area, and we know he has my daughter. We'll find that bastard and bring him in dead."

They rousted a couple of mule deer as the afternoon dragged on, and there was more and more complaining. They were spread out, covering a lot of ground but not finding anything until Jimmy Autry yelled out, "Got something." He was up a slight hill in heavy forest and climbed down from his horse. "We got him," he yelled again. He walked through the trees into an open area and climbed back in the saddle.

"Oh, yeah. Here we go," he hollered out again. "Just fall in behind me, boys. He's making like a crow for that ridge there." Autry put his horse in a trot and the expanded posse cleared the ridge in minutes. They were looking down on a small line-shack with a corral. There was smoke coming from the chimney but no horse in the corral.

"Easy now," Henderson said as he and Autry led the group down toward the cabin. "Ain't the right time to die, boys."

"You're right," Wilkinson said. "Let's dismount, Nils, you hold the horses, and we'll spread out and walk in slow and quiet. He'd be shooting if he saw us, so let's not let that happen."

They spread out through rocks, brush, and trees, and slowly made their way off the hillside. When they were less than twenty yards from the cabin, Wilkinson spotted the trail that Jacob Best had left earlier that morning. Damn, it," he said. "He's gone, boys." He yelled back at Nils to bring those horses down.

Inside, they found the bloody rags Best had used to clean Cynthia's wounds. Clarence Wilkinson was in a rage and almost raced for his horse. "Wait," Autry yelled. "We'll all ride that bastard down."

"Look at this," Jimmy Henderson howled out. "Holy damnation, would you look at this?" He had two canvas bags emptied on a cot. "There's thousands of dollars here. Is this Sonny Kinkaid's money?"

Autry walked over and looked at cash, coin, and some sheets of paper. "It is Kinkaid's," he said. "These are receipts from the sale, in his name. This is the robber's nest but Corcoran said that Jacob Best couldn't possibly have been involved in Kinkaid's killing."

"You're right," Henderson said. "Corcoran's sure it was the Cannon brothers what done that. But, I remember him also saying that the Cannons and Best were good friends."

"There's only one track leading out and I'm on it right now," Wilkinson said. He'd heard enough talk.

"Grab the money, Autry, and let's ride that bastard down." Henderson whacked the stockyard owner on the shoulders and ran for his horse.

They were on the trail in minutes, working through a myriad of game, buckaroo, and hunter trails, slowly coming down the mountain. "If you came to that cabin often," Jimmy Autry said, "you would know these trails well. There is a pattern to them that if you rode up here often, you would know how to get to that cabin without having to do a lot of cross-country."

"The man we're following knows where he's going and doesn't seem to care whether anyone might be coming along after him." Henderson and Autry were riding side-by-side on a well used trail. "Doesn't this trail lead to Hell's Canyon? Seems like I've hunted elk on this trail many more times than once. The trail splits about half a mile in front of us, one side going deep into the canyon, and the other along a narrow trail across the face of the canyon wall."

"Yeah, about five hundred feet up that wall." Autry gave a shiver thinking about that trail. "This is the steepest most dangerous part of the Diamond Mountains. Lost a lot of buckaroos in this country. And hunters," he said.

"What's the hold up?" Clarence Wilkinson rode up to where Henderson and Autry were talking. "This the trail to Hell's Canyon?"

"Sure is, Clarence. We were talking about the high route. I hope that bastard didn't take it."

They stayed on the trail to where it split. "Going the high route, boys. If your horse ain't perfect, turn around here." Henderson had the posse around him. "This is narrow, footing ain't good, and it's a long damn way to the bottom." He turned his horse and led off with Toby Erikson right behind him.

Sheriff Connors and Deputy Corcoran led the men onto the Palisade Road at a lope, following the fresh prints left by James Cannon. "Watch for him to leave the road," Corcoran yelled out. "This is his country, knows it well, and probably has someplace to run to. He's much more apt to run into the Diamonds than back into the Cortez Range. It's for damn sure he ain't gonna ride to Eureka."

It was less than half an hour later that Skitters saw where Cannon ran off the main road onto a smaller trail. "Here we go," he yelled out. Connors and Corcoran, who had been leading, turned back through sage, never losing stride, and joined Skitters, already at a full run.

"Ease her back, Skitters. Let's not kill the horses." Corcoran rode up alongside the skinny little deputy. "We'll be climbing fast, old son. Ease her off." They settled in at a solid trot, slowing to a walk every several miles to let the horses catch their breath.

They found that Cannon would leave one trail, go cross-country for a short time and join another trail, always climbing, higher and higher. "That boy knows where he's going." Ed Connors was leading the pack now. The trails evaded the heavy timber and large rock outcrops, wove through steep country, all the time climbing for the clouds. "Bet we've made fifty or more switchbacks," the sheriff said.

"Is that smoke?" Connors was pointing to the top of a ridge where a wisp of smoke could be seen through the heavy forest. "Must be a cabin on the other side. Let's not clear that ridge, boys. We'll tie it up this side and walk in, slow and ready. Corcoran, you lead us in."

There were jumbled rocks along a saw-tooth ridge they had to climb over, but the rocks and scattered alpine trees gave plenty of cover for the small posse. Corcoran knew they were making a lot of racket going through the loose and scattered rocks, but knew also there was nothing that could be done about it. They covered the wind carved ridge-top and looked down on a pleasant little meadow surrounded by heavy forest. A natural spring fed a small creek that tumbled out of the high country, searching for the valley below.

James Cannon rode fast and hard for hours always stopping for just seconds to check the trail behind him and let his horse catch its breath. He cleared the ridge and was looking down at his cabin. "There shouldn't be smoke coming from the chimney." He tensed, crouched, and quietly made his way down. Did Jacob

Best come back? Are there hunters down there? He was within a few hundred yards of the cabin when he spotted the tracks of several horses leaving out from the place. They cleared a ridge almost due west of the cabin. He came in from the north.

Rifle in hand, he stepped off his horse, tying it to a tree, and slowly worked his way to the cabin. He saw hoof and boot prints, figured there must have been at least five, maybe more, men in and around the place earlier. It was getting late, would be dark in a couple of hours. Would they be back? He needed to grab that sack of money and get out of there.

"Oh, my God, is my money still there?" He was almost in a panic, thinking about that. That was more money than James Cannon ever thought even existed. He had the small pickings from the stage robbery tied tight to his saddle, but they were nothing compared to what should be in that cabin.

For three years he and Willy had used the place for their 'hideout' and only once or twice had anyone just showed up. Now, five or more men had been there? Who were these people? Willy was dead, the sheriff must know that James was his partner. Maybe Willy wasn't dead. Maybe he told the sheriff about the cabin. "I gotta get out of here."

The door of the cabin wasn't pulled to and he

pushed it open with barrel of his rifle and eased in-side. The cabin looked like it had been trashed and Cannon made a dash for the cot, under which, there should be a large canvas bag full of money. His cut and Willy's too. "No," he cried out when he turned the bed over and found nothing there. "Some bas-tard's stole my money."

He made a quick search, under the other cot, in boxes and cabinets, and was almost sick at what he felt was his lost money. He found the bloody rags and they didn't make any sense, either. "I gotta get out of here. Elko, that's where I'll go, get enough money to make Denver."

Corcoran and Skitters worked their way down the hillside to the makeshift corral and moved Cannon's horse out. "Take it back and tie it off somewhere." Corcoran said, and moved toward the cabin. The door stood open but it was too dark inside for him to see anything. He heard scuffling, not of men jostling but of someone moving things around.

"He's getting ready to run," Corcoran murmured. He had his rifle at the ready, stood to the side of the open door and yelled. "You're surrounded, James Cannon. This is Corcoran, Terrence Corcoran. Come on out and you'll live."

He was answered by two quick shots from inside. Corcoran saw the flashes of gunpowder and fired his rifle at them. He was answered by howls of pain and rushed inside in time to see James Cannon fall forward onto the floor, clutching his stomach. "Now, you ain't gonna live." Corcoran grimaced, knowing what a terrible wound that was. "It's gonna hurt and there ain't nothing we can do about it."

"Who do you suppose all those other prints out there belong to?" Ed Connors was inside the cabin, knelt down next to Corcoran and Cannon. "More than six or seven people were here earlier."

"They stole my money," Cannon tried to say.

"Your money?" Terrence Corcoran stood up with an ugly look on his face. "Your money? You ain't never had more than a half eagle in your life, James Cannon." Corcoran looked around the cabin and found some papers on the floor. He handed one of them to Sheriff Connors. "Sonny Kinkaid's money, you filthy killer. You'll be dead before morning, Cannon, and that's a shame because I really would rather see you hang."

Connors got the outlaw's shirt open enough to see the terrible damage that rifle bullet did and closed the shirt. "I'm afraid Corcoran's right, boy. Ain't nothing we can do about a wound like that. Who do you suppose was here? You're gonna die, son, so you might as well tell us who it is took the money."

James Cannon was in horrible pain, terrified of dying, and spat it out. "Jacob Best."

"Dean, you stay with him, keep the cabin warm, and bury him in the morning." He had a forlorn look on his face as he continued. "I'm going to ask you to do the worst job in law enforcement, Dean. I should do it, and I think everyone here would agree that I need to continue being on the chase."

"After you bury this piece of filth, I want you to ride to Emil and Rose and inform them that both their boys are dead. I'm afraid that Rose will be difficult, but they have to know how and why Willy and James are dead."

"I will, Sheriff. I'd rather it be you, but Jacob Best needs to be caught and you need to be with Corcoran when he is."

Connors nodded his thanks. "Corcoran, Skitters, Let's ride. We've got a few hours before dark. Let's get close to that bastard, Jacob Best." Connors was out the door that fast with Corcoran and Skitters right behind.

"Why would Best be riding with a bunch of other men?" Corcoran asked not expecting any kind of answer. "He killed Zack Bennett and Jack Hopkins but never ran with a gang, unless you call Willy and James a gang."

"We'll ride that bunch down, Corcoran, and you can ask him before we hang the bastard." Riding in the high country, trying to follow a trail, isn't easy, but following the trail left by seven horses isn't that difficult, even if it is in some of the roughest country in Nevada.

CHAPTER TWENTY-TWO

"I ain't one to go out on that ledge when the sun's going down," Autry said and got more than one piece of agreement from the gathered posse.

"It would be too dangerous," Wilkinson had to agree. "I'm going to go a ways out on foot, at least I might see something."

"I'll go with you, Clarence," Jimmy Henderson said. "Even on foot, this trail is most dangerous." He looked back at the gathered men. "Make up a good camp. We'll be back and continue on in the morning."

The trail across the face of that canyon was carved out of the natural rock and hoof prints were hard to come by. Just a scrape here and there, a small patch of mud with a fresh print in it, was all the two men saw as they carefully walked along. The mountain dropped away, vertical for several hundred feet, then sloping out with great slabs of broken rock, but still steep.

"This trail saved a full day's travel when the prospectors opened this country," Jimmy Henderson said. "More than likely the big horn sheep and Ancient Indians used it regular. Imagine leading a mule train along here."

"I'd rather not," Wilkinson said. "Why would Jacob Best abduct my daughter and bring her along this trail?" He instinctively knew why. He knew they would look over the rocky edge and see the girl's broken body, hundreds of feet down. What terror had that foul creature caused that beautiful little girl? Rage was building, even Jimmy Henderson could see it in the man's face, hear it in his angry voice.

"Maybe we should go back, wait until morning, Clarence. It's getting dark and mighty dangerous out here." It would be the sensible thing to do, Clarence knew.

Toby Erikson had a good fire going, there were lean-tos set up and the horses were in fair grass when Henderson and Wilkinson got back. Nothing was said, the men understanding that nothing had been seen. "We'll move out in open daylight," Wilkinson said. "You mentioned that you've hunted this country for years, Henderson. Does that trail that leads down into the canyon follow along this rock face down there?"

"Same general direction but well out from the wall. Rock slides, debris, timber, would get in the way if you tried to follow. It turns and follows the terrain down the canyon. What are you thinking?"

"I guess nothing," Wilkinson said. Henderson saw it, though. Wilkinson already believed they would find his daughter's body at the base of that cliff. "We'll leave when it's light enough to see and walk out on that trail safely."

"It's getting too dark to see," Skitters said as they worked their way down a winding, brush filled trail. "Need to camp up, Sheriff."

"I know," Ed Connors said. "I want to catch up to those men we're following. Need to know who they are, why they were at that cabin, who has Kinkaid's money." It was a sad Sheriff Ed Connors who had to call it a day. A long day, one outlaw captured, trailing what he thought was another. "Find us some grass for the horses, Skitters, and we'll call it a day. Been in this saddle for a hunnert hours so far today."

Corcoran had been riding well out in front of the two and called back. "I think we found 'em Sheriff." He was pointing down the hill where the faintest hint of a camp fire lit the surrounding trees. "Half a mile down there."

"Let's go easy, Terrence. There's a bunch more of them than us." Connors urged his horse forward and the three walked slowly down the trail. "We think it's Jacob Best and who the others are, who knows? They will have guns, Best is wanted for open murder." He was setting the stage for the possibility of a wild, in the dark, gunfight. As they got closer they could smell meat cooking, hear voices, and were able to see shadowy figures moving about. "Not too close now," Connors whispered.

Corcoran stepped off his horse and handed the reins to Skitters. "Wait for me," he said and moved off into the trees and brush. He was about twenty yards out when he spotted Jimmy Henderson and Clarence Wilkinson standing near the camp fire. A second cooking fire had three men near it, and others were scattered about, already eating.

"Hello the camp," Corcoran yelled out. "This is Terrence Corcoran yellin'. Don't shoot the sheriff."

"What the hell are you doing out here?" Henderson hollered out.

"I'll tell you all about it," he answered, turned, and hollered out to Connors and Skitters to come on in. "It's a long damn story, Jimmy and I think it's about to get longer. What the hell are you doing out here?"

There were ten men standing around that fire instantly, all talking at the same time. It was Wilkinson who got things quieted down. "I ought to shoot you where you stand, Sheriff." He was once again in a rage and Corcoran stepped forward, standing between the two men.

"No, you won't, Clarence." He reached out slowly and eased the rifle from the mine superintendent's hands. "We just killed the man that robbed the stage coach yesterday, we ain't gonna be doing anymore killing today. What's this all about?"

"Stage coach robbery?" Wilkinson hadn't heard anything about that.

"Everybody settle down," Sheriff Connors said. "Corcoran, tell these fine gentlemen what we've been doing and when he's through, Henderson, you tell us what you've been doing. Ain't that often a bunch of men from Eureka get together in Hell's Canyon for a little chat. No guns, no anger."

Corcoran told them about the stage coach robbery, about Willy Cannon's death and the chase to capture James, only to have to shoot the boy. "The most interesting part was finding a receipt from Jimmy Autry's stockyard sale made out to Sonny Kinkaid. James Cannon admitted the robbery but said he thought Jacob Best had stolen the money."

"He didn't," Autry said. "He stole Wilkinson's

daughter, Cynthia. We have Kinkaid's money." Autry went on to tell their story and when he was through Ed Connors walked over to Clarence Wilkinson.

"I understand your anger, Clarence. I hope you understand why I wasn't in the office to respond to Cynthia's abduction."

"I do now, Ed. Sorry about the rifle thing." The two men shook hands.

"We'll all finish this search and capture that bastard tomorrow," Connors said.

Best didn't know the country as well as the Cannon boys but he had spent most of his young life on the run and wasn't afraid of being alone in a strange forest. His plan, even if it took two or three days, was to get back to Eureka, steal a horse and supplies, and make for other country.

After several hours he found himself deep in a canyon that hosted a small creek spilling down one side and made a small camp under an outcrop. He hauled his saddlebags with him the whole day and took this time to find out just what he had. "Flint and striker is good, small canteen is good, and only a few slices of dried meat. That ain't good," he muttered. He had his rifle and sidearm, a good knife, and that's it.

"Bedroll's still on that damn saddle," he groused. He made up a small fire in front of the outcrop, drank some water, and laid out on leaves and grass, glad it wasn't winter. There was just a hint that sunrise might be on its way when he left out. He filled the small canteen when he crossed the stream, and followed the canyon down.

It was late in the day that he spotted the young fawn and shot it. He roasted the liver on some hot rocks and ate most of it. He cut away the back strap. "That's enough to get me to Eureka. He didn't stop moving until he realized just how dark it was, found some trees to sleep under. Didn't bother to light a fire, just ate the rest of the roasted liver.

Morning came and Jacob Best took the time to try and figure out where he was in relation to the valley and the town of Eureka. He was in the rolling foothills, probably five to seven miles out from and above the Palisade Road, and maybe ten miles north of the stockyards. "I can have a horse before dark," he muttered. That would be a very long walk in difficult terrain. He roasted a piece of meat and enough to eat on the trail, and lit out, staying in the foothills, toward the stockyards and a sure horse.

There was never a thought in his mind that he might be followed, that Wilkinson might put together a posse to save his daughter, that men with rifles were out to kill him dead. His little camp sites were just left, his tracks were deep in mud in many places. A man with bad eyesight could follow his trail.

"This is a big group of men," Connors said. They were standing and sitting around the morning fire eating biscuits and drinking coffee. "We know Best and Cynthia left out across that rock face, and that's all we know. I'd like to split us up into two groups, one to follow across the top of the canyon, and the other to take the low road into the canyon."

"Why would you want to do that?" Jimmy Henderson walked around some, anxious to get started. "What sign there is points out that he went across on the high trail."

"I know, Jimmy, and I can't tell you why, but I just have a hunch that his plans were changed for him and we need to cover all the areas. I'll take a few men down the lower trail, and Corcoran you follow from the top. If I come across something, I'll send a runner. Corcoran, you do the same."

This wasn't a suggestion from Sheriff Connors. It was the way it would be and no one argued. Connors was in his second term as sheriff, had done superb work keeping Eureka safe, and wasn't going to let this murdering, kidnapping bastard color his reputation. "Let's get moving. It's going to be a long day, I'm afraid."

Henderson, Skitters, and two of the cowboys from the stockyards rode with Connors, while Wilkinson, Autry, and the others rode with Corcoran. The morning was cool at their altitude, but they knew it would be a blistering day in the valley. They were lucky the previous night, not getting swamped by a thunderstorm, but would that last?

"Stay off your horses and walk them along this cliff," Corcoran said. "Keep your eyes open for some kind of sign. It won't be like in mud, dirt, or grass, just something out of place or doesn't look right."

It was single file, plenty of room between the men, and each man was fearful that his horse would be the one to throw a fit, or would slip and go over the edge. It was Autry who spotted the turned over rocks, scrapes in the hard surface, and signs of a fuss of some kind. "What would make those marks, Corcoran? Look how the scrapes on the rock are."

"Those are the signs of a terrified horse, Jimmy." Corcoran spent a long time going over the marks, which were spread out over several yards. Wilkinson was right alongside him the whole way.

Toby Erikson made the discovery when he followed one set of scrapes close to the cliff's edge. "Oh, no," he cried out, falling to his knees. "No, no."

The girls body was slightly up the rock slide from the horse's, and neither was moving. They were several hundred feet down the cliff. Wilkinson was on his knees peering over the side and Corcoran stood directly behind him, just in case.

"Toby," Wilkinson said, quietly. Ride your horse hard, find the sheriff, and bring him back." He slowly got to his feet, tears running freely across his dirty face. Corcoran slipped an arm around him and held him tight. "I'm all right, Corcoran, but thank you. How will we get her out of there? How is it she and the horse are down there, but that bastard isn't?"

Corcoran knew but this wasn't the time or place to say what happened. He could see it in the scrape marks in the rock. The horse being terrified, on purpose, in some way, and forced to fall from the cliff. "We'll have to come up from the bottom of Hell's Canyon, Clarence. We'll get her." He squeezed the man's shoulders. "And, we'll get him. He's on foot now, Clarence. We'll get him."

Corcoran saw a big problem and took a minute or two to work it out. Jacob Best wass on foot, he knew, but which way did he go? Nobody had looked for boot marks at the edge of the cliff where the trail started. Nobody had gone to the other end of the cliff to look, either. He motioned Autry over.

"Take someone with you to the end of the cliff and look for boot marks. Fire off two shots if you find them. Best is on foot but we don't know which way he went."

"On my way," the stockyard boss said, motioning for one of the buckaroos to follow him. Corcoran motioned for everyone else to follow him back off the cliff face, where it was safer.

"Our man is on foot, gentlemen. We probably ruined any prints he might have left if he went back this way. If Mr. Autry finds prints, he went that way. If not, we will have to carefully spread out and look at this end. This will slow us down a little bit, but we'll get him."

Within fifteen minutes they saw Jimmy Autry and his man walking back toward them having not fired a shot. "Damn," Corcoran said. "All right, spread out and be careful. We need to know which way he might be going."

CHAPTER TWENTY-THREE

"Look here, Sheriff." It was Skitters, pointing at the ground some fifteen feet or so from a rock overhang. "Looks like a man-nest to me. Ain't no horse prints around, either. This man's on foot and I'd bet your salary it's our man."

"You men stay put for a minutes." Connors hollered at the two who came with them. "Don't want to mess up any sign that might be here. Skitters, see if you can find out which way this yahoo lit out." Connors went over the area where Best spent a night, but didn't come up with anything.

"He's in for a long walk, Sheriff. Easy to follow, though. Rains have left the ground nice and damp and his prints stand out. Probably heading for the valley floor. Looks like your hunch was a good one."

"Ride back to Corcoran, Skitters, and bring that

bunch down here. We'll keep going and you catch up." Skitters rode out and Connors showed the two men who would be with him the prints and where they started out.

"Let's ride that bastard down boys." They made good time following prints that Best hadn't given thought to hiding. It was past mid-day when they found the remains of the young deer and the fire he made, and they found his little cave. Before it got dark.

"Gotta remember to tell that feller thanks for leaving us such a good supper," one of the buckaroos from the Autry's sale barn said. "We gonna make camp here, Sheriff?"

"We're making good time but we're still well behind him," Connors said. "Let's keep going. We can make another few miles before it gets dark and Corcoran can catch up with us tomorrow."

"I'll just tie this little critter up and we can finish butchering it out when we do. Shame to waste this much good meat."

Skitters was climbing back toward the top of the canyon when he heard a rider coming down hill. He got behind a large spruce and waited, stepping out just as the man got there. His rifle aimed at the man's chest, he hollered for him to stop.

"Riding down to tell you the girl's been found. They want the sheriff back up there," Erikson said.

"We found Best's trail and I'm riding to bring Corcoran and you folks down for the chase. I'll ride up with you."

They reached the camp site quickly and Skitters told his story. "Good work, Skitters," Corcoran said. He gathered everyone around the fire for some planning. "We have two jobs and we have enough people to do both. The sheriff is on the trail of Jacob Best and I'll be leaving with Skitters shortly to join him. I'll want to take a couple of you with me. Best is a slippery bastard and we'll need to overwhelm him."

"We also have the task of recovering little Cynthia's body. That won't be an easy chore but it must be done."

"I'm staying with Clarence Wilkinson," Jimmy Henderson said. "We'll come to her from the bottom of the canyon and care for the remains properly." Clarence reached out and grasped Henderson's shoulder in thanks.

"It won't be easy, Jimmy," Corcoran said, "But find out whether she died in the fall or was dead before. We will need that for evidence in court. We have a lot of daylight, so whoever is coming with me, let's go."

"Does that mean you're planning on taking Best alive?" Wilkinson hadn't given that any thought at all. In his mind, this chase was to kill Jacob Best on sight. "I want that man hurting bad before he dies."

"My job is to capture criminals and bring them before a court of law, Clarence. If at all possible I'll be bringing Best in alive."

"You don't want me with you when we catch him, then," Wilkinson said. "Not after what he did to my little Cynthia. That man needs to hurt bad."

The men standing around all nodded and Corcoran knew, deep down, that he would almost be willing to step aside and let that happen. "Jacob Best is the worst kind of outlaw. He's a bully and coward, and that means he takes pleasure in hurting people. I agree, Clarence, the man deserves to die hard, but I will do everything in my power to see to it that he gets a fair trial. Situations like this, Clarence, are one of the reasons many men get out of wearing this old tin badge. Catch 'em and kill 'em ain't the way the law reads."

"I'm just an old tramp miner, Corcoran," Wilkinson said. "And that was my daughter. I'm not wearing a tin badge and right now I don't give a hoot in hell about what the law says."

"We'll stay with you," Jimmy Henderson said. "Corcoran, go chase that bastard down, and I hope he fights back and you kill him dead." The grumbling ended with that comment and Corcoran mounted up.

Henderson, Wilkinson, and Toby Erikson stayed and would work their way to Cynthia's body. "Kill that bastard, Corcoran," Clarence said. Corcoran tried to hide his smile as he rode off with Skitters alongside.

"Mr. Wilkinson is more right than we are, Terrence," he said. "Maybe not according to the book, but sure as hell according to my heart."

"I know, Skitters," Corcoran whispered. "That's what makes it so hard."

Jacob Best stayed in the lowest fringes of forest, about a mile up in the foothills from the Palisade Road. He could see the road and anyone on it but it would be almost impossible for anyone to see him. The day was boiling August hot, thunderstorms were a definite possibility, and he hadn't filled his canteen when he had the chance. "I ain't gonna die like this," he swore, but was getting more anxious about the situation.

"I'm a good seven miles or more from the stockyards and I'm sure there ain't no springs between here and there. Ain't much shade, either," he muttered. "Don't want to, but I gotta sit down and rest. Tired," he almost whispered. He found a ravine with some heavy brush along its crest and settled in the skimpy shade. "Catch my breath, that's all."

His last drink of water had been at the little springs where he spent the night. That was more than twelve hours ago and he'd been walking though rough country, climbing over rocky outcrops, and flailing his way through downed trees. He was asleep in minutes and didn't come awake until great splashes of water wakened him. The increasing crashes of thunder had no affect.

"Water," he murmured, and got slowly to his feet. He raised his face to the torrent and opened his mouth wide. "I'm gonna drown," he laughed. He scrambled out of the gully instinctively, and found where a small stream was emptying into the ravine. He filled his canteen first, then drank at least three tin-cups full of cold rain water.

He was soaked to the bone, it was pitch dark, and he knew he couldn't climb back in that gulch, now slowly beginning to run with water. It could be running full in minutes. He started walking, hoping to find a big tree, a rock outcrop, anything to get under. A flash of lightning and a cottonwood exploded, close enough that he actually ducked. Burning pieces of tree were thrown about and Best headed for what was left of it.

"It's always best if someone else makes the fire," he chuckled. He found a large branch already burning, added to it, and got as close as he dared, letting the fire heat him up. He spent some time gathering more wood, kept the fire high, finally laid his head down to sleep. "I'll be at the stockyards early, boys. Hope you'll have a good pony waiting for me."

His dreams were filled with horror. He saw Cynthia's dead face looking at him every time he closed his eyes, saw her and the horse crash through the rocks after the long fall, and worse, saw a posse riding down on him at a full gallop. He was up far earlier than he planned, tired and angry. "I'll have a horse today."

"I don't think we have to follow these prints at all, Sheriff." Terrence Corcoran was looking downhill to the west, and then south. "He's making for Eureka, and there's no doubt. Why don't you, Skitters, and Autry ride straight down to the valley and then back to town and wait there for him. Get the town riled some and watching for him.

"I'll stay on his trail and hope to catch him before he gets to town. He'll be looking for food and a horse. Don't forget that."

Connors didn't have to think twice about Corcoran's idea. "We'll pinch him off, Corcoran, you behind him and us waitin' for him. Let's go Skitters, time's a wasting."

Corcoran had to chuckle watching them ride off cross-country for the valley floor. They would be there in two or three hours and be in Eureka just a couple of hours after that. He had another few of pounds of deer meat left from what Best had shot, so he was in good shape for the rest of the chase.

"If I were Best," Jimmy Autry said, "I wouldn't go to Eureka. I'd ride to my feedlots and steal a horse. There are always saddled and bridled horses tied off for the corral riders. He could just walk in, get on a horse, and be gone before anyone knew he had been there."

"Damn, right," Connors said. "But not if we're there waitin' for him." They made good time riding out of the mountains, not having to keep on someone's trail, and were on the Palisade Road just about the time the thunder storms roared in. "Gonna be a wet night, damn it." Connors bellowed over the fury of a clap of thunder. "Rocks over yonder," he pointed and they rode hard and fast for them. "Like clockwork, ain't they? Just about the time you're feeling good about the day, they try to drown you out."

Skitters wasn't laughing, Autry had a wry smile, and Connors continued to bellow his frustration. The horses had good grass, the posse was crouched under some rocks, and thoughts of Jacob Best in irons made for a better night. "We're not ten miles from the stockyards, so we can get there fast in the morning," Connors said, striking his fire stick at some wet wood.

CHAPTER TWENTY-FOUR

"My God, that bastard bashed her head in. This didn't come from the fall," Wilkinson said, cradling his daughter's cold body. It was still partially wrapped in bloody shreds of a blanket, and there were pieces of bandage stuck to the head wound. "Killing him is too easy on him. Too good for that fiend." He held Cynthia tight, rocking back and forth, tears cascading across his cheeks.

His eyes darted about, first looking into Cynthia's battered face, then at the men standing around him. It was a wounded and forlorn father they saw. He wanted to say something and they wanted to, as well, but no one said anything as the large mining engineer sat, rocking slowly back and forth, cradling what was left of his daughter.

Clarence Wilkinson was a ferocious man in most

of his employee's minds. They had seen him with a double jack, single jack, seen him work a muck stick and move tons of rock. None had ever seen this side of the man. His frail wife could testify to his softness. She's seen him weep at her sicknesses, seen him be as soft and gentle as a goose down feather. Cynthia was his only child, the only child they would ever have. "She's gone," he whispered.

Jimmy Henderson carefully got Wilkinson to his feet, slowly took Cynthia's body from his arms, and led the man to a small fire that had been lit. "We'll have coffee shortly, Clarence. I think it would be better all the way around to bury her here."

"Her mother won't like that, Jimmy, but I know you're right. We're still two days or more from home and it is summer." Wilkinson's voice was flat, no emotion left in the man. He didn't have to bring out hot temperatures and a cold body. They knew and he knew. "Yes it is best that we do that." Wilkinson looked around at those standing by the fire. "Will you help?" He asked the men who had spent the day working their way to the girl's body.

"Of course," one said. A rock cairn was built and Cynthia was carefully laid in. Her wounds had been washed as clean as Clarence could make them, and he used his own bedroll to wrap her. The men stood back as he said a few words, so softly they couldn't hear most of them, and then the rocks were used to cover her, and protect the body from animals.

"This canyon was named right," he whispered, sitting down next to the fire. "Hells Canyon is the proper name. He had two small tree limbs tied together as a cross and stood it up near the cairn, great streaks of mud running down his haggard face. "Corcoran better not let me anywhere near that man," he whispered.

Henderson moved the men and camp away from the burial site. "We'll camp down the canyon some," he said. "We can leave out early in the morning and be home in a couple of days."

"Should we try to hook up with Corcoran and the sheriff? I want to get home as soon as possible, but I want to know that man is caught. Know that he will hang."

"If Jacob Best is on foot, they'll have him before we get there. We'll know it," Henderson said. "Let's make the best time we can for the Palisade Road. Hell's Canyon is steep, but we'll have a fair trail, good water, and good grass all the way down." He got no arguments and the men were packed, saddled, and moved to their new camp within the hour.

Corcoran was up before it was light, had a quick coffee and hard biscuits, and looked for Best's prints. "Damn that rain," he said. All he could come up with was mud. He slogged through wet grass and deep mud until mid-day, simply following the natural terrain. He stepped out of a large stand of pine and looked out across a rolling sidehill, hoping to catch sight of a walking man.

What he saw, several miles in front of him was Jimmy Autry's stockyards. "If I were on foot and needed a horse," he spoke right out, "that's where I'd go." He touched Dude with spurs and rode at a strong lope toward the corrals and sale barn. There were cows and horses in the corrals, and as he got closer he could see men moving about, seemingly in a hurry.

He raced in at a gallop and found Sheriff Connors in a heated discussion with a buckaroo. "Corcoran," Connors yelled out. "Get over here. Best can't be five minutes ahead of us. Took the road to Austin. His prints will stand out like a wildfire at night. Go, Terrence." He pointed west and Corcoran was on the road in seconds. "We'll catch up."

The buckaroo, still angry as a hornet, still bleeding about the head from the hit from Best's rifle butt, and still furious at the loss of his horse, shook his fist at Corcoran. "You get that bastard, Corcoran. You get my horse back."

"I know where he's going, too," Corcoran muttered. He had Dude at a hard trot, found where Best hit the main road west, and was glad to see there hadn't been any other traffic. "He's heading for that damn shack I never could find."

Best had his horse at a gallop but Corcoran kept his at a steady trot and it wasn't long that he saw Best had to ease off too. Best was riding at a walk now and Corcoran kept scanning the road and country on both sides. They had already covered several miles and Corcoran knew the big mine would be coming up shortly. "He's got to be cutting for those mountains to our south, but when," Corcoran muttered.

To the north, the broad valley opened up with deep gullies, large rock outcrops, and open plateaus, while the mountains rose quickly to his south. Those were the mountains that held Wilkinson's mine and the line shack where Best had hidden before.

Best jumped off the main road where a gully crossed, and rode the rocky bed for some time, then up through brush and trees, around large rocky areas, and into other gullies with their rocky bottoms. He was using all the tricks to throw off anyone who might be chasing him. He ran up one gully and into another, climbed out and stayed in tall grass before moving higher into the mountains.

"You're slowing me down, boy, and that just makes me a more angry man when I catch you," Corcoran growled. He and Dude were at a walk, staying on the trail. Best came to an area where great slabs of rocks had peeled from its face well above, and worked his way through, weaving, turning hard where no print was left, riding east for five or six minutes and climbing south before turning west for ten minutes. The tumbled rock-fall was filled with danger for the horses. A simple slip could bring a broken leg that fast.

It was a jumbled mess of rocks, few areas where a horse's print could be seen, and Corcoran was left groping about, searching for any sign. "This area must be close to where that line shack is. I've been in this rock field before. That line shack can't be above me," he murmured. "That's where this mass of rocks fell from, so it's either east or west."

Jacob Best had no trouble stealing the horse. He snuck up behind the buckaroo tying it off and bashed him across the side of the head with his rifle. He was surprised when the buckaroo who owned the horse actually took a couple of shots at him. He set the spurs and rode hard on the Austin highway for at least an hour before getting off the road to work his way to that cabin. "There's some food there, but I'll need more in order to get out of this country."

Best assumed there would be people chasing him but never saw anyone. He let his mind stray to what he'd done and knew he had to get as far from Eureka as he could, and as soon as he could. He saw her dead face, saw the horrible head wound, saw the horse go over the cliff every time he tried to rest or let his mind get off the race to get away.

Desperation was driving him but he fought to keep in control, to concentrate on making good his escape to the cabin. He dodged about through the rock fall and made his way west to the cabin. It was almost hidden, tucked under a massive rock and surrounded by pine trees and brush. The roughed in brush corral seemed almost natural to the setting and would hold his horse while he got what was there packed. "I gotta get into Eureka tonight and get supplies and food. Old Harry Martin at Martin's Supply would have just about everything I need."

The stolen horse had a bedroll tied on, empty saddlebags, which Best filled with what he had at the cabin, and a slicker. "Could have used this last night," he snickered. When he left the cabin, he rode through the trees, climbing high up the mountain side, and toward Eureka. "I'll find a downed tree or something and get some sleep, and hit that big old store after midnight."

Corcoran rode to the east edge of the large rock fall and could look down on Wilkinson's mine. He rode back and forth along the two or three miles of rock and knew he had picked the wrong side. "Not a trace," he said. It would take hours to work back across the rock field and then search that side and he knew he would run out of daylight before finishing the first part of the ride.

"I'm just a few miles from town. A hot bath, a hot steak supper, and a good night's sleep, and I'll find that yahoo tomorrow." When he worked his way back down to the main road he was met by Sheriff Connors and Skitters. He spent several minutes telling his story and the three turned back for town.

"I'll put together a ten man posse in the morning and we'll scour that mountain, Ed." Corcoran was angry, knew his boss was upset, and was worried about being able to catch Jacob Best.

"You're the best I've ever worked with, Terrence. Don't get yourself worked up to the point you're not thinking. Let your mind do its job." Ed Connors was upset. But not at Corcoran, just at not catching the outlaw. "You're far better than he is, Corcoran, and you're the best at using what little sign is left. I'm sure you're right that he is on this side of that rock fall. He's gonna want to get out of this area."

"What we don't know, Ed, is how much he might have as far as food and supplies at that shack. He could be loading up and getting ready to move out right now." Corcoran was frustrated.

They rode into town at a walk and pulled their horses up at the sheriff's office. Three tired, tin-star wearing men, duped by a young killer. Frustration and anger along with that fleeting thought of failure. "Go have a cold beer, Corcoran. Let your mind do its work. That's when you're the best."

"I'll have one with you," Skitters said. "I've chased a few outlaws with you, before, Corcoran, but this guy seems to be able to disappear. If he came out on the east side of that rock slide, he could have climbed high and around, and be sitting in those trees right up there, watching us."

"Well, Skitters, I wouldn't doubt that he is. If he has a full pack, though, come dark he will leave and we won't catch him. If he ain't, he's got to get one. I'm gonna work on that second thought." They took a table at the Bonanza Club and motioned for cold beer. "I need you to be rested and ready to spend most of the night working with me. Meet me at the office right after midnight, and have your horse saddled and ready for a long ride if what I'm thinking happens."

"You think he's coming to town tonight? Would he dare?"

"If he needs food and supplies, he will, Skitters. If you see Shorty Rogers, tell him not to be surprised to see us moving around through the shadows late tonight. We don't need him shooting at us, too."

"I can almost hear him cackling if he did," Skitters said.

Cindy Cook had a huge rib steak for the man, filled him with cold beer and tucked him in under a thin summer's sheet. "Wake me before midnight you sweet little darlin'. I got a lot of work to do tonight."

"I'll wake you in the way that I know best, Terrence. I'll just roll over and kiss you all over. You need to spend a lot more time under my love and care," she was whispering in his ear and it was a moment or two before she realized the big man was already asleep. "Oh, Terrence, if you only knew." She wrapped her arms around him and let his rhythmic snoring put her to sleep.

Jacob Best rolled out of the bedroll to a sky full of stars. "I hate those thunderstorms but I could have used one tonight. Nobody hears a breaking window when the dishes rattle around from crashing thunder." He packed the stolen horse with what little he had, mounted, and slowly walked it downhill, through heavy timber, and to the edges of Eureka.

Charley Stone's supply store was along the main road, same as Jimmy Henderson's Bonanza Club, but he had loading docks behind the store as well. They were set in from the back street far enough for large wagons and teams to be able to work up to and around the docks. There was little light and Best walked the horse right up to a hitch post.

He and Willy Cannon had spent several days learning everything they could about the store, entrance ways, escape routes, and had figured on using the docks as the best way into the large supply store. There were man sized doors that opened within the sliding warehouse doors and windows in several locations along the long back wall.

Getting in would pose little problem for Best. It was the getting out with supplies, getting them loaded, and making a quick getaway that bothered him. The other side of that back street was lined with homes and where people lived, there were often dogs. Barking dogs brought men with guns to the street, so Best had to be more quiet about his work than he had ever been.

Best was good at stealing things but he usually did it at the point of a gun or through physical violence followed by intimidation. This was different and his method of perceived terror was't in the plan.

He used his knife to slide the keeper from a window and got it open, slipped inside and made his way to the man-door in the sliding door to unlatch it. "I can walk right out of here with my sacks of food and not have to crawl out." He headed to the dried food section of the store. Charley Stone had everything from dried beans to blasting caps and fuse, noodles to steam powered jack drills. Best was looking for food more than anything. So far, no yapping dogs, no drunks making crazy noises, no deputies checking doors and windows.

CHAPTER TWENTY-FIVE

"Brought a friend of yours, Corcoran," Skitters said. "Town's about as quiet as I've heard it in a long time."

Tom Harris walked into the sheriff's office with Deputy Skitters. "Good to see you, Corcoran. Glad you got that Cannon boy. Told Skitters I'm open to helping you get this Best outlaw, too. I have met the man," Harris said. "If you think I can help, that is."

Harris was in the coach, protecting Jimmy Autry's livestock sale receipts when James and Willy Cannon held it up. A long, tall buckaroo, Harris had helped maintain order at the stockyards for several years. Whether making a rowdy buyer or seller more peaceful, or calming drovers anxious to get to the saloons, Harris was the man Autry called on.

"Ran into Tails McGee from Kinkaid's, Corcoran. He's at the Bonanza Club. Probably be available for whatever you have planned. Count me in for a full hand."

"Tails is in town? Probably doesn't know what's going on. Looking for answers on his boss's death and drinking all the good whiskey Henderson has."

"We talked," Harris said. "He's damn angry. Anyway, I'm yours if you want me."

"Might get lively, Tom. You're welcome, though. I've seen you in action. Pour a cup and listen up, both of you." He settled in behind Sheriff Connors desk and put his feet up. "Jacob Best might be coming into town tonight to fetch supplies for the long road he hopes to ride. There's only a couple of places that would carry what someone would need for a long ride."

"You're meaning Charley Stone's place and maybe Hank Arrow's?" Harris smiled. "I'd pick Stone's myself. Hank carries heavy stuff for putting down a claim or moving a lot of people."

"I agree," Corcoran said. "Shorty Rogers has his eyes on Arrow's Mercantile, and we'll have ours on Stone's. We'll keep our horses with us, but walk with them as quietly as possible. Tom, you walk your horse to the east side of the building, away from all the lights from Henderson's saloon, and tie it off. Try to stay in the shadows, listen for anything, and get a look in those dirty windows if you can."

"He keeps 'em dirty on purpose you know," Skitters chuckled.

"How do I get word to you if I see or hear something?" Tom Harris thought with him on the main street and outside and them inside with the killer, it might get nasty fast.

"That's the glitch in my plan, Tom," Corcoran said. "Stone's is a big building and we'll be separated by distance and substance. Any kind of noise we would use would of course be heard by Best and light is out of the question.

"What do you think, Skitters? Just holler out?"

"Sounds reasonable. Just yell something like, Stop, or Freeze. And then follow up with This is Deputy Sheriff and you're surrounded. And hope to hell whichever of us is on the other side hears it."

"Guess we better pin this on you, Deputy Tom," Corcoran said. He swore him in. "Let's get it on, then." Corcoran was already heading for the door. It was an easy walk for Tom Harris, just across the street where he tied off in front of the store next to Stone's. Corcoran and Skitters split up, worked their way to the next street over and met again near the back entrance to the supply store.

"See anything?" Skitters moved to the far side of the street from the back of Stone's warehouse.

"A couple of rowdies at the Bonanza and that's all." Corcoran moved to join him. They were standing under a large tree in front of a residence across the street from Stone's. "Probably Tails. He'd be a good man to have with us if he ain't likkered up."

"That's the only reason I didn't say anything when Tom Harris brought it up. Tails McGee is a wonderful fightin' fool, Skitters, but not when he's been drinking." Corcoran said. Corcoran held in a chuckle thinking that Tails would probably say the same thing about him.

"Is that a horse near the west end of the building?" Skitters was pointing but cloud cover made the night as dark as dark can get.

"Might be. Move your horse down another house or two, I'll tie off here and move that way. It'll be hard to see each other, so if things get busy make sure you have some idea of where I am and I'll do my best not to shoot you."

"Thanks," Skitters laughed. He walked his horse down the street a couple of hundred feet.

Corcoran kept low and ran across the street into the warehouse complex property and toward the west end. "That old man's got good eyes." Corcoran slowly moved up to the horse, put his hand out for the horse to smell. "It's all right, fella, I ain't gonna hurt you." He slowly undid the cinch and lifted the saddle from the animal. He pulled the head stall and let the animal loose.

"There's good grass across the street, buddy. Go have some." He watched the horse wander off and then turned his attention to the supply store. "The only thing I know is somebody brought that horse here. Is he in there? Alone?"

Skitters moved to the other end of the building and made his way to the loading dock. He ducked down and used it for cover as he slowly walked toward the middle of the high platform area. "Sliding doors are closed but that man-way looks to be ajar." He saw Corcoran moving toward him and motioned for him to look at the man-door. Corcoran nodded and slipped up onto the loading dock. Skitters stayed below and moved more toward where Corcoran was.

Corcoran walked to the side of the doorway and motioned for Skitters to come on up. With one on each side of the door, they listened for a minute or two. "Hear that?" Corcoran stepped into the building and knew he was in the receiving storeroom. He moved toward what sounded like someone moving large and heavy boxes.

He motioned Skitters to follow and slowly crept along a corridor of crates piled more than six feet high. Skitters stayed about ten feet behind him. The closer to the entrance to the store itself they got, the louder the scraping became. *What the hell's that man doing? Best way to find out, Terrence Corcoran, is to go in and look.* Corcoran almost chuckled and moved toward the open door.

Tom Harris tied his horse off and stepped up onto the board walkway, trying to stay in the deep shadows. Light from the Bonanza Club on the west side of the building, partially lit the walkway but did cast shadows in places. A light midsummer night's breeze wasn't strong enough to make the dust fly, and the heavy clouds moved slowly overhead hiding the moon and stars.

Harris was pressed to the side of Stone's building, working his way toward the first of the big windows that were always filthy. He had to chuckle remembering what Stone told him when he asked why he never washed the windows. "What people can't see they won't steal," Charley Stone said. He remembered the conversation like it was yesterday.

"I tried to tell him that what they can't see they won't buy, Charley. He just looked at me." It brought a smile to his face, but Tom Harris couldn't see a thing through the windows. He moved to the big double door, locked tight, and tried to press his ear to where the doors came together.

"Somebody's moving around," he murmured. "And I'm locked out here. Damn." He decided the best bet was to continue listening and move only if something inside happened. It wouldn't do a damn bit of good to yell out if he couldn't get through those doors and he might get Corcoran or Skitters shot.

Two shots rang out from inside the store followed by a yowl of pain. Harris heard Corcoran yell stop, and Jacob Best came rolling through the dirty windows, glass and framing flying everywhere. Best rolled off the boardwalk, jumped to his feet, and ran the short distance to Harris's horse. The outlaw jumped on and made for the desert. Harris had his revolver out, fired twice, and watched the horse go down in a heap. Best was thrown clear, got to his feet and raced for a nearby house, Harris was fast on his tail.

"Damn, damn, damn," Best yowled, feeling intense pain in his already wounded leg. It wasn't fully healed, walking through the Diamond Mountains for two days didn't help it any, and now, jabbed with something when he came through the window, it hurt like hell.

Corcoran came through the broken window, saw Harris shoot his horse and the two were in a hard run down the middle of the street. "Don't let him get out of sight," Corcoran yelled.

People erupted from the nearby Bonanza Club, guns in hand. All they saw was two men with drawn guns chasing another man down the street. "Somebody robbing old Charley Stone's place," a man yelled. "Must be them," and he fired off a couple of shot, not hitting anything.

"Quit your damn shooting," Jimmy Henderson yelled. "Idiot. Who you shootin' at?"

Jacob Best crashed through the front door of the Henry O'Keefe house, a look of panic in his face. O'Keefe and his wife Margie were sitting in arm chairs reading, and the elderly man jumped to his feet, taking a chunk of lead through the middle of his chest. Margie screamed and fell into a faint.

Best grabbed the woman up and held her as a shield. Who the hell shot at him? Who did he shoot? Gotta get out of here is the only thing he could think. "You got a horse, woman?" She couldn't answer and he let her drop to the floor. He heard shots on the street and boots racing toward the house, grabbed the woman up, and dragged her with him into the kitchen. He ducked behind a table just as Harris and Corcoran burst into the house.

"Back out or the woman dies," Best screamed. He took a wild shot that only put a hole in the wall.

Corcoran could see he held a pistol to her head, knew he would shoot her, and motioned for himself and Harris to back out of the house.

"Go around to the back, Tom. Run." Corcoran stood at the side of the door, could hear movement and tried to get a quick look. The bullet missed his head by less than an inch, he thought, and dropped to the porch floor. From that angle he could see O'Keefe's body sprawled across his chair, gathered his feet under him and waited for Harris to make a move.

He could hear a stampede of people on the street near the saloon. "No, no," he murmured. "That's all I need. A hundred drunks telling me how to catch this fool. On the other hand, I hope one of them is named Tails McGee. I could use him right now."

CHAPTER TWENTY-SIX

Tom Harris ran hard for the other side of the house, had to climb over a wooden fence that surrounded the back of the house, fell through some plants with large thorns, and finally got to the back porch. He found the kitchen well lit and he could see Best holding the unconscious body of Margie O'Keefe. If he made one wrong move, Best would be sure to blow the woman's head off. He had to get in closer, keep under cover, and get this bastard.

"Jacob Best," he called out. "This is Deputy Sheriff Tom Harris. You're surrounded. Give it up. There's no way out. Give it up and you'll live."

Best whirled and fired his Colt twice, breaking a window but missing Harris by yards. Corcoran took that minute to dive into the living room and get behind O'Keefe's chair. He couldn't see into the kitchen enough to know where Best was and moved to the wall separating the rooms.

"This is Corcoran, Terrence Corcoran. You will live if you give it up," he yelled out. "There's no way out, Jacob Best. Give it up."

Best saw Tom Harris move and fired his last two shots at the man, knocking him to the ground. He dropped Margie O'Keefe and ran hard, blowing through the flimsy back door and across the yard, jumping the fence but crashing to the ground on the other side with a bullet hole, high in his shoulder, and leg bleeding hard again. Harris had managed to get to his feet, got one shot off, but fell back.

Best scrambled to his feet and crept or limped slowly into shadows along the side of the road, found a door to a carriage house unlocked and slipped inside. It didn't have a latch, which is why it was half open in the first place. Corcoran was fast enough coming through the house to see Best go over the fence and fall down. He knew Harris made a good shot. When he got to the fence, he saw Best slip into the carriage house.

I've got two men down and Jacob Best wounded but inside another building. I should have allowed for more men to be with me. Maybe I was wrong not getting Tails McGee in with us. Corcoran looked at

Harris. "Gotta ask you to take care of yourself, Tom. Gotta get that guy."

"Go," is all Harris said He was already working to stem the blood flow from his leg. "I'll catch up."

Several men from the saloon had reached the O'Keefe house and moved into the back yard. Tails McGee was among the first to kneel down next to Tom Harris. "It's Tails, Tom. Was that Corcoran going over the fence?"

"It was. Good to see you, Tails. Go help him. I can't."

Tails called a couple of the looky-looks over to help Harris and jumped the fence to run to where Corcoran was. *That crazy bastard's gonna try to do this all by himself again. Never have understood that man. Well, okay, Terrence, my friend, Tails is gonna come along and save your sorry butt one more time, and you better be ready to buy me a drink when this is over.*

"What's all the shootin'?" Jimmy Henderson was in his upstairs office and ran down to the Saloon's main floor. There were only a few late night customers and they were gathered around the bat-wing doors. "Let me through, damn it," Henderson said. He pushed his way to the street in time to see Corcoran come through one of Charlie Stone's broken front windows.

He stopped the one fool from continue shooting, saw the dead horse, the broken window at Stone's, and heard a voice inside cry out for help. "Skitters," Henderson said. "What the hell's going on? What are you doing in there. My, God, man, you're bleeding."

Skitters came out through the broken window, holding his side. Blood was running through his fingers and he collapsed onto the board walkway. Henderson was at his side immediately.

"Quit talking and listen. Jacob Best was in here. Shot me. Corcoran's chasing him now. Get some help and catch that bastard."

Henderson started to get Skitters to his feet but the old deputy pushed him away. "I'll be fine. Get help and catch that fool."

The saloon owner stepped back through the broken glass to face a small crowd of late nighters. "Skitters is hurt. Somebody get him some help. He needs to be taken to Doc Sanford's. Corcoran is chasing the man that killed Jack Hopkins and Cynthia Wilkinson. Anyone want in on this, follow me."

Henderson raced off in the direction he saw Corcoran running, saw the busted up door at Henry O'Keefe's place and ran inside to find O'Keefe's body. Margie gave a groan from the kitchen and Henderson spotted Tom Harris lying on the ground in the back yard with Tails McGee helping him. He helped get Margie O'Keefe onto a kitchen chair. Three men had followed and one got her a small glass of water.

"What the hell?" The man said. "Were you hit, Mrs. O'Keefe?"

"No. Oh, poor Henry. Oh, my poor Henry," she said. She laid her head on the table, sobbing.

"Stay with her," Henderson said and ran out into the back yard.

Tom Harris had a rag tied around his leg and was doing his best to get to his feet. "Corcoran went over the fence after Best. McGee is following him. I lost sight of him because of the fence. He'll need extra guns, Jimmy." Henderson motioned for the two men with him to follow and went over the fence.

Corcoran spotted McGee and waved, catching his attention despite the dark of the night. He motioned where Best was and Tails moved up to nest with him. "That's Jimmy Henderson coming now," Corcoran said, and waved him over. Henderson had one of the men with him and ran to Corcoran.

"Henderson, I've got Best trapped in there. Take your men and run around to get behind the carriage house. "This guy's a killer, so be as careful as you've ever been."

Andy Sinclair was a miner at the big mine, had gotten off second shift and was in the Bonanza Club for a cold beer when the ruckus broke out. He was well aware of Cynthia Wilkinson's murder and the hunt for Jacob Best. He was twenty-two years old and threw ten by ten timbers around like they were toothpicks. "I'm gonna tear that man limb from limb, Mr. Henderson. Let's go get him."

They moved through the yards of the house next to the little barn and found shelter behind a tree. There was a back door to the carriage house and they could see it plainly from the tree. "Doesn't look like that's been opened for a while," Sinclair said. Dirt and debris had piled up around the bottom of the door. "Side windows are closed and not broken out. If he ran in there, he's still there."

"Let's ease up to that door, Andy, and just listen. Corcoran will call the shots. Stay calm and let him make the decisions. We'll get this fool."

Sinclair moved like a cat, quick, soundless, and was standing next to the sliding door in seconds. "It's got a cross bar inside, Mr. Henderson. We can't get in, but with all this junk in the runners, he ain't gonna get the door open."

"We'll just sit back there in the shadows and watch, then," Henderson said.

"Sean Morgan, didn't know you were back in town. Glad to have you alongside." Corcoran watched the gambler run up to where he was hidden behind a hedge at the side of the carriage house. "Gettin' crowded out here," he chuckled. "This is Tails McGee. McGee, Sean Morgan." The two nodded to each other. "That's Jacob Best inside there. None of the windows are broken and Jimmy Henderson is on the back side. Watch those windows as I move toward the building."

"I'll shoot anything that shows a face," Morgan chuckled. He hunkered down and was able to see the front of the barn through the hedge without showing his head to whoever might be inside looking.

Corcoran ran the thirty feet or so to the side of the building, darting, one way then another, coming up alongside the sliding double doors. They were locked with a cross-beam from inside and he worked his way around to the man-door on the side of the building. He motioned for Morgan and McGee to stay where they were and crept up to the door.

Corcoran was aware that in most carriage houses there would be one or two stalls along one wall with an area set aside for tack. The center would be taken up by a wagon or buggy. Corcoran knew there was a window on the opposite side of the building, which meant this door would open between the stall or stalls and the tack area. It probably also meant that would be where Best would be cowering and watching for someone to come after him.

Corcoran looked about, found a length of baling wire and attached one end to the door, which still stood ajar after Best ran in. He stood back and to the side, and jerked the door open wide. Two quick shots came from inside, Corcoran saw the flashes, and fired at them, but didn't hear a howl of pain.

"He's behind a post or something," he murmured. "He'd see me in an instant if I moved toward that door." He moved back into deeper shadows and to the side, advancing on the open door from the side. He was about to crawl closer when the home owner, Terry Bingham came running from the house with his shotgun.

"Don't move or I'll blow your head off," Bingham yelled at Corcoran. Before Corcoran could say anything, Jacob Best put two bullets in Bingham, one in his arm, and he dropped the gun, and the other in his leg, just above the knee. Bingham fell to the ground, screaming in pain.

Corcoran fired into the barn and rushed to Bingham's side, grabbed him under his arms, and dragged him to the side before Best could shoot again. "Bad timing, Terry. This is Corcoran. We've got that bastard Jacob Best trapped in your barn. Let's see what we can do to keep you alive, old man."

"Corcoran. Damn, that hurts. Best you say? Killed that little girl? Wished I'd knowed it was you."

"Tell me what's in your barn, Terry. Do you have horses? Saddles?"

"Yeah, sure," Bingham said. "You've seen that beautiful stallion I brought from Kentucky. He's a pacer and I got a fitted-out two-wheel cart. Pacer ain't broke to saddle but he sure can pull that high wheeled cart. You think that fool would try to break out of there?"

"I know he will," Corcoran growled. "Andy Sinclair," Corcoran yelled out. "Can you hear me?"

"You bet," Andy answered.

"Find Doc Sanford and send him here. Then get the sheriff and Dean Berry over here. Hurry." He turned the other way and hollered out for Sean Morgan.

"I can hear you," Morgan answered. "No movement over here. Shorty Rogers is here with me now."

"Good," Corcoran yelled back. *That makes Tails, Morgan, and Shorty on my side of the barn, and Henderson with a couple of drunks on the other side.* "Shorty, get around to the other end and don't let that bastard out. He's shot his last man."

Shorty cackled and pumped his fist, hobbled as fast as his one good short leg and his wooden short leg would take him around to the other side of the building, hiding behind a tree. "Old Jack Hopkins was one of my best friends," Shorty mumbled. He had his double barreled shotgun in one hand and laid his revolver in the grass next to him. "Come on out, Jacob Best" he hollered. "I got something for you."

"Glad you're here, Shorty," Jimmy Henderson said. "Got a window on the side over there, and this double sliding door at the end here. Corcoran's got the other end."

"Good," Shorty said. "I haven't shot at a man for a couple of years, but I am ready to shoot this one." He couldn't hold the cackle back. "I'm laughing at you, Jacob Best," he howled. "You've killed your last."

Best answered with a string of foul language and those outside could hear him kicking something. There were sounds of something being thrown and more cursing. "I'm gonna get you," Shorty cackled.

He was surrounded and knew he had to make his escape before even more people showed up. The horse in the stall was a young stallion that was already in a fit because of the gunfire, was pawing hard at the walls and gate. He wondered if he'd even be able to saddle that wild eyed stud, more or less ride him out of the barn.

"I ain't gonna let them get me. They ain't," he vowed. "They'll get tired of yelling at me, and burn me out, sure as hell. Maybe that's it. They ain't gonna burn that stud alive. No they ain't." He had a little snicker stick in the back of his throat as he thought about being inside a burning barn.

On each end of the building were the big double, sliding doors, braced from inside. The west side of the barn held a small window, but big enough for a man to jump through, and there was a doorway on the east side, with several guns pointed at it. "Fire to block that door and a good run at that window, and I'll be a free man," Jacob Best said. "When they see that fire, the only thing in their minds will be to save that horse."

CHAPTER TWENTY-SEVEN

Ed Connors slowly fought his way through the clouds of sleep when Andy Sinclair started banging on the door with the handle of his forty-four. "Sheriff! Wake up! Corcoran needs you." Still in his night shirt Connors made his way in the dark to the front door and got it open.

"Andy. What is it got you so riled?"

Sinclair told his tale as fast as he could while Ed Connors got dressed. "At the O'Keefe's?" Connors asked.

"No. He ran from the O'Keefe's to Terry Bingham's place. Best is holed up in the Bingham's carriage house. Corcoran needs you Sheriff. He wants me to find Dean Berry and send him over, too."

The sheriff nodded and Sinclair took off to find the other deputy while Connors made the short run to the middle of town and the Bingham home. His mind was still fighting sleep but remembered that Terry Bingham brought that beautiful Standard Bred pacer in last year and kept it in that little barn. " My God, that man will do anything to protect that stud."

It took just a few minutes to make the run and he slowly advanced on the property, not wanting to make himself a target for Best or to be shot by one of his own deputies. "Corcoran," he yelled out. "It's Sheriff Ed Connors. Where are you?"

"Around on this side, Sheriff. There's an open door and Best is inside. Don't make yourself a target."

"Who's on the other side of the building?"

"I'd like it to be you, but we need to talk first. Come in low and slow, Ed."

Connors sidled up to Corcoran, saw Doc Sanford working on Terry Bingham, and settled on his haunches. "Nasty business, Corcoran. Sinclair said people hurt. Who?"

"Skitters is in Charley Stone's store with a bullet in his side, Henry O'Keefe is dead, and Tom Harris has a gunshot wound to the leg. And, you can see that Terry Bingham was shot, too. We have people all the way around the building, but if Best feels trapped, God knows what he'll do to escape."

"What's your thought on it?" The sheriff preferred Corcoran to make these kinds of decisions.

"Looks to be tough to get in without losing people."

"Too many already hurt, Ed. I'd like to set up a revolving group of people, and wait him out. He'll get hungry and thirsty, Particularly when the sun comes up. We can wait in the cool shade of these trees and eventually he'll have to either give it up or make a break for it."

"Sounds good. When Dean Berry gets here, I'll send him to the Bonanza Club to get that organized." Sheriff Connors gave Corcoran a good punch to the shoulder and moved back and away from the building. He worked around to the other side and came face to face with Shorty Rogers' shotgun.

"Don't shoot the sheriff, Shorty. Glad you're here."

"Got to let people know you're coming, Sheriff. Damn." He was shaking, scared, and worried all at the same time. "I coulda kilt you." There was no cackle, no joy from a man who some say smiled twenty four hours a day. Shorty was a deputy sheriff whose only job was to rattle doors late at night.

Thirty years ago, he was a fighting machine in a Union uniform, but with a peg-leg on one side and a gimped up leg on the other side, he hadn't raised a weapon on a man in a long time. He was intense, wound tight as they say.

"Henderson's right around the back," Shorty said.

He had himself back under control. "There's double sliding doors there, and barricaded from inside. Figure that outlaw would make so much noise trying to get then open, he wouldn't try. Makes this window a prime route of escape."

"Corcoran said he thought the man was wounded. Heard anything from inside?"

"I'll say," Shorty cackled. "That fine stallion Bingham brought in has been raising all kinds of hell in there. We gonna charge that fool? It'd be better to just burn him out."

"It would, Shorty, but we'd probably kill that stud in there. No, we'll just sit out here, all comfortable like, and wait him out. No food or water in the middle of summer? It'll be a short siege, my friend."

Dean Berry arrived and was detailed to the Bonanza Club to put together a group of men who would occupy the positions now held by Corcoran and his group. "You set it up, Dean. They'll need to babysit this murdering fool for five or six hours at a time." Sheriff Connors wiped some sweat from his face. "Hard to say how long Best will hold out, but without food or water, it won't be too long."

Jacob Best was trapped and knew it. His only way out was going to be far more than just dangerous, it would probably mean his death. "Dyin' is okay, but gettin' caught and then bein' hung ain't," he muttered. He was laying a stack of old dried hay near the doorway and had some scrap lumber that would go on top of it. Anything dry that would burn went on the pile.

His shoulder was bleeding bad and he had some dirty rags tied around as best as he could. The bullet went in high and to the outside of the shoulder, ripped meat and muscle, but didn't break any bones. That bullet had eyes as it missed the collar bone and the clavicle.

He was limping, knew his leg wound had opened up again, and wondered if he would be able to jump through that window. The pain hampered his ability in stacking the hay and wood. The high-strung stud continued to whinny loud and long, kicked at everything, and the noise was having an effect, too.

"Shut up!" Best threw a chunk of wood at the horse, which brought a whole new chorus of noise and another scream from the outlaw. Best paced the distance from where the fire would be to the window, judged how fast he would have to run to launch himself through it, and got his striker out. "Gotta let the fire get a good start. Let those people out there understand that this fine horse is gonna die soon."

He let his hand run down the side of his leg, felt the warm blood and cringed. "I ain't gonna make it," he muttered, then looked again at the window. "Just one good jump and I'm through it."

He opened the base of a lantern, poured coal-oil along the base of the straw pile, and hit the striker. It was just seconds and there was a roaring fire inside the old barn. The horse went crazy, busted the old wood of the stall, and was about to break out. An old rusty hasp is all that held it together. Best stood up, waited until the cry went up from outside, and ran as fast as he could for the window at the same instant the horse broke free.

The horse knocked Best to the ground. It was kicking, screaming in terror, racing from one end of the barn to the other, and Best was cowering behind one of the wheels of the cart. The horse kicked the cart three of four times, doing serious damage, but also knocking Best to the ground again.

Bruised from the kicking, bleeding from two wounds, Best was cowering from the horse's hooves and a raging fire. "I gotta get out of here," he almost hollered, jumped to his feet and almost hobbled to the window. Terror was building in the killer, the horse was kicking what was in the barn to shreds, and Best knew there were men outside waiting to kill him. "Now," he yelled, took two steps and dove for the window.

Shorty Rogers saw the flames and knew what would be next. He pulled his shotgun to his shoulder and let go with both barrels when the window exploded in front of him. The blast hit the wooden wall but the wall exploding hit Jacob Best so hard it stopped his flight, and the murderer fell to the ground, dazed but not hit by the shotgun.

"I got him!" Shorty Rogers could be heard all over town. "I got that bastard, Sheriff." He stood up, almost dancing on his short legs as he reloaded and waited for the others to join him. "By God, I earned the right to wear this badge tonight," the old man cackled.

Best, hurt but not out of the fight, crawled the short distance to the old deputy and knocked him to the ground, grabbing the shotgun. He hit Shorty Rogers again, across the head with the scatter gun, and made his way further out from the burning building. "Gotta get away, get out of sight, find a horse," he said, over and over.

He tried to run but couldn't. The best he could do was a fast hobble, and he moved quickly away from the fire, away from any light. Homes along the street were being lit up as all the noise and gunshots awakened those inside. "Gotta find a horse," Jacob Best kept saying.

Corcoran saw the fire as soon as it was lit and raced for the door, his Colt belching fire of its own.

He burst through the flames in time to see Jacob Best fly through the window and heard the shotgun blast. "Good for you, Shorty," he murmured. "Gotta get these doors open and get that horse out of here."

The flames were already attacking the dry walls of the carriage house, would move to the stall in no time. Corcoran ran to the north set of double doors and yanked the plank away, but the doors wouldn't come open. "Help me." He yelled it out and ran to the other end of the carriage house. The horse was screaming in terror, racing back and forth, kicking everything. The flames were eating at the straw on the floor and the wood of the stall, the heat was intense, and Corcoran had to protect himself from flailing hooves.

Tails McGee was with him at a dead run and they fought to get the heavy doors unstuck. McGee rammed his large body onto the doors, over and over, while Corcoran fought to get them moving on the rails. The horse in the meantime, free of its stall, was dancing, kicking, and pawing at anything and everything.

The horse was still inside the barn, though, which was becoming an inferno, and his terror hadn't cooled a degree. He ran from one end to the other, kicking, screaming in fright, lashing out, and was a danger to everything inside the barn.

"Gotta do it now, Corcoran, or run for our lives. That stud's gonna kill one or both of us." Tails McGee gave another body slam into the door and Corcoran heard the roller wheel drop onto its rail.

"Got it, Tails," he hollered. They pushed as hard as they could, felt the door slowly begin to move and were able to side-step the fury of the young stallion as it made its get-away. "That's one fast and terrified horse. He'll make Utah before he needs to catch his breath," Corcoran laughed. He and McGee were spread out on the ground, gasping for breath.

"You're free," Corcoran laughed, getting to his feet. "Gotta get out of here." The fire had one wall fully involved, was moving up the roof line quickly, and it was just about all over for the barn. "Let's make sure Shorty really got that guy. Best is the most slippery outlaw I've ever had the pleasure of killing. And you noticed, I'm sure, that I ain't killed him yet, McGee."

Tails McGee and Terrence Corcoran ran to where Shorty was spread out on the ground. "Damn it," Corcoran hollered. The two knelt down, found Shorty still alive but unconscious, and looked around quickly.

"He has Shorty's shotgun, Tails. If it was me, I'd run for those trees and make for somebody's barn. He needs a horse bad."

"We're alone, Corcoran. Everyone's fighting that fire. Let's move as fast as we've ever moved." Tails was on his feet, Corcoran alongside, and they ran for the trees and shadows along the side of the road. "There," Tails yelled. He was pointing down a dark street at the silhouette of a man several hundred yards away, hobbling as quickly as he could.

"That's him," Corcoran howled, and took off at a run.

CHAPTER TWENTY-EIGHT

The cry, "Fire!" In a mining camp brings everyone. The fire boys brought their hand pumper, the hose wagons raced to the scene, and men started a bucket brigade as well. The neighborhood cistern was opened and water was pumped through the breaks to the nozzle, but that barn was searing hot. Andy Sinclair yelled at the nozzle men to save the house.

"The barn is gone, boys. It's time to save Bingham's house." The hose crews turned their nozzles to the home, the bucket line moved to the house, and every effort was made to make that house wetter than the deepest pond in Nevada. Working the pumpers was hard, could wear a man out in minutes, and those on the breaks worked in teams.

The barn slowly caved in on itself and the fire boys let it burn out, but kept pouring water onto the house. Terry Bingham watched in horror. Doc Sanford had two men carry Terry away from the conflagration and all effort was made to keep the flames away from the Bingham home. Edith Bingham was crying out for Terry, Terry was howling for his horse to be saved, and it was general chaos in the area.

Connors found Sean Morgan and Jim Henderson kneeling over Shorty Rogers, who was just beginning to come around. "Where's Corcoran?"

Morgan jumped to his feet and pointed down the street. "He and Tails McGee went that way, Sheriff."

"Take care of Shorty, Henderson. Come with me, Morgan," and Connors took off at a high lope down the dark street. People were out in their yards or standing on their porches, some crowded out into the road, watching the fire-boys at work. Some had ventured too far out onto the roadway and had to be evaded when the men passed.

"Damn fools," Connors howled. "Get out of my way. There's gonna be shootin'. Get off the road." Some had to jump out of the running men's way, others got bumped aside.

One or two had seen the wounded man hobble by and watched Corcoran and McGee fly pass, and pointed the direction out to the sheriff as he and Morgan ran by. "Thank you." Connors called out to them without slowing down.

"Looks like they're heading for the main street, Sheriff," Sean Morgan said.

"Looking for a horse would be my guess," Connors said. They continued running, letting the men and women on the street point which way Corcoran went.

"Another couple of blocks and he'll be on the main street, Tails. If he finds a horse he'll be gone again." They were racing, caught glimpses of Best and knew they were catching up fast.

"If we get too close, he just might grab a hostage, Corcoran."

"If we're that close, it'll be time to shoot him dead," Corcoran hollered. "There, he ran into that house. Damn it, McGee, we can't let someone else get shot tonight."

The two raced into the yard where Best ran and found a man and woman on the ground, but not gunshot. "What the hell's going on?" The man helped his wife up, glared at Corcoran who hustled the two into some bushes.

"Stay down. That's a killer knocked you down. We'll get him," Corcoran said. He watched Tails McGee slowly advance on the house, using every bush, tree, or yard decoration for cover. Corcoran moved toward the side of the house in time to see a window being raised and put a shot from his Colt through it. His shot was answered by two quick shots from inside.

McGee used that to move quickly to the front door of the house, still standing half open. Corcoran moved along the side of the house toward the open window as McGee stepped inside the open door.

"Gotcha surrounded again, Jacob Best," Corcoran yelled out. He put another shot through the window keeping Best occupied while McGee moved inside. "Give it up so we can hang you or fight back so we can kill you here. Your choice, killer-boy."

"Killer-boy? He called me killer-boy? I'm gonna make you hurt bad, Corcoran, before I kill you." His rage and mad run to find a horse left the man out of breath, in pain, and screaming at everything.

People were gathering around the little house, Corcoran knew somebody sure as hell would get shot if he didn't get them away. On the other hand, if he left where he was, Best would see McGee and shoot him. "Damn looky-looks," he muttered. "Come on, Jacob Best, I'm right here." He yelled at the open window. "Come on you coward, come on and face a real man."

McGee moved slowly through the living room of the small cabin and toward where Best was in the front bedroom. He edged up to the open door but couldn't see anything inside the room. He could hear Corcoran taunting the man and was able to catch some mumbling from the outlaw. It was hard not to chuckle but he didn't try to hide the smile.

Corcoran put another bullet through the open window, Best cussed long and hard, and emptied the shotgun, blowing the whole window and frame into kindling and shards. "You missed, killer-boy," Corcoran laughed. "I'm coming for you, better run again. You ain't good enough to face me."

"That's a lot of shooting, Morgan. We gotta hurry." Ed Connors and Sean Morgan were just half a block away and started shooing people off the street as they ran toward the house. "Get inside where it's safe and stay there," he yelled. "Hurry, Morgan."

They got to the house, saw the front door standing open and heard Corcoran taunting the trapped outlaw. "Corcoran," Connors yelled. "I've got Sean Morgan with me. Where do you want us?"

"Hear that, Jacob Best? That mean old Sheriff Connors is here now. You man enough to face both of us? Give it up you stinking killer-boy. I've got the front and this side, Ed. Why don't you and Sean take the other side. His killin' days are over."

Connors motioned for him and Morgan to move around the house but took a couple of minutes to shoo all the onlookers away. "You people understand that's a killer in there? He don't know you ain't some damn deputy. Now get back somewhere safe."

The windows were closed on that side of the house and Connors saw that the back door was pulled to as well. "I hope that means the people who live there are out and safe. Sean, watch those windows, I'm going to see if I can get in the door."

Using all the shadows of the night, Connors moved to the back door, had to climb three steps onto a small porch, and slowly turned the handle. It opened, and without any noise. He motioned for Morgan to move up to one of the windows to see if he could see anything. Connors edged into the kitchen of the cabin, an oil lamp still burning.

"Wish that was out," Connors mumbled. He moved around the big wood stove, slid up to the door that opened into the living room, and saw Tail McGee, pistol in hand, at the side of the bedroom door. McGee caught the movement and whirled, recognizing Connors just in time, pulling the heavy revolver up and not firing.

Using his hands, McGee let Connors know where Best was in the room and Connors slipped into the living room to stand on the other side of the doorway from McGee. They could hear Best moving around and cussing as he was trying to do something. They didn't dare try to look.

"I gotta get out of here now," Best muttered. He had the cylinder of his revolver empty and was trying to re-load. His shoulder and arm were slowly becoming useless, his leg hurt just to stand, and he had multiple glass cuts on his front and back. It took all his effort to get one round at a time in. Corcoran's taunts were working and Jacob Best was in a rage. More bullets fell to the floor than went into the cylinder.

Is the house really surrounded? Are there other law-men just waiting for him to make a move? How was he going to get out, anyway? Jacob Best finally was re-loaded, closed the trap door on the gun and moved toward the door that led to the living room. Maybe there would be a horse in the barn. Maybe he could sneak out the back door.

McGee heard the footsteps coming toward the door and motioned the sheriff to get back. He got down on his knees and as close to the wall as possible, saw Connors do the same thing, and had his weapon at the ready. Two quick shots, a scream of pain, and Best fell through the open door, dropping his gun as he fell.

"Told you I'd get you," Corcoran said. He climbed through the broken out window frame, walked up, and kicked the gun away. McGee and Connors had to chuckle, watching the display.

"You got him," McGee said. He and Connors got to their feet catching Corcoran by surprise. "We let you get him, Corcoran. Thought it would make you feel better." Tails laughed and cuffed the big deputy.

"Ha!" Corcoran had to laugh at the two. "Wondered why you two were being so quiet. Not like you, Tails."

"He ain't dead, Corcoran," Connors said. I'll go get the doc down here."

CHAPTER TWENTY-NINE

It took hours for Doc Sanford to get the wounded tended to. He did most of the work right where they fell but had several tucked into beds at his home, which doubled as a hospital when needed. Skitters leg wound was such that he could walk around some and refused to be put to bed.

Tom Harris's wounds, on the other hand, were much more severe, as was the head wound suffered by Shorty Rogers. Old man Bingham was in his own bed, at home, tended by a tearful Mrs. Bingham. His prize stud had wandered back to the property after just a few hours of freedom and was being tended to at the sheriff's corrals.

"I'm not putting Best in there, Doc, and that's final." Corcoran and Doc Sanford were standing at the front door of the doctor's home while Jacob

Best was laid out on a platform, readied to be carried somewhere. Terrence Corcoran had fought this battle before, and usually Sanford won.

"This fool has slipped out of my hands too many times. You can tend to him in a locked cell, Doc. I'll have Skitters and his leg wound right with you. You can take care of both of them that way. Skitters owes the man a good two or three bullets, so you'll be safer than out on the street."

Sanford growled some but realized Corcoran was probably right. "In the long run, Terrence, my boy, I'd rather not have him in my house. All right, gentlemen," he said to those standing by to help, "Take him to jail, but be careful. He's hurt really bad." A couple of men mumbled obscenities about just how much Jacob Best should hurt, and Corcoran's thoughts were more toward what those men might represent than what they said.

Would there be an attempt to lynch Best? After all, Corcoran was thinking, the man killed several of Eureka's most loved residents. His attack on a young girl would be enough in most communities to bring on an attempted lynching, add on all the other killings, robberies, and fires, and the possibility gets boosted.

If Clarence Wilkinson got the miners fired up over his daughter's abduction and death, this damn old town could explode. I gotta sit down with the sheriff and talk about this right away. Corcoran had a deep frown on his face as he helped get the wounded prisoner inside.

Several men had Best on a platform and were working their way through the big doors at the jail when Clarence Wilkinson rode up in a cloud of dust. "That bastard dead? If he ain't, he's gonna be." Wilkinson had a shotgun in hand as he baled from the horse. Corcoran dove across the wide wooden walkway and the two fell to the dirt and mud of the street.

Tails McGee jumped onto the wreathing mass of fighting men, trying to wrestle the shotgun away. Fists hammered, feet kicked hard, and McGee came up with the scatter piece. "Damn it, Clarence, you ain't gonna kill that man," Corcoran said. The two men clambered to their feet, glaring at each other. "I've known you a long time, Wilkinson. You're a good man, you have every right to be as angry as a bear, but the law is the law, and that man will stand trial."

"I want him dead, Corcoran." The anger and fury exploded in a string of foul language, then a slow cooling down. "What he did to my little Cynthia needs to be answered with his blood. Dead, do you hear? My Amelia hasn't stopped crying since I got home with the news, Corcoran."

"I'm pretty damn sure the judge and jury are going to feel the same way, Clarence. Let's you and me go have a cold beer, and talk about this. My jaw hurts." The two men, muddied and bloodied, walked across the street, one still mostly angry, the other trying to stave off chaos.

The sore jaw comment brought a chuckle from the mine superintendent. The Bonanza Club, filled with people following all the commotion, was abuzz, and Corcoran feared this where any problem would start. Funny how fires, mid-town shootings, and lawmen racing up and down the streets brings life to a community on a hot summer morning. Corcoran hoped it didn't bring more death.

The equally muddied Tails McGee was already standing at the bar, a bottle in one hand and a flagon of beer in the other. "Damn it, Corcoran, I was just getting a glow on last night. That's when you forced me into helping you nab that little killer boy, as you called him. Why can't you just do your job and not make all of us help you?"

Corcoran motioned for McGee to follow and took a table near the front window of the large saloon. "You're a good man, Tails, and so are you, Clarence. We're about to put closure to some damn serious crimes. Sonny Kinkaid's murderer is behind bars, Tails. And, Clarence, Cynthia's abductor and murderer is too." He poured about half a glass from McGee's bottle and settled back in his chair.

"I'm sure that Judge Mallory and his jury will find Jacob Best guilty and we'll have a hanging shortly. After all these years, Clarence, and I've worn this old tin badge a long time, I'm pretty sure I know how you and Amelia must feel. You know you'd be wrong, know you'd be held for open murder. And, you know I would have to be the one to hold you. I ain't gonna let that happen."

"Better save some of that lecture for me, Corcoran." McGee took a pull on the whiskey, straight from the bottle, and looked back and forth at the two men. He chuckled. "I was in here when you started this fight. You know why? I was getting all primed to kill that boy. Then, you invited me to the party."

"Wish I'd been in town," Wilkinson said. "I know you're right, Corcoran, and that's part of what irritates me the most. Cynthia was my daughter and I can't say I did anything to help stop that fool."

"My God, Clarence!" Corcoran almost jumped out of his seat. "You sounded the alarm. You were the first to give chase. You led the posse chasing Best. You did everything and more that a man, a father, could possibly do. We would never have caught that bastard if it hadn't been for you. Don't you ever say anything like that again, in front of me."

Wilkinson sat quiet, let the words fight their way into his head, and for the first time in a long time, tried to smile. "I hadn't thought of any of that, Corcoran. Thank you." It was quiet at the table and each man, in turn, picked up the whiskey bottle and took long pulls. Who really needs a glass?

"Thank you," Wilkinson said again, got to his feet, and walked out the door. "Amelia needs me."

"There's a very proud and broken hearted man, Terrence," Tails McGee said.

Sheriff Connors was behind the desk, Corcoran was sitting in a cane-back chair, and Skitters was limping around the stove, pouring coffee and cussing loud and long. "I gotta listen to that damn idiot every time Doc Sanford comes to work on his wounds. You gotta get to be a better shot, Corcoran. All you did was make more wounds on him for the doc to work on. Next time, shoot to kill and I won't have to listen to any of this."

"It's good training," Corcoran laughed. "Actually, I was shooting to kill, but so was he. Judge Mallory says we should make him ready for trial next week. I stopped in this morning to make sure we had all the paperwork in. The judge is bringing in a young lawyer from Reno to defend Best. Should be here tomorrow."

"That's what's missing," Connors said. "Good. A young, hot-shot, book carrying lawyer to gum up the works. Maybe we'll get lucky and Best will kill him."

"It might get worse than that, Sheriff." Corcoran finished his coffee and stood up. "There's a lot of talk of a lynching. Some of the hot-heads at Wilkinson's mine have been coming to the Bonanza getting things riled. Town people are furious at the killings, fires, and robberies. Shorty's out, Skitters, you're moving slow, and all we have right now is crippled Kenny Johnson and Dean Berry."

"I'd like to have Tom Harris and Sean Morgan wearing badges," Connors said. "Ain't the right time to be short-handed."

"Sean might be available, but Tom is busted up pretty bad. Leg won't be right for a while. I'll take a ride down to the stockyards and talk to Jimmy Autry. Might get a couple of his buckaroos to work with us. If we have a problem, it would probably be while we're getting Best from here, one block up the hill to the courthouse. A few well-placed rifles would do the job."

CHAPTER THIRTY

"You're wrong, Emil. My boys were never criminals. They would never hurt a fly. You're a horrible man for saying something like that, and I'm going to do something about it. How dare you tell me my boys were killed committing a robbery. Why, they were there to stop it. Certainly. That's why they were there."

"Justification, Rose. From the day Willy was born, you have tried to justify every single wrong move the boy has made. He was blown off his horse, wearing a mask, by the stage coach guard." Emil glared at his wife, paced some, and sat back down.

Emil Cannon almost expected that kind of reaction from Rose, but not the so-called justification of actually being there to stop the robbery. "It's past time you faced reality, Rose. Willy was killed by the messenger on the stagecoach and was identified by many on board. James was killed by Deputy Sheriff Terrence Corcoran after James tried to kill him. Those boys of ours have never been anything but trouble. Now, they are called dead outlaws and killers."

Cannon's leg and back hurt more and more every day, it seemed, since Dean Berry rode onto their small ranch to tell them Willy and James were dead. "The sheriff has asked that we come to town to tell them what we know of the boys' activities, particularly as they relate to Jacob Best."

"Never." Rose exploded, paced around the kitchen, and sat down at the table. She thought about what Emil said, and slowly put together an idea that would have pleased her son James. She could walk right up to that uppity Deputy Corcoran and shoot him dead. "How dare that Deputy Corcoran call my son a criminal? How dare he kill my son?" Rose Cannon was in tears. "James was still a baby, Emil. He could never be a killer."

Emil knew that no matter what he said, it would mean nothing. Never had before, he knew. His boys always had the protection of their mother, and their mother never recognized what little terrors they were. "Sheriff Cannon will provide you with all the proof you'll need to understand that our boys went bad, Rose. We have to go." His eyes were pleading with the large woman and she finally nodded her head in agreement.

"I'll harness the team."

"We gotta have a talk, Sheriff." Dean Berry poured some coffee and sat down across from the sheriff, a sad but determined look on his face. "I ain't cut out for this job. I sat in the cabin and listened to James Cannon cry himself to his dying breath. It wasn't something I want to do again."

"A man gets gut shot like that, hours from the nearest medical treatment, there isn't anything else to do but let him die. Try to move him, you'll bring him even more pain. He'll still die before you can get him anywhere. Think of it as bringing him some comfort in his last hours."

"I hadn't thought of it that way, Sheriff, but I still don't ever want to have to that again. Ever."

"As long as you wear that badge, you'll have to. Just hope that it isn't too often," Connors said. "Thank you for riding to the Cannon place and giving them the bad news. They'll be coming to town soon to talk with me. I'd like you to be there."

"Sheriff, I just can't wear this badge any longer. Being a lawman just ain't in me. I thought Mrs. Cannon was gonna shoot me. Called a liar, she did. Said Corcoran was a murderer. It was horrible." Berry reached up to remove his badge, but Cannon put his hand up.

"Hold on a minute, Mr. Berry. Inside of one day you had the two hardest jobs there are in this old business we're in. You helped a wounded man over that last bridge, gave him a bit of solace, and then passed on the word of his death to his parents. Ain't nothing harder to do wearin' a badge."

"No, Mr. Berry, you've been a fine deputy and I want you to stay. Hell, man, you even slept on the rocks while we were chasing Mr. Best." Cannon laughed right out and the memory triggered a chuckle from Dean Berry. "You go on over to the Bonanza and have a cold beer, Deputy Berry, and think about the good you've brought to Eureka."

"I think that's about it, Sam. The judge said to have Best at the courthouse well before ten tomorrow morning." Corcoran brought a large envelope filled with information on all the crimes he believed Jacob Best was to be tried for, to District Attorney Sam Atkins.

"Thank you, Terrence. How are you getting along with Best's attorney. He's a smart Alex for sure."

"Sylvester Paine needs a good ten minute session behind the barn, Sam. A willow switch or black leather harness strap across his fat ass would be my choice. He's filed half a dozen complaints with Judge Mallory in just the three days he's been here. Doesn't like the jail, doesn't like what we feed Best, and has demanded that Skitters not be allowed in when the doc is working on the prisoner."

Sam Atkins was laughing hard and at the same time knowing that Paine had filed complaints against his office as well. "Welcome to the club, Terrence. The paint on his shingle hasn't had time to dry and he's defending a murderer in front of a judge who thrives on murder cases. This is gonna be fun."

"Fun, Sam, only if I can get Jacob Best to the courthouse alive. It'll be a real chore."

"What kind of plan are you putting together." Sam Atkins carried a badge in Humboldt County for several years before getting his law degree, understood the possibility of a town's uprising, the threat of a lynching.

"Ed Connors and I will get our small staff together early tomorrow morning to put it all together."

"Kind of waiting 'till the last minute, aren't you?" Sam Atkins had been Eureka County District Attorney for almost twenty years, and knew Connors and Corcoran well.

"On purpose, Sam. Ed and I know the plan, but no one else, and no one will be able to know what time we're going or how we're gonna get there." Corcoran had a big smile on his face as he walked toward the door.

"See you in court, Sam." Terrence said, and headed out of the courthouse for the office.

"I don't want to do this, Emil, but I will, just to prove to that fool sheriff that my boys were not there to rob any stage coach or kill anyone. Why, the idea of James killing someone? That sweet boy? He would never, never, do anything like that."

Emil drove the few miles from their small holdings to town, did his best to hold his tongue, and knew it would be useless to say anything. Justification for every misdeed had been this way from the time the boys were born and got worse following his accident. Over protective didn't cover the subject, he almost snickered, thinking about it.

"They are taking Jacob Best to court this morning, Rose. You'll have the full story from Sheriff Connors when we get there. I think we should consider selling our little ranch and moving into town. I could work for Charley Stone part time and with the income from my mining stock, we'd be fine."

"I could never live in that town, Emil. Not after all the lies that have been spread about my boys.

Filthy old biddies have said terrible things, according to Clarence and Amelia. Just terrible. Saying that James and Willy were close friends with that murdering Jacob Best, that they killed Mr. Kinkaid, that they killed a man on that stage coach."

"No, Emil. If we sell the ranch we would need to move far away from all these lies." Rose was sitting straight up on the seat of the buggy alongside Emil as he drove the team at a brisk trot toward Eureka. Emil had a cigar clamped tight and kept his eyes straight ahead, on the road.

"Just the five of us? Ain't enough, Terrence." Ed Connors was sitting at his desk, scowling at Corcoran and Skitters. Andy Sinclair and Sean Morgan were seated, drinking coffee. Corcoran had to hide a smile watching Connors act his plan out. It was the morning of the first of the Jacob Best trials. They would deal with the murders of the two Eureka men, then the abduction and murder of Cynthia Wilkinson.

It would be a complicated time and this morning would just be the beginning. Late summer heat boiled from the dirt streets of the little mountain town, almost as hot as some of the rumors that flooded any gathering of people. One indicated an army of miners coming to vindicate little Cynthia, another predicted Sonny Kinkaid's buckaroos, led by Tails McGee were going to burn the town out.

A petition with several hundred signatures was handed to Sheriff Ed Connors demanding that the army be called out to head off an invasion of righteous individuals from Utah, coming soon. District Judge Tim Mallory was demanding extra security, and there were reports that the governor was most upset by the bad publicity generated by the killings.

The sun shone brightly on this morning, belying the intrigue. Little currents of summer air moved the dust around on the porch of the sheriff's office, and the calm inside was barely skin deep. Every man inside knew there would be more deaths before Jacob Best's trials were over.

Ed Connors again suggested that five deputies simply wouldn't be enough to hold off a horde. "I have Boots Cahill and his wagon out back," Corcoran said. "He'll drive and Skitters, you ride in the back with Best. Keep that shotgun aimed at him at all times. I'll be on Dude riding escort with my double-barreled monster, and Ed, I'd like you to be on the steps of the courthouse when we get there."

Corcoran looked over to Andy and Sean. "You two are the kickers," he chuckled. "Andy, you need to be about a third of the way from here to the courthouse. A hundred yards, maybe. Sean, about two thirds of the way. Everybody carries shotguns and please understand that we are there to keep that foul bastard back there alive. I don't like it any more than anyone else, but that comes with the badge."

"He got any friends that will try to break him free?" Sean Morgan asked.

"No, not that I know of," Corcoran said. "Any trouble makers will be there to lynch the fool, not set him free. It is possible that someone with a rifle might take a long shot at the boy. You do your best to keep him huddled under a blanket close to the wagon seat, Skitters."

Skitters had been through trips to the courthouse like this more than once. He lost a prisoner when the wagon was simply overwhelmed by a mob. Two blasts from the shotgun and three shots from his Colt hadn't slowed them down half a second. "Wish this old fouling piece had fourteen barrels, Terrence."

"We will leave here at nine thirty sharp." Connors said. Everyone checked their watches, and the sheriff continued. "Sean, you and Andy need to be in position well before that so you can know the crowd near you. Better take off right away." Ed Connors was pacing around the office. "What have we forgotten?"

"It's pretty well covered Ed," Corcoran said. "Skitters, get back with your prisoner. We'll come for you. Sean and Andy, take off now." He watched them all leave and motioned Sheriff Connors to sit down. "You need to relax just a little, Sheriff."

"Thought we were gonna talk about those bucka-roos from the sale barn." Connors said.

"They're on the roof-tops, Ed. Didn't want those boys to know that. Sure as hell, Andy and Sean would be looking around to see them, giving it all away. Only you and I know this."

"One of Sam Atkins' deputies will be standing with me on the courthouse steps when you ride up. To receive the prisoner, Atkins said." Connors had a worried look on his face. "Sam will be in the court-room waiting. Have you gotten any kind of feedback from Sylvester Paine?"

"I spent an hour and a half explaining why we're taking these precautions getting Jacob Best to the courthouse. His only answer was to proclaim Best's innocence. Innocent or guilty makes no difference to a mob, Ed. You and I know that, but this fat twit is too young to be out without supervision."

Ed Connors laughed and walked over to pour some coffee. "Well, Terrence, you got me to relax just bit with that one. He's not planning to ride in the wagon with Best, is he? I won't allow that. No, sir, that won't happen."

"It was mentioned, Ed, but I told him that, because of safety, we couldn't let that happen, that it would be hard enough to protect his client without having to protect him, too."

Sheriff Ed Connors was about to say something when Emil and Rose Cannon walked in.

CHAPTER THIRTY-ONE

"Good morning Emil, Rose," Connors said. "I'm glad you came. Please, have a seat. Can I get you some coffee? I'll make this as short as I can. We have to be in court in an hour. First, my apology for not being the one to bring you the bad news about Willy and James. Mr. Berry will be along shortly."

Emil stuck his big hand out to shake with the sheriff and Rose turned her back on him, to face Terrence Corcoran. Her handbag was held in one hand, the other was stuffed in a pocket of her heavy coat. Was it instinct? Did Corcoran see something? He side stepped quickly toward the pot belly stove as she pulled a small single shot pistol from her coat and fired, all but point blank at the big deputy.

Corcoran roared his pain and tumbled to the floor, almost falling into the hot stove. Emil twisted his back to the point of losing his balance and fell into Ed Connors. Rose stood quiet, the smoking gun held tightly, still aimed at Corcoran. Terrence had one hand covering his bleeding side and scrambled to his feet, slamming a huge fist into Rose's face, wincing from the pain.

Rose fell to the floor, the little gambler's special slid across the floor, and Corcoran grabbed it up. He pulled his big Colt and stood pointing it at Rose as Skitters came charging back into the office. "What the hell?" He helped get Connors and Emil Cannon untangled and on their feet, grabbed a chair for Corcoran to slide into, quickly got Rose Cannon to her feet, her hands behind her back, and into cuffs.

"Don't know what's what, Miz Cannon, but if Corcoran's bleeding and pointing a gun at you, you're going in cuffs. Sit down." Skitters pushed her into one of the cane back chairs.

Rose was screaming obscenities at everyone in the room and Skitters threatened to whack her if she didn't shut up. "Shut your mouth woman. You're under arrest, so shut up!" Skitters looked at Corcoran, then to Ed Connors, and finally saw Emil Cannon simply sink to the floor in horrible pain. "I'll put her in number three, Ed, away from Best. Somebody better get the doc for Terrence."

"We kicked everyone out too soon, Terrence." Connors wanted to chuckle in the worst way, but continued. "I'll go get the doc and then go see the judge. We gotta get a postponement on the trial. Don't die on me while I'm gone."

"I'll wait till you get back, Sheriff," Corcoran laughed, breaking the heavy curtain of tension hanging over the office. "It's just a scratch, but don't tarry either." Corcoran found some clean rags used to wipe coffee cups, opened his shirt and saw the gash in his side for the first time. "Don't stop and get in conversations, Ed. It is a bleeder."

For the first time in minutes the room was quiet. Corcoran was tending his wound, the sheriff was putting on his hat. Andy Sinclair walked into the office with Sylvester Paine in tow. "Got a problem here," Sinclair said. He stopped so fast that Paine bumped him.

"What the hell happened here? Corcoran? Sheriff?" He just stood there, half in the doorway, watching Corcoran try to patch up the hole in his side.

"Been a problem. Run for Doc Sanford's and bring him back. Paine, come with me." Connors moved toward the door. "We gotta see the judge."

"No, sheriff, I'm here to see my client and make arrangements to get to the courthouse."

"No, my young barrister friend, you'll come with me, now. I'll explain on the way. Move it," and the sheriff turned the attorney around and led him out the door. "Run, Sinclair, get the doc." Connors all but marched the young and very overweight Paine up the hill to the courthouse, talking a mile a minute about the Rose Cannon attack.

"You got all that? You and I are going to talk to the judge and get today's proceedings postponed. You better understand something right now. I'm the sheriff of this county and my best deputy just got shot in my office. At this moment, I don't give a damn whether your client lives or dies, so you better play my game or ride out of town."

"We'll talk to the judge," Sylvester Paine mumbled, cowed by Connors fierceness.

"Rose Cannon shot you?" Doc Sanford's eyes widened and his mouth dropped when Corcoran told him. Sinclair couldn't tell him what happened because he didn't know. He only told the doc that Corcoran had been shot. "What the hell's going on in our little community? More gunshot wounds in the last month than I've seen in five years."

"Go back in the cells and get Skitters," Corcoran told Sinclair. "You can sit with the prisoners while he's out here. Doc, when you get through with me, you got-ta take care of Emil. He twisted that busted up back of his something fierce when I got shot. He ain't moving."

Emil Cannon was still on the floor, near the wood stove, softly cursing and moaning. "I can't feel my legs, Doc." The look on his face was one of sheer terror at the thought of being paralyzed. There were other thoughts rambling through his mind too. His wife just shot a deputy sheriff, his boys both dead and known forever as killers and outlaws, and him with forty acres of rocks and unable to walk.

Doctor Euel Sanford had been an army doctor in his younger years, even saw duty during the big War Between the States, and knew firsthand the terror a man felt when told he would lose his legs. Being paralyzed was the same thing. He moved over to Emil's side, got right down on the floor next to him.

"We'll do everything we can to make them work, Emil. Just relax now and let me probe about some. Yell out if it hurts." Sanford turned him over onto his stom-ach and worked his hands up and down Cannon's back, as if giving the man a massage. He knew it was working, hearing almost sighs coming from the old miner.

"That rock fall moved things around in your back, Emil. Of course you know that, but this tumble you just took, moved things a bit more. Did Rose give you back rubs like this? I suggested it to her."

Emil winced some when Sanford probed a bit deep. "Easy there," he said. "No, she never did. She was supposed to?" The boys antagonized Emil constantly and Rose let them. She was told to give him massages and never did? And now, she's behind bars and he might be paralyzed. "I don't much care for this life of mine, Doc. Maybe we need to talk about that."

"Actually, Emil, your life's gonna be pretty good from now on." Sanford prodded even harder and Emil cried out. "Much better, I think. That little bone just slithered right back where it was supposed to be in the first place. I want you to lie quiet now, take a nap if you want."

The old doc stood up, motioned Skitters to get a blanket for Cannon, and sat down next to Corcoran. "There are some nasty people in this old world of ours, Terrence. If Rose had massaged his back years ago, that spine bone would have nested itself and he would never have had all these years of pain. He's gonna be fine." Anger and compassion were evident in his words and the look on his face.

"That's where we are at the moment, Judge." Ed Connors was sitting in a wingback chair in front of Judge Timothy Mallory while Sylvester Paine paced around the large and rather elegant office. "I'd feel much better if we could postpone this trial for at least three days. With this kind of chaos, I couldn't get that prisoner here on time today no matter what."

"Your point is well taken, Sheriff. Mr. Paine, We're moving this trial one week forward. On Monday next, ten a.m. sharp. No argument. Inform your client, and Sheriff, tell Corcoran he has one week to heal."

Connors was laughing with the judge as he walked from the chambers. "You got the word, Mr. Paine. Might even have a new client in Mrs. Cannon, if you play your cards right."

Connors found Corcoran sitting behind the sheriff's desk, Emil Cannon laid out in front of the wood stove, and Skitters making a fresh pot of coffee. "Nice and cozy, eh? Well, Mallory gave us a week, Terrence."

"Good. Doc says I'm gonna live, and Emil's probably going to be able to run his little ranch. How did our Sylvester Paine take it?"

"Gunfire right in the sheriff's office pretty much convinced him that when we say something is dangerous, it really is. Boy might be smarter than we gave him credit for. Is this really over?"

"No, Ed. We still gotta get that boy to the court-room, and then get him to the gallows before the mob does."

"It sounds like you have an idea." Connors took a cup of coffee from Skitters and filled the cup the rest of the way with some fine bourbon. "You have any idea why Rose Cannon walked in the office and shot you? I can sure understand being upset about learning that her angelic sons were killers, but to shoot you?"

"We'll talk about it in the morning, Ed. I'm gonna find pretty little Cindy Cook and let her get me healed."

CHAPTER THIRTY-TWO

Some in Eureka were looking forward to seeing Jacob Best ripped from the grasp of the sheriff's men and strung up at the nearest cottonwood tree. Others were fascinated by the story they heard about Rose Cannon shooting Terrence Corcoran, while still others were disappointed at not being able to attend the court hearing. Among those was Jimmy Henderson, owner of the Bonanza Club.

"Judge, well damn it, I was all primed to hear your pontificatin' this morning. Now you tell me I have to wait a week. I even brought up an extra barrel of my best whiskey for the celebration."

"The celebration? You mean the killing of a human being? That's what a hanging is, you know."

"Justified killing of a filthy low-down, murdering human being, judge. You gettin' soft in your old age?" Henderson loved jabbing the judge, and in the past, the judge always jabbed back.

"Justified, surely, Mr. Henderson, but in truth, I've never found it pleasant sentencing someone to hang. It needs to be done. They must face the consequences of their actions, but it is hard to do. No, not getting soft, and damn you, not getting old."

"That calls for a drink, then," Henderson said. A bottle was produced along with some glasses. "To next week, your honor."

"You're feeling better this morning, Terrence?" Connors was surprised when Corcoran showed up at the office.

"Yes, I am, Ed. Skitters here?"

"In the back with the prisoners and Doc Sanford."

"I'll be right back. Gotta talk to him." He wasn't walking the walk of a tough deputy sheriff, more the walk of a man who hurt bad as he made his way into the cell area. "Morning, Rose. How's that jaw? How do, Jacob? You don't look well."

He turned to Skitters and motioned for him to sit down. "I can't ride, Skitters. Doc says a ride would tear the wound wide open. I want you to ride to Clarence Wilkinson's place and bring him here. Tell him everything's that's happened, but bring him here. He and Jimmy Henderson are the keys to keeping the lid on this old town of ours. Don't take no for an answer."

"On my way, Terrence." Skitters was out the door and Corcoran turned back to the prisoners.

"You two getting along, are you? Splendid. Judge Sanford will hear your plea before the end of the week, Rose and I'll be there, too. For your information, I don't like getting shot, so don't look for me to telling nice stories about you."

He turned to the next cell. "Mr. Best, you'll be talking with the judge next Monday. I'll be there for that, too. This will give you a full week to think about what your future might be. Lot of dead people in your past got to be atoned for. Have a good day, now."

"Thank you for coming, Clarence," Corcoran said. "I want you, me, the sheriff, and Jimmy Henderson to have a nice lunch together. They're waiting for us at the Bonanza."

"Is it true, what Skitters said about my sister shooting you? Is that why you're limping?" Wilkinson had a genuine look of concern on his face. "I hope you don't think I had anything to do with that."

Corcoran had to chuckle. "Not at all, Clarence, no, not to worry. It's the current mood of the town that has us so concerned. There have been too many good people lost, Clarence. Don't need to lose any more."

Henderson had a table in the back set up for the luncheon and little Cindy Cook was busy bringing bowls and platters of food out as Wilkinson and Corcoran came in. "Oh, Terrence. You must be hurtin' something awful," she said.

"Nothing you can't cure, little darling," he said. "Looks like you outdid yourself on our meal. Gentlemen, let's talk some."

Corcoran waited until plates were filled and drinks were poured before he started. "We've got us a boiler getting overheated and a lot of people's lives are going to be changed for the worse if we don't get it cooled down. Ed's the county sheriff, but it isn't a lawman who the people will listen to, I'm afraid. Jimmy, you've been a voice of reason in the past, people look up to you, listen to what you have to say."

"And Clarence, you're the leader of the mine and the grieving father of little Cynthia. The men at the mine look up to you. Ed Connors and I are asking you two to pinch off the fuse that's been lit by Jacob Best. The town is close to a riot, blood is going to flow like cold beer after a long shift if we can't calm things down."

The only sound was Cindy walking among them, pouring coffee, exchanging plates. "Leading citizens of our community are dead because of Best," Ed

Connors said. "Jimmy, I'm asking that you spread the word that Jacob Best, like every citizen of this town, will get a fair trial before he is hung. I won't stand for a lynching."

Corcoran looked at Wilkinson. "The men at the mine will follow your lead, Clarence. Cool them down. Don't force our little department to have to shoot our own citizens. And you know we will."

"You're asking a lot, Sheriff," Wilkinson said. "On the other hand, without you, Jacob Best would still be running loose, killing others. I'm an intelligent man, compassionate at times, but I want that man hanged. I want him to die hard, Sheriff. I can tell you this," he said.

Wilkinson stood up and paced around the table for a minute, putting his thoughts together. Pictures of his little daughter danced in his head, ugly, sinful pictures from the bottom of that cliff. He had sweet memories, too, of that girl dancing and laughing through the thirteen years they had her.

"I'll do everything in my power to cool off the men who work for me. I can't order them, only reason with them. But, hear me now, if the judge does not order Best to be hung, I will probably lead the lynch party." He had a deep frown on his rugged face as he sat back down. "Couldn't live with myself otherwise."

Both Corcoran and the sheriff already had that figured out. "I'm as sure as anything, Clarence, that Best will be found guilty and sentenced to hang," Corcoran said.

"The people that stupid boy killed, hurt, and stole from were good friends of mine," Jimmy Henderson said. "Long time friends. Good people. But this is my community, Terrence. I'm one of the first people to open a business when gold and silver were struck. I love Eureka and won't watch it be destroyed by hate. I'll do everything you ask to ease the pressure."

Between good thinking, good food, and plenty to drink, the tension at that table eased considerably. "Anyone want fresh peach cobbler?" Cindy Cook asked, and all hands were raised.

The few hot-heads at the mine who were stirring up trouble were calmed down, possibly with threats of future employment, and Wilkinson was able to tell Sheriff Connors that there would be no trouble on trial day. Only one, Hans Spreckles, didn't sign the paper Wilkinson asked them to do.

"Hans, I know you and Cynthia were friends. This isn't how justice is served. You can't take the law into your own hands. We have laws, judges, trials, and justice is served. You will not be helping me, my family, or Cynthia's memory by killing Jacob Best as he is transported to the courthouse."

"You can't tell me what to do when I'm off work, Mr. Wilkinson. That man needs to die and I will kill him."

"You're going to be killed, Hans, and maybe others around you. You're wrong. I beg you not to try to create a riot. Too many people are already dead." Wilkinson's words fell on deaf ears and Hans Spreckles rode off the mine property, giving up his job, and Wilkinson feared, also his life.

Henderson spread the word that he had given his word, too, and it appeared that many of the townspeople felt the same. There were still hot-heads, but the talk of lynching, of mob violence was quieted, if not subdued.

Monday morning blossomed forth with summer winds telling all that thunderstorms would be the order of the day. Massive clouds were building by nine o'clock, winds were blowing dust and scrap everywhere, and the pounding of thunder could be heard in the distance.

"I hope the weather isn't telling us what we're looking at in that courthouse," Connors said.

"Wilkinson is sure that Spreckles feller is going to try to kill Best as we take him to court this morning." Corcoran's side was still sore as all get out but healed enough that he probably wouldn't tear it open riding a horse. "We'll follow the same plan, Ed, but we do have a couple of extra people that Henderson has vouched for. They'll be along the route, mostly watching for Spreckles."

Skitters and Dean Berry came in from the cell area as Tails McGee walked in. "Riding with you, Corcoran. Can't protect yourself from a wild woman, figured you'd need me."

"Glad to have you." He ignored the slam, saw the sheriff chuckle, and continued. "Sean Morgan is on the street now, along with Gerald Sinclair. That wagon out back, Skitters?"

"Ready to roll, Terrence. Just give us the word."

"Wish we could just hold court right here," Ed Connors said. "I'm heading for the courthouse, Corcoran. Give me ten minutes and start the process." He pulled his hat on and walked out into a blustery morning. There was a considerable number of people out on the streets, considering the weather.

Sheriff Connors nodded to many, spoke to a few, and let his eyes roam through the throngs. It was a long block and a half up the hill from the main street, and Connors had to fight to keep from searching the rooftops for the riflemen that Corcoran had in place.

He expected to meet with an investigator from the district attorney's office on the front steps of the courthouse, and they would escort the prisoner to the courtroom.

"Bring him out, Skitters. We'll chain his hands and feet out here. I'll ride Dude on the right side of the wagon, you ride on the left, Tails." He watched Skitters leave, and continued. "Nobody knows this, but I have men with rifles on rooftops along the route, also. Don't be looking for them."

Tails McGee chuckled. "That's why you didn't tell the others, eh? Well, I'll do my best." It was an easy walk out the back of the jail and they hustled Jacob Best into the wagon. Skitters climbed in and sat facing the prisoner, that shotgun aimed and just inches from Best's head.

"My fingers are all itchy this morning, Corcoran. Hope we don't hit any big bumps." Corcoran laughed and motioned the wagon driver to start off. "Eyes wide open, now," he said.

CHAPTER THIRTY-THREE

The wind seemed to pick up as the wagon slowly made the short jaunt to the courthouse, and dust was blowing about, small dust-devils sprang up and made things miserable for those in their path. Corcoran and Tails McGee rode in close to the wagon so that anyone wanting to shoot Jacob Best would have to shoot them first. Best was huddled down as close to the wagon bed as he could get, staring into the double barrels of Skitters' scatter gun.

They made the first half block and across an intersection as a dust-devil moved through, almost with them. A rifle cracked and Tails McGee's horse reared up and fell back to the ground, flailing about in its last seconds. McGee jumped clear, holding onto his rifle and Corcoran yelled to the wagon driver to "Run like the devil for the courthouse."

Sean Morgan spotted the man, shooting from the doorway of the apothecary's, and pulled his shotgun up. *No, too many people. Damn it, get out of my way.* His thoughts were only on stopping that man from shooting again. Three fast steps, pistol in hand, and Morgan knocked a buckaroo out the way and put two quick shots into the closing door.

They were answered by a wild shot from inside the drug emporium, and Morgan shot twice more as he slammed through the door. He caught a glimpse of a large man dashing through another doorway and gave chase. It led him into a back storeroom where he saw the shooter trying to get a window open.

"Don't move." His command was ignored, and he saw the man turn with every intent of putting a rifle slug in Morgan. The shotgun belched its grayish white smoke and young Mr. Sprekles died, splattered onto the window he was trying so hard to get open.

Tails McGee jumped to his feet in time to see Sean Morgan begin his chase and stepped into the middle of the street, his rifle at the ready. The wagon was racing for the courthouse, protected by Corcoran, so McGee put two quick rifle shots into the air, getting everyone on the street's attention.

"Stay calm. This ain't the time to be foolish." He

was shouting, trying to see exactly where Sean Morgan went. A man yelled and pointed at the apothecary shop, and McGee made a run for it. He got there in time to see young Spreckles die.

"Good job, Mr. Morgan. Let's get up to the courthouse. This fool may have friends." The two men ran from the shop and up the street, doing their best not to knock the bystanders down. Jacob Best was already inside when they got there. "Go tell Corcoran what happened," McGee said. "I'll stand guard out here."

"That was the only incident then," Corcoran said. All the deputies, Jimmy Henderson, Clarence Wilkinson, the sheriff, and Tails McGee were crammed in the sheriff's office. "We'll have the hanging on Wednesday, so there shouldn't be any trouble from anyone. Thank you, each of you, thank you."

"You owe me a horse, Sheriff." Tails McGee wasn't smiling. "That was a fine stock horse that fool shot out from under me."

"Weren't worth five cents a pound, Tails, and you know it," Corcoran said.

"Oh, no," Sheriff Connors yelled out. "We ain't gonna get that started. Find a good horse, Tails, buy it, and the county will reimburse you. Damn it, Corcoran."

"Weren't," Corcoran laughed. Tails scowled, but just for a moment.

"Were," he said.

"First drinks are on me," Henderson said.

Emil Cannon picked that moment to walk in. "Just wanted to thank you for getting that boy and getting him a trial. Corcoran, can we talk, alone, for a minute?"

"Sure, Emil. You boys go on, I'll catch up."

Corcoran walked around Connors' old oak desk and sat down. Emil took the chair in front of the desk and Terrence saw hurt and fear in his eyes. "What is it, Emil?"

"All these years, Terrence, Rose protected those boys, and I wasn't aware that she also cut me down in front of them. When Doctor Sanford told me that he had told her to give me massages, my heart splintered. That day, me on the floor right there," and he pointed, "he gave my back a simple massage and the pain disappeared. He's given me three more, Terrence, and I feel like a new man."

Tears rolled down Emil Cannon's face. "Such a simple thing. Why? Why didn't she do it? Why did she tear me down in front of the boys? My, God, Terrence, our life would have been so different."

Corcoran let him talk, knew there was no one else

left in his life to talk to, and also knew he had no an-swers for the man. How could he answer questions like that? He couldn't talk about Rose because he still couldn't understand why she shot him. "It's a time to rebuild, Emil. Some questions in life simply can't be answered. There was something very differ-ent about Rose, something that we'll never be able to understand.

"You're still a young enough man to make a good life for yourself. You own your property and you're get-ting your health back. It won't be easy, of course, but you also have friends, many friends, willing to help."

"When will Rose leave for prison, Corcoran?"

"We'll put her on the train in the morning. Do you want one more visit?"

"No, I'd rather not ever see her again. I'll drive the buggy back to the ranch, I think, and do some long-range planning. Thank you, Terrence Corcor-an. You are a friend, indeed."

It was a quiet crowd that gathered Wednesday morning behind the courthouse. Judge Timothy Mallory made a short speech about rules, laws, jus-tice, and duty, and called for a prayer, which was led by a young man trying to get a church organized in the town. He kept it short, and the judge gave Jacob

Best a chance for his last words.

"I ain't got nothin' to say." The hood was placed over his head, the noose adjusted, and he fell to his death. Corcoran jerked when it happened, as he had so many times.

"Why?" Corcoran quietly asked himself. "What makes young men like James and Willy Cannon go bad? Why did Jacob Best hate women? Why did he have this burning desire to kill? There are no answers, I know that." He kicked some dust, watched Doctor Sanford pronounce Jacob Best dead, and turned toward town. "There are only little boys who go bad and big boys with tin stars to catch them before they do too much harm." He wanted Cindy Cook to come running, to fling herself into his waiting arms, and started walking toward the Bonanza Club.

A LOOK AT OUTLAWS, HERE, THERE, EVERY-WHERE: A TERRENCE CORCORAN WESTERN

An outlaw gang is ravaging the small White Pine County mining camp of Ward, Nevada. The sheriff is grievously wounded in a battle with the gang and puts out the call to near-by counties for help.

Eureka County Deputy Sheriff Terrence Corcoran responds. Corcoran finds a community needing help but not helping and discovers far more criminal activity than he rode to help with.

"You will find yourselves completely engrossed from beginning to end, and unable to put the story aside until the final paragraph has been read."

AVAILABLE NOW ON AMAZON

ABOUT THE AUTHOR

Reno, Nevada novelist, Johnny Gunn, is retired from a long career in journalism. He has worked in print, broadcast, and Internet, including a stint as publisher and editor of the Virginia City Legend. These days, Gunn spends most of his time writing novel length fiction, concentrating on the western genre. Or, you can find him down by the Truckee River with a fly rod in hand.

https://wolfpackpublishing.com/johnny-gunn/